Gypsy Soulmate

MARANDA MARKS

Nina,
Enjoy!

Maranda
Marks

This is a work of fiction. Any resemblance to real people or events
is coincidental. Gypsy Soulmate is Book One in The Destiny Series

Copyright © 2014 MARANDA MARKS
All rights reserved.
ISBN: 1505 216508
ISBN–13: 9 781505 216509

For Toni, my family, and all my friends who have taught me anything is possible and never let me give up. Special thanks to everyone who gave their input and expertise.

—

"There is a legend among the gypsies of a very powerful potion that would link true lovers' souls together through lifetimes. Only a few true healers have known the secret. But it is said that if it were their destiny to be together, then neither time nor death could separate their love."

Gypsy Soulmate

PROLOGUE
Present Day, Florida

He was real, flesh and blood, not just a man in the sepia photo she had found years ago. Rose sat near the water's edge,
burying her toes in the moist gritty sand. Closing her eyes, she
inhaled deeply, feeling the brisk salt air enter her lungs. Absently she wrapped her fingers around the antique jewel that hung
from a gold chain around her neck, needing to feel the familiar
warmth that emanated from the stone. A damp tendril of shoulder length brown hair whipped its way into her eyes. She
brushed it aside and hugged her knees tightly to her chest, cradling her chin on her forearms.

Staring out into the indigo night, she envisioned his face. So
many nights she had dreamed of this man from a nineteenth
century photo. Then earlier this evening she saw him; she was
wide-awake, and he stood across the room. He was rakishly
handsome and assured of himself, just as she imagined he would
be. A chill ran through her. Rose shivered, less from the misty
air than from remembering him watching her, even for that brief
moment.

The breeze had picked up and what moments ago seemed to
be an endless void now became a bright line as the pinkish or-

ange began to light the sky. Unwinding her legs, she stood and walked up the beach towards the villa. Reaching the gates, she turned towards the sunrise for one last look. A vague outline of two fishing boats far in the distance sounded their foghorns. One, then another answered as they signaled their passing. Within the melancholy sound, she thought she heard a whisper... *Roszalia*, and she almost expected to see him. Instead, only the large red fiery ball of the sun rose to greet her. A determined smile crept onto her lips as she murmured,

"I *will* find out who you are. I now know you are not just in my dreams."

CHAPTER ONE
1873 County Kerry, Ireland

Caitlin O'Connor Anders stood at the side of the east wing lawn, her slender hand shading her eyes from the morning sun. She watched as her two energetic children ran through the newly trimmed grass, giggling as they chased imaginary butterflies. Smiling, she called out, "Children do try to keep clean, and stay close," knowing her words would not be heeded.

It was late spring in the countryside, as a brilliant flora burst from the abundant gardens, spilling across the lawns of the O'Connor Estate. The distant blue–green mountains and azure sky provided a pristine backdrop for the three story grey stone mansion, which has stood solid on this land for over two centuries. In the pastures, the family's horses grazed on the green satin ground as a thin veil of morning fog was lifting.

Caitlin closed her eyes and inhaled the scents that she knew so intimately, fresh oats, lavender, and heather. A slight breeze rippled through her waves of burnished copper hair, which she hastily secured atop her head.

Her daughter's voice interrupted her thoughts as she ran towards her. Thrusting a handful of wildflowers at her mother, and with a bright smile said, "I picked them for you momma!"

Caitlin took the cluster from her fist. "They are lovely Elizabeth, thank you." Receiving a quick hug, off her daughter went in search of her brother. Looking at the wildflower bouquet, she remembered playing in these very gardens with her own brothers and her mother's smile as she brought her daisies and buttercups. An almost inaudible sigh escaped her lips as she spoke softly, "Mother, I so wish you were with us." Allowing herself a moment of grief, wishing, as always, that her mother had lived to see her grandchildren happily playing in the gardens she loved so dearly.

Closing her eyes, she thought of how beautiful, and vibrant of a woman her mother had been. Katherine O'Connor was known throughout the southwestern region of Ireland for her quintessential parties and holiday events. She had a kind heart and helped whenever a family was in need. Katherine had always told her daughter to be kind and care for all people, no matter what social status they held, never take for granted anything you have, especially family. Caitlin had inherited her mother's compassion for caring for her family, and one of her main concerns was finding suitable brides for her two older brothers. Her brother Devon was entering his twenty–second year and Gavin his twenty–third year. Neither seemed the least interested in any of the women she proposed for them or entertained the idea of settling down. She worried if left up to them they would end up dour old men, never finding a mate to bear their children and carry on the family name.

Today was the day her father, William O'Connor the Second, and brothers, would be coming home after a long absence. Her father had sent a telegram letting her know of their arrival. After Gavin had graduated with his degree in business from Cambridge University in England, he returned to run the family's fishing and shipping companies, both on the peninsula and abroad. He was returning from a meeting in Iceland with information on a partnership with a new ship building company. Conveniently, Devon returned a day prior and was staying at the Harbour Bay Inn, after another of his undisclosed trips abroad.

A frown came across Caitlin's lovely features as she thought of her brother Devon. He had always been arrogant and aloof. When the family would go to visit friends, Devon kept to himself, never socializing with the other children. He was only close to their mother and after her funeral he seemed to withdraw from the family entirely. He would disappear for extended periods and return angry and secretive, often staying in Dingle for days. There were rumors of his reputation as a high stakes gambler, and of his questionable business partners.

Her father, Barrister William O'Connor had been in Tralee at his law office. Now retired, the barrister still took on Samaritan cases for the people who could not afford representation. He helped those who lost everything during the terrible time of the blight. Many of the neighboring landholders whose crops were ravaged, and with no other income source, were no better off than their tenants. Due to the O'Connor family's foresight to diversify business and invest in partnerships abroad, the family and estate remained financially sound.

William decided since both his sons would be in town at the same time, the three men would meet at the family's country manor, to discuss business. They were expanding their trading territory and adding passenger transportation. This being the opportune time since travel to America was growing. Gavin was the first to arrive at the country manor, located just on the outskirts of town. The home was small, compared to the Big House at the estate. With twelve rooms, the two story house sat on fifty lush green acres, a sentinel overlooking the Dingle Peninsula. As far as the eye could see the beauty and serenity of the lush green hills lined the eastern side of the valley. In contrast to the far west, the jagged cliffs plummeted down to the ocean's violent salty surf. The manor was the birthplace of Katherine Callaghan O'Connor. It was the residence where she and William resided after their marriage. When Kathrine was with her first child, they moved to the family estate inland. William's practice in Tralee and the shipyard business made it necessary for him to be on the peninsula quite often. Since the estate was only a few hours from the country manor, Katherine would often accompany her husband and shop or visit friends in town while he attended his business. When the children were young, the entire family would vacation there during the summer months. After Katherine passed away, William rarely visited the manor, unless his business required him to do so. The home remained staffed and guests or business associates were always welcome to spend the night. Often Gavin would stay at the home when he was in Dingle working at the office or shipyard.

Caitlin brought her mind back to the yard as she heard her children, Edward and Samantha giggling with merriment, and then squeals of glee as they caught a glimpse of the carriage entering the long drive.

"Mama!" Edward said excitedly, "Grandfather is home!" Caitlin looked down the drive and saw the dust from the horses' hooves and the carriage wheels. "Children, quickly, come to me." Motioning them to her side, she took her handkerchief and began dabbing at the dirty faces that stood squirming before her. "Oh my, you two are a sight." Finally giving up the fight with a sigh, she quickly smoothed her own hair down and followed as the two ran ahead. The carriage pulled through the gate and stopped at the front entrance.

William O'Connor slowly began unfolding his body, wincing as he stepped out the small door. He thought he would soon have to cut back on these long journeys, for he was not as young and healthy as he once was. Soon he hoped to relinquish the companies to his sons. In seconds, the children were upon him, hugging their grandfather as they asked a barrage of questions. With a smile on his face, he hugged each child saying in his daughter's direction,

"Ah my Caitlin, every time I leave for a week and return, it seems these two youngsters have grown a foot!" Making an exaggerated gesture of his grandson's height, then scooped Samantha up, she giggled and kissed him, he then let the squirming child down to run after her brother.

"Oh father, I am so glad you all are home, the children and I have missed you."

The older man gave her a light kiss. "Do not fret my lass," he winked and his love for his daughter reflected in his tired eyes.

"We are home now and all is well." He looked past her and with concern and asked, "And your husband?"

"Andrew is still in Cork, the Board of Guardians have enlisted a number of physicians in the area to help with their new duties of maintaining health and welfare. He is at one of the workhouse facilities." She looked distressed, hesitating only a moment. "He has been gone for two weeks but he will be home soon." Again, she hesitated. "That is if all goes well, I hear stories that these are horrible places." Her father hugged his daughter, seeing her concern.

A shuffling behind her made her turn as Devon brusquely barreled past and nodded. He had his usual scowl on his otherwise extremely handsome face as he headed straight for the house. Devon's spruce manner of dress showed off his handsome physique. He took after their mother, with deep piercing grey eyes and a thick stock of dark auburn hair meticulously groomed. As he rumbled up the steps and through the front entrance into the house, a straight whiskey, and the chambermaids were the only things on his mind.

Caitlin followed her brother with her eyes and feared for the evening chambermaid, Evelyn, would be the one her brother would seek out. But the girl was no longer at the Big House. She had married one of family's demesne gardeners and moved to his cottage. She had come to Caitlin in fear, believing if Devon found she had married, that he would evict her new husband from their land. Assuaging the girl's fears, Caitlin told her father of the situation, and William assured them that Devon did not have the authority to do such a thing. Both Caitlin and her father agreed it best that Evelyn resign her position at the Big House and help her new husband with the gardens. Caitlin knew Devon would be furious. He had been away from home for months and was not aware of the changes.

Turning back to the carriage, she was startled to see Gavin standing before her with his ever–charming smile.

"So, little sister, I see you held our home together while I was away?" Gavin's grin mocked his own question, for his sister knew that he had little interest in the running of the estate. He loved the adventure of the sea. There was nothing here at their home that held his interest. Yet, being the eldest son, he was destined to be the next landholder of the O'Connor Estate, a title he would gladly give up to his brother if it were not for family and honored tradition.

"You are incorrigible. When will you realize I cannot even manage my own children, let alone handle our entire staff and home?" Gavin gave a quick laugh. This he knew to be just the opposite, his sister was excellent at the running of the estate. The children, their small hands grasping their grandfather's, were dragging him towards the house, telling him of everything that happened while he was away. Gavin hooked his arm with his sister and they followed.

The help was waiting attentively for the three men to arrive, everything was perfect, and every detail looked after. This was what Caitlin took her pride in, and she was unquestionably the driving force behind the elegant appearance of their home, just as her mother had been. As they entered, Carlson, their butler greeted them,

"Master Gavin, We are so pleased to have the entire family back under one roof. We will have your bags brought to your room right away," taking their cloaks, he set out with the door attendant to bring in the luggage.

Caitlin, coming to her father's side, said with a beaming smile,

"Papa, I have arranged for a small dinner party to celebrate your return and..." William put up his hand and sighed,

"Caitlin lass, it has been a long, tiring journey home for your brothers and I, we may want to keep things quiet this evening."

"Oh, but Papa, it would do you all good to see old friends, you can rest now and be fresh for this evening." Caitlin had a stubborn look on her face and her father was too tired from the journey, and dealing with Devon's attitude to argue anymore on the matter.

"Very well, but I am retiring early, guests or not," her father said in a faux stern voice. For he knew he would attend this for his beloved daughter and stay until the last guest left.

"Thank you Papa!" Caitlin beamed, and with a light kiss on his cheek, left to make sure the party preparations were on schedule. Gavin had been leaning against the foyer's doorframe as he saw his brother come out of the library. Whiskey in hand, Devon headed up the large main staircase to shed his traveling clothes and seek the company of one of the chambermaids.

Gavin shook his head and thought, *Poor girls.* He then caught a glimpse of a female figure in the passage to the kitchen; she had dark hair pulled tightly back with a ribbon. He did not recognize her as one of the staff. Curious who this may be, he headed towards her.

The girl, suddenly realizing he intended to speak to her, turned to retreat towards the kitchen. Before she could take a step, she felt a warm hand gently grasped her forearm, as she spun around she was looking into the handsome face of Gavin O'Connor.

"And just who may you be lass?" Gavin said with his deep Irish brogue. He could see she was nervous and thought with irony– *Just be glad I spotted you before my brother!*

Roszalia stared intensely at this man who held her arm gently. She had seen him three years ago when she and her mother had been visiting her aunt who was in the O'Connor employ. She held her breath for fear she would scream or worse yet, say something inappropriate. She had dreamed many times since she saw him last of what a real meeting would be like. She would be dressed as a princess and he, the lord of the estate. He would take her hand and gently kiss it like a lady. Now with his fingers on her arm, all that she could do was blush deeply. Coming out of her daydream, she realized Gavin was speaking to her.

"So shall we play a guessing game? Let's see," Gavin stroked his chin and narrowed his eyes in mock concern. "Maybe you are here to steal the silver and the fine china?" Roszalia eyes opened wide as she shook her head.

"Of course not, I jest lass. Well then, maybe you are here to steal my heart." He gave her a smile, then, with a frown, placed his hand on his chest in mock hurt gesture, releasing her arm as he did so. Realizing he had possibly frightened or offended her, he softened his tone, "Now if you please, do you have a name?" His smile was genuine.

"I am Truda's niece, my name is Roszalia." She did not cast her gaze down as he spoke. Instead, she looked directly into Gavin's amber eyes. Trying to project a confidence she did not feel. "I came to live here under the care of my aunt since my mother passed on recently." Her voice became quieter, "Lady Caitlin told my aunt that it would be acceptable. I will assist the governess in the children's language studies, I am fluent in English, Gaelic, French, and Hungarian, and I read and write Latin and have an understanding of many others." She added, "Language is a gift I have." Still meeting his gaze, she would not let him see her discomposure. The place where Gavin's fingers touched her arm was tingling with the sensation only a young woman's imagination could know.

"My apologies, please forgive my callous remarks." A small pain shot through his heart for this girl, he knew what it was, not to have a mother's guidance, and he still missed his own mother's presence terribly. Studying her more closely now in the sunlight from the kitchen, he noticed she was well proportioned and the signs of womanhood were evident. She wore a simple grey skirt and white pinafore apron with ties around her small waist. Yet, the satin gold ribbon in her long, mahogany brown hair was not part of the uniform. Her wide innocent eyes captivated him, a curious array of brown, gold, and green set perfectly on a heart shaped face accented by small but full red lips. Hungarian gypsy breeding, he surmised since he knew her aunt had lived in the camps on the peninsula prior to her position as head pastry chef. However, this girl seemed very different, she was educated, and she held her head high and spoke with perfect diction. Intriguing, he thought. Gavin felt his heart stir as he realized this girl was genuinely stunning. He would have to make sure his brother stayed away from this one.

"Pardon Sir," Roszalia said softly, for she was extremely uncomfortable under his scrutiny. "May I go now?" Finally averting her eyes from his gaze.

Realizing he had been staring too intently at the girl, Gavin tried to ease the moment. "Of course, but you may not call me Sir, you will learn I am not fond of formalities," he paused, "Please, call me Gavin."

Roszalia smiled and finally fidgeted in a nervous fashion saying quietly, "Yes, Gavin." As she heard his name exit her lips, a warm feeling flooded within her. Turning, not wanting him to see her discomposure, she made haste down the hall towards the upper level and the servants' quarters, leaving Gavin watching her retreat.

When Roszalia reached her new room, she found herself alone. Kicking off her shoes and dropping down on a small bed, oh how handsome he is, she mused. She let herself indulge in the fantasy of a young woman. Gavin would ask her to dance tonight at the party. He would hold her as she had seen him dance with other ladies of status, and they would swirl to the music. Resting her hand on his broad shoulder, he would swing her out into the gardens where he would take her in his arms and confess his love for her before his tender kiss covered her lips. Suddenly the door to her room flung open snapping her from her fantasy. She sat up quickly.

"Who are you?" Devon's voice raged at her, surprised that Evelyn was not in the room.

Roszalia could only stare at him. She knew this was Gavin's brother, and she had heard terrible stories from the other maids about his behavior. He was also very handsome, but in a different way than Gavin, *a dangerous way*, she thought.

"I am Truda's niece Sir, I will be staying here on the premise, helping the governess," she said softly, wishing her aunt would come to check on her. They had moved into a new larger suite so Roszalia and her aunt could share the space. Devon's eyes narrowed, noticing she was alone in the room. His steel grey eyes bore into her making her feel uncomfortable.

"Where is Evelyn? This is her room." Fear began to creep into Roszalia, she tried to inch off the bed towards the door, but Devon stood square in front of her.

"I am sorry, but I do not know an Evelyn. This was the room that I was told my aunt and I would share," Roszalia managed to

11

say in a shaky voice. Devon was staring at her hungrily, looking her over from her stocking ankles to the neckline of her blouse. Feeling helpless and now frightened she was still on the edge of the bed; she watched as Devon began to come around the side towards her. She stood and headed for the door, instantly feeling a tight grasp on her wrist as Devon grabbed her.

"And where do you think you are going?" Devon said, swinging her towards him. Roszalia could smell whiskey and tobacco and felt her head began to swim. Devon pulled her close, holding her wrists so she could not fight him. "I am going to welcome you to the estate. Do you know who I am?"

Roszalia gave a small cry as he pulled her head back. She knew what would happen next, she had seen some of the men and women in the gypsy camp after a night of celebration. Her mother tried to shelter Roszalia. Knowing her life may be difficult at times, but only give her body to the man she loves. That is why her mother made arrangements that she would live with her aunt when she knew her illness was terminal, for a young girl in the camp alone with little skills would only have one mean to survive. Wanting to scream out, but knowing she could not, she was a member of the staff, she shut her eyes, too proud to let Devon see her tears. Roszalia waited for the feel of his hands on her flesh, when suddenly, she heard a much different voice, low and deadly serious.

"Devon, remove your hands from the girl!" then with more force, "Now or so help me, I will break your arm in doing so myself." As she opened her eyes, she saw Gavin standing behind his brother. Devon turned his attention from the girl to sneer at his brother,

"Not to worry brother, she is a gypsy wench, they start early, I'm sure there will be plenty of fire left for you."

Gavin's anger flared, and he grabbed Devon by the neck, easily pushing him towards the open door. Devon staggered back, glaring at his brother.

"Damn you Gavin, take her!" But before Devon stumbled off in search of a more willing partner, he looked directly at Roszalia and said in a steady, stone cold voice, "Be warned wench, some day it will be just you and me!" He strode off rubbing his chin and cursing his brother.

Roszalia finally exhaled and fell into Gavin's arms. He held her for a moment feeling her tremble, then gently pushed her back and looked at her to make sure she had not been hurt.

"Are you all right?" A strand of hair had escaped the ribbon and he gently brushed it from her face.

Roszalia looked into Gavin's eyes, he was genuinely concerned, and she felt an overwhelming feeling in her heart. Then remembering her station, she straightened and moved away, embarrassed.

"Yes, thank you, how did you know he was...?" She choked off the last words.

"I was just passing the stairwell when I heard his bellowing. I surmised he was after one of the maids again. I came up to see if the situation needed my intervention, apparently I was right." Gavin gave a sheepish smile to try to lift the girl's spirits. He could see she was very upset. As Gavin began to leave, Roszalia touched his arm and said quietly,

"Gavin, I want you to know, I grew up in the gypsy camp, and I know what people think. But I have never bedded a man." He was taken aback by her innocence and honesty. Not knowing how to reply, he nodded. "I will have my father speak to Devon. Now remember to lock your door." He said in a serious tone, for he did not like the threat his brother gave the girl. After leaving the room and hearing the lock catch, he surprised himself by thinking how beautiful the young girl really was, and for the short moment she clung to him it felt so right. He needed to go have a hot bath and get ready for Caitlin's party. He was confident his sister invited every eligible female in the county. Nevertheless, his mind kept wandering back to the girl that he held just moments ago.

Immediately locking the door as Gavin had instructed, Roszalia wearily sat down in the chair next to a small writing table, taking a moment to recall all that had just taken place. Devon was a real threat. He was an angry man, and she would need to be careful and try to avoid him if possible. Her solemn mood softened as she thought of Gavin, his scent and his firm chest when he held her made her feel safe. He was her secret love and tonight he became her protector. She felt a warm feeling begin to flood her insides as she pictured his face and his tall, well–built body. She was in her sixteenth year and had been having womanly feelings now for some time; many of the girls her age in the camp had been earning their living by bedding the wealthy men of the area. Many others were already married within the camp and were busy raising their children.

Her thoughts went to her own mother, Marguerite. During her childhood, her mother would make her promise that if something should happen and they were no longer together, she wanted her to get out of the camps and make a better life for herself. Some of their family lived in town and had businesses, or worked at prominent homes that could take care of her. Often when she spoke of this, Marguerite's eyes would cloud over and as she fought the tears from the thoughts of her painful past.

Roszalia never knew her father. When Marguerite became gravely ill, she finally told her daughter the story of the only man she ever loved, Joseph Danyovok. When Marguerite was a young woman living in Hungary, there were few professions a gypsy girl with little education could have. Gifted in the art of premonitions, sight, and healing, Marguerite practiced under the tutelage of her aunt Agnes, who was respected in the community for her trade. After time, Marguerite's potent mixtures helped many of the wealthy families in the town with their ailments. One family in particular sought her help for their youngest daughter's bouts with a breathing illness. Marguerite would make the trip daily to the wealthy patron's home to aid the child. Within a few months, the child's symptoms decreased and her parents rested easier. In appreciation for her help, the family offered her to stay at their home where she would continue with their daughter's treatments.

Marguerite was a stunning young woman, slender of figure with porcelain skin and dark dancing eyes. Many men lusted after her, one in particular, Joseph who was the eldest son of the prominent family where she was residing. She was young and found his attentions flattering and soon she made the ill–fated mistake of falling in love with him. He told her he returned her feelings and they would wed. He insisted their differences in social status meant nothing to him, but when his father heard of the plans his son had of marrying the gypsy girl, he threatened to renounce him and leave him penniless. Soon after, Joseph was sent on a business trip abroad, and immediately after his departure, Marguerite was sent away. Roszalia's father never came after her mother. After Marguerite left the home, she realized she was with child. She was too ashamed and scared to stay in town. She decided to travel with the roaming band of gypsies. It was not an easy life and soon after the birth of her daughter, Marguerite decided that living close to her relatives was a better life for them both. She moved to the camp where some of her family lived, on the coast of Ireland. Marguerite continued selling her herbal medicines earning a meager living for herself and her daughter, determined to protect her child from the same life that had befallen her.

For as long as Roszalia could remember, her aunt Truda, was a pastry chef employed at the O'Connor Estate. On certain occasions when the family would be entertaining, Marguerite would fascinate the women with her tarot readings and gift of predictions while the men retired to the parlor. At a party arranged to introduce the O'Connor brothers to the eligible women of County Kerry and beyond, Roszalia was brought along and told she could help her aunt in the kitchen. But being a child, she was easily bored, and her aunt told her to go sit in the hall. When she entered, she could hear the music and the sounds of laughter. Unable to resist, she hid in the shadows of the large drapes and stole a look into the grand ballroom. That was the first time she saw him.

Gavin O'Connor, he was such a handsome young man, tall, perfect physique, clad in a cream linen shirt with maroon velvet waistcoat and black tight trousers. His hair was dark brown, cropped to just above his collar. Gavin dutifully bowed as he held each young woman's gloved hand in line. He would smile as they giggled and played their coy games. Roszalia watched from her hiding place, her young heart fantasizing about being one of the women that Gavin would choose to dance with. She would have stayed in that location all night, but her aunt's voice called her back to the kitchen.

Roszalia brought her mind back to the present. Sitting at a little table in her new room, she shared with her aunt, blinking to stop the tears of her reality. When Gavin held her, she trembled more from his strong warm touch than from fear of Devon. She knew that it was impossible for Gavin to love her, she a gypsy and he one day to be the master of the estate. Moreover, she winced at the thought that all her mother did to protect her. She was still just a gypsy wench. A woman's voice softly called her name through the locked door.

"Roszalia, it is Caitlin, I would like to come in and speak with you." Wiping her eyes, for she had not realized tears had been leaking from their corners, she unlocked the heavy door to let Caitlin enter. She stood with her eyes cast down. She suddenly felt shameful, as if she was the cause of Devon's unscrupulous behavior...or was it her thoughts of Gavin, she feared would be discovered? "Roszalia dear child, Gavin told me of Devon's behavior. I am so sorry, please let me be your friend, and if you ever need to talk to me about anything, even my brothers, feel free to seek me out." Caitlin's warm and heartfelt words touched Roszalia, the fear, and shame that she had withheld rushed out, and she began to sob. Caitlin reached out, took the girl in her arms, and rested her head on her shoulder.

"There, there, cry if you need to," Caitlin said as she stroked Roszalia's hair.

After a moment, Roszalia backed up, giving Caitlin a waning smile and said in a small voice, "Thank you, I do not want to cause trouble." Caitlin gave her another hug, producing a handkerchief and dabbed the tears from her eyes.

"I am sorry this happened. You are a beautiful young woman, but there is no excuse for ill behavior. So go freshen up, I would like you to help me. I have so many last minute details for tonight's party. The children's governess has taken ill and is in her rooms. I need someone to entertain the children for me while I tend to the preparations. Can you do that?"

Caitlin's sincere smile made her feel grateful for a chore to occupy her thoughts. Roszalia's said she would be happy to help in any way she could.

"Good, now freshen that beautiful face." Caitlin left Roszalia to get herself cleaned up. She was honored that Caitlin thought her worthy of watching her children and for a moment, her mind was taken away from the O'Connor brothers.

Samantha and Edward had taken to Roszalia the moment they met her a month ago to help with their languages, and were excited that she would be with them this evening. As promised he kept them busy as she told Caitlin she would. They played games and sang songs. The hour was getting late, and the children had utterly exhausted themselves with their new friend. It was time for their maid to take over with their nighttime bed preparations. Closing the door behind her as she left, she intended to head up to her room, but she paused as the sound of flutes, pipes, and strings from the festivities below caught her attention. Unable to resist, she went down the back stairs, stopping outside the great room.

The estate was set up on three levels. The second housed the bedrooms and living quarters of the family. The west wing was dedicated to the children's sleeping rooms, with adjoining rooms for their governess. Caitlin and Andrew's quarters were directly across. A narrow set of stairs led to the third floor where the servant's quarters were. Roszalia and her aunt Truda were now in the largest of the rooms and shared a bath with the other rooms on this level. At the end of the hall, another narrow set of stairs led down to the east wing of the home. This area was the living chambers of Barrister O'Connor, consisting of a den, a large bedroom, and a private bath with dressing room. Past these were guest quarters, followed by Devon and Gavin's rooms with a bath at the end of the wing. Another set of stairs led down to the main floor where a vast library housed hundreds of leather bound books, heavy mahogany furniture and large paintings of the O'Connor family. A large painting of Kathrine and William

O'Connor the Second hung over the mantel of the massive fireplace. The main hall led to the parlor to the right and a large dining room on the left. The ballroom was straight back from the two curving staircases with its twenty foot ornately carved rich hardwood ceilings. Exquisite furnishings and a massive chandelier graced the ballroom, tall windows with cut prismatic glass allowed bright, warm light to shimmer and dance upon the walls. This had been Katherine's favorite room to entertain.

Tonight the home was bustling with guests attending the welcome home party that Caitlin had arranged for her father and brothers. The women wore the latest fashions, their dresses in glorious colors and fabrics. Some of the younger women wore the new French designer gowns with daring low décolleté. The men sported their best waistcoats and breeches. Roszalia hung in the shadows and watched as more guests entered. Near the entrance, she could see Caitlin looking stunning as always. She wore a deep emerald gown with her fiery hair swept up and fastened with a gold and emerald comb, her energy apparent as she greeted every guest exuberantly. Roszalia searched for Gavin, from the very place she had many years prior, but could not find him. She did spy Devon, and involuntarily retreated further into hiding. He was flirting with two young women, hardly older than she was. His eyes stayed glued to their bodices, and she blushed as she noticed that he took no shame in his lustful stare. Just as Roszalia dared to step further from her hiding place to look to the other side of the hall for Gavin, she turned as a noise behind startled her.

"They look like a bunch of fancy peacocks strutting about." Gavin whispered next to her ear, so close she felt his warm breath and could smell his intoxicating shaving soap. Confused and embarrassed she had been found peeking at the guests, Roszalia tried to hide her face as she spoke. "I was just going back to the kitchen, and I, well," she stammered off in her explanation. Head down, she felt trapped, a child, and humiliated, the man she had been searching for was behind her. For how long, how could she have not heard him?

Gavin chuckled. "Do not look so glum, I despise these parties that my sister insists on having. Here, let me point out the people to you." Gavin steps further from their hiding place, "Over there is Aunt Marianne and Uncle Charles, stuffy, and she smells of too much powder." At this comment, Roszalia had to stifle her laughter. "Ah, and over there in the yellow dress, dear cousin Sallie, and her many suitors, trouble that girl is….not yet sixteen and well…" Gavin made a motion with his hand and trailed off. "Oh yes, see that woman in the deep blue gown? This would be the woman my dear sister is playing matchmaker for me this evening, Vanessa, Barrister Burke's daughter. She's a very proper match," he imitated a stuffy old man.

Roszalia felt a pang of jealousy. This Vanessa woman was stunning: tall, flaxen hair, aristocratic cheekbones, and of the wealthy class.

"She is beautiful. I cannot see why you would not fancy her?" Roszalia asked rather slowly, secretly wishing he preferred dark haired girls.

"Not my type," Gavin answered briskly and before she could respond, he grabbed her hand and led her to the back hall leading to the galley and the kitchen area.

"Gavin, what are you doing? This is your party, you will be missed!" Roszalia protested, flustered. "And what would your guest say? I am employed….."

He cut her off, "Ah lass, you will learn, I do not put people into classes, and besides, you look like you need a dance. These women are loud, conceited and after only my name. So, shall we?" Gavin bowed and held his hand out to Roszalia. For a moment she stood shocked, this could not be possible. To dance with Gavin, surely, she would awake at any moment. His deep voice brought her attention back.

"Will the lady break my heart and forgo me this dance?" Gavin said with a mock frown.

"Oh no," Roszalia said, as she smiled and curtsied back. "It would be my pleasure." Gavin took her small hands and as the next waltz began, he swirled her around the hall. Roszalia kept up fine, her mother had taught her all the finer dances and manners for her to one day be accepted in society. As she faced

Gavin, he was smiling.

"I hope you are feeling a wee bit better about being here, and I am sorry for the earlier events with my brother. We are not all cads, but now lass," he said, bowing low and doing his best dandy impression with a devilish grin. "I must attend the festivities and see whom my sister can throw at me." He rolled his eyes and gave an exaggerated groan. "No more lurking in shadows eh?" Gavin bowed and kissed her hand, turned, and strode off in the direction of the party.

Roszalia stood for a moment, her heart beating furiously, her skin tingled from the feel of his lips. At that moment, she knew she would never love another as she would this man.

Chapter Two

Gavin was home from months of travel at sea. William O'Connor had relinquished the shipping trade to his eldest son, taking great pride in Gavin's sharp business sense and negotiation abilities. He was often gone for weeks or even months at a time, and each time Roszalia would anxiously await his return.

She was now in her eighteenth year. The children's governess had taken ill and could no longer stay at the estate. Roszalia enthusiastically accepted the position when Caitlin asked her and told her there was no other candidate that she would even consider filling the position.

Most of her time was spent with the children on their lessons, and when she was not with them, she was helping her aunt with chores. Men from town would come to call on her from time to time, or an old friend from her youth attempted to court her, but she always politely refused their attentions. Most women her age were married with children of their own. It did not matter to her; there was only one man in her heart. Taking extra care in her appearance today, she brushed her dark hair until it shined. Choosing a deep blue skirt and over blouse of matching color, she tied her long silken mane up in a bun securing it in a tortoise shell comb. Now ready for the day, and hopefully an encounter with Gavin, she headed down the stairs from her quarters to the large laundry area where her aunt was speaking with one of the maids folding the fresh linens and towels.

Truda gave her a warm smile. "Roszalia child, please gather the towels for Master Devon and Gavin's rooms. I am helping Rosa today but I did not have a chance to place fresh ones in their chambers, and the chambermaids have taken the linens to the other wing. The masters have already gone out, so you may place them on the wash stands."

Roszalia's face fell and her carefree mood felt heavy. How could she have missed him, it was not yet breakfast, where had he gone so early? Containing her disappointment as best she could, she gave a soft sigh and nodded.

"Yes Aunt Truda, I will take care of the linens." Hesitating but needing to know she asked, "Did you by chance overhear when Gavin would return?"

Truda had known Roszalia was infatuated with the eldest son for some time, and she gave her niece a look and a friendly warning. "Roszalia, child, you speak with too much familiarity of Master Gavin. Take heed, a heart is a fragile thing." Truda was thinking of her sister, Roszalia's mother, and how much pain she had been through by falling in love out of her class.

Still feeling forlorn, Roszalia assured her aunt that she knew her place and carried the large pile of fresh towels up the stairs to the east wing where Gavin and Devon's quarters were. The children did not have lessons today, so she had time to help her aunt. Although Devon was out in the stables, she did not dally in his quarters. In the event he returned unexpectedly, she left the door open while she placed the towels on his washstand and straightened the pillows on the divan, then left closing the door. She crossed the hall, opened the massive oak door to Gavin's quarters, and stepped inside. This time she gently closed it behind her. Roszalia stood for a moment taking in his room, breathing in deeply, inhaling his scent. Walking over to the washstand, she placed the clean towels next to it. Gavin's large four-poster bed was across the room from where she stood, a warm blush rose to her cheeks as she imagined him lying in it.

On an impulse, she picked up Gavin's tortoise handle brush and took the dark strands of his hair from its bristles stuffing them in her apron pocket, then ran her fingers lightly over his shaving instruments. So deep were her thoughts that she barely heard the handle of the heavy door turning. Panicking, she quickly hid behind the heavy drapes next to his wardrobe. Gavin swung the door open with ease, shutting it behind him, and then headed towards his dresser.

Gavin's chiseled features and deep tanned skin only added to his rugged good looks. Undoing the buttons and removing his sweat–drenched shirt, he threw it over a chair. His bare chest revealed dark, crisp curls spiraling down to his navel. He had been out for a morning ride on his favorite stallion, Samson. The sweat glistened in his hair and a damp lock fell into his amber eyes, he absently ran his fingers through it to put it in place.

Roszalia caught her breath. She had to stop herself from groaning at the sight of his handsome physique. Now only clad in his leather breeches and riding boots, she marveled at his broad shoulders and well–muscled abdomen. Her eyes followed down to his narrow hips and his muscular thighs. Blushing, she thought of how she wanted to feel his body under her touch. She felt ashamed, she knew she should not watch him disrobe, yet she could not look away.

As Gavin pulled off the second boot, a rustle behind the drapes caught his eye. He saw small feet behind the material, then noted the fresh linens next to the washstand and whiffed a slight lavender scent in his room, Roszalia's scent. Amused that she was watching him undress, he inwardly smiled. Then the thought that had been plaguing him resurfaced. Lately every time he returned to the Big House, he was seeking her company, even just to gaze upon her. With this thought, another feeling began to stir in his loins, one that he did not think she should witness. Standing up, he cleared his throat then said absently as if to the air,

"Shall I finish removing my trousers or shall I wait until I am alone in my room?" He turned and stood facing where she hid. Roszalia realized Gavin had spotted her. Humiliated, he knew she had watched him disrobe, and now stood in front of her, picturesque in only tight breeches. She came out from behind the drape, averting her eyes from him. She began to stammer an explanation, sounding foolish to her own ears,

"Gavin, I was... that is, the children do not have lessons this morning, and I was speaking to Truda, she was busy so I told her I would help put fresh towels on your wash stand. When I heard someone coming, and…"

He put his hand up to stop her. He had made the poor girl suffer enough. "Do not fret, no harm done, but another moment and I fear you would have seen more of me than either of us had intended. Then, I would be the one to blush."

He smiled and came towards her. Instinctively she backed up as if an electric current was in the air between them. She could not handle him so close and revealed. She suddenly felt she needed to leave before events took a turn.

Gavin too sensed the sexual tension between them and backed up, the smell of lavender and the mahogany lights that seemed to dance in her hair were intoxicating. Feeling his desire begin to arouse, it was all he could do to keep from grabbing this girl and kissing her right there. How had he not noticed just how beautiful she was? He ran his fingers through his hair and then moved to open the door. In a voice a bit too harsh, trying to mask the lust in it, he cleared his throat once more and said,

"I must finish dressing for breakfast, please excuse me." Roszalia nodded and scurried out and down the hall that lead to the servants' level, only stopping when she reached the stairs. She sunk against the wall, her legs were weak, and her eyes stung from the tears that threatened to fall. She felt cursed for loving him and even worse for being such a coward and not letting him know her feelings. Roszalia knew she could never be more than his mistress, but for her, that would be enough. She mounted the narrow stairs to her quarters where she removed her good dress and put on her daily attire. She would not impress anyone today.

Closing his door he thought how she affected him. Her scent drove him mad, and the desire to hold her, stroke her hair, kiss her ruby lips and make her his was almost unbearable. He had thought of her far too often on his voyages. He did not care that she was employed by his family. Never being one for peerage. This morning he had ridden early, in hopes he could clear his head. His father was not well, and his sister was pressuring him to stay at the estate more to tend to events that he would need to know about when he took over the running of it. Being tied to one place was something he did not relish. The adventure of sailing was in his blood. Yet, the thought of his brother running the estate was unimaginable. Devon with his gambling, women, and drink would ruin the name O'Connor and all who held it. He could never allow that to be placed upon his father or his mother's memory.

Then the thought of gazing upon Roszalia everyday crept into his mind, and it made his imminent duties seem tolerable. Gavin shaved and dressed, as he opened his door, his brother stood in front of him in the hall. Devon was the last person Gavin wanted to see right now.

"Well, well. The favored son has returned. I saw the gypsy wench leaving your room, I must admit I didn't think you would have her first, but then you are always first, eh brother?" Devon said, his voice dripping with sarcasm and his steel grey eyes held his resentment.

"What do you want Devon?" Gavin was exasperated with his brother's endless jealousy.

"Want from you? Nothing, however, I could not resist watching as the wench scurried out of your room. I noticed she was not smiling. Disappointed her maybe?" With that comment, Devon turned and walked away. Roszalia had been at the foot of the stairs and heard Devon's comment. She decided to wait before entering the hall and avoid both of the brothers.

Gavin purposely lagged behind, hoping he would meet Roszalia coming down from the third level. As he passed the stairs and she was not there, he headed for the dining room and told himself he would ask her to ride this afternoon with him.

The previous evening, Caitlin had told her she would get the children ready and down for their early meal herself in the morning. She was feeling rested and wanted to spend time with them. Roszalia breathed a sigh of relief as she remembered this. Due to her delay in Gavin's room, she was late and the servants had already begun preparing the family's morning meal. Hurrying into the kitchen, her aunt gave her a scolding look,

"Goodness child where have you been, we have finished breakfast long ago." She shook her head at her niece's folly. However, this morning she could not concentrate on her duties, her mind jumping to the image in her head of Gavin clad only in his breaches. Thoughts of him were none the innocent, but she did not care. She purposely stayed in the kitchen hoping that she might see him again this morning. He sometimes came into the kitchen to talk to the help after his meal or to escape the chatter of the family at the morning table. Gavin did as he pleased and was never formal about his friendship with the staff. However, Roszalia wished it were possible for much more than his friendship…she ached for his love.

Gavin's entered the large dining room on the other side of the swinging door to the kitchen. He headed towards his sister and gave her a morning kiss on the top of her head. Although he was only four years her senior, he had always felt protective of his younger sister. He was there during her first riding lessons, worried and watchful that she did not fall. He would carefully scrutinize the fellows that would come to court her. He was so very proud of the woman Caitlin had become. Even through the difficult weeks after their mother passed, knowing it was often stressful keeping everything at the estate running smoothly, she never complained. "Good morning, dear sister," he then went to each of the children and gave them a hug. "And who will be up for a ride today with me?" Gavin winked at Caitlin already knowing the answer.

"I will uncle Gavin!" chimed Edward.

"Me too, can we go to the open fields and pond today please?" little Samantha pleaded. Gavin pretended to think about the child's question, then, with a wide grin said,

"Well why not, we will take a picnic. I would like to invite Roszalia along if you two agree?"

"Oh yes," both children said in unison. They began to chatter about the day ahead and forgot their uncle was behind them.

Caitlin gave Gavin a smile and said, "What an excellent idea, I do believe that poor girl does nothing but work, she needs to have some fun and explore the countryside. Now children settle down, your grandfather will be here any moment and then you may eat." Gavin noticed Devon was not present, he briefly wondered where he had gone after the meeting outside of his room, but decided it was much too peaceful to ask, lest he would be summoned. He sat next to his sister and scooped a generous helping of eggs and toast onto his plate. Feeling good, he would ask Roszalia to a picnic today.

Overhearing the conversation from the kitchen door, Roszalia's heart fluttered, a picnic with Gavin, she could barely swallow when she heard. She quickly washed her food down with a glass of milk, hugged her bewildered aunt, and took off to her room with a skip to wait for her invitation to the outing. She would feign surprise, but she would be ready.

William O'Connor entered the dining room and said his good mornings to all. Noting Devon's absence, he had become much more secretive, unruly, and headstrong as of late. Devon's questionable acquaintances were getting him an unsavory reputation. Although both his sons were now adult men, William did not want this taint to the O'Connor family good name. He made a mental note to have a long talk with his son, and with this in his mind, he took his seat at the head of the table.

"Ah, another fine day! Gavin, will you be accompanying me on my trip into Tralee today? I must speak with Barrister Ausby. I thought we might take care of some business at the same time." William had asked before he stuffed a fork full of sausage in his mouth. He noticed a change in Gavin's disposition. This was not like his eldest to hesitate on a trip to Tralee he thought.

"Father, of course if you need me to accompany you, I will." His plans to spend the afternoon with the children, and yes, Roszalia, would have to be canceled. *Foolish*, he thought. It was only a ride.

"But Uncle Gavin," Edward whined, "You promised to take us on a ride today."

"And a picnic!" Elizabeth chimed in.

William O'Connor looked at the two stricken faces of his beloved grandchildren and turned to Gavin. This, he was sure, was not the only reason for Gavin's hesitant behavior and sudden downtrodden attitude. "I will go to town and take Devon, perfect opportunity to have a discussion on his behavior of late."

"Father," Gavin began, but his father put up his hand.

"No more said, you will take these poor children on their picnic, and will there be anyone else going?" Gavin looked up in surprise at the small smile behind his father's remark.

Before he could speak, the children both sang out, "Roszalia is going with us!"

William raised an eyebrow and continued to pay extra interest to his food to hide his grin. Gavin wondered why this outing meant so much to him. Yes, he enjoyed Roszalia's company, and there was no denying she had become a beautiful woman, that set certain feelings off in him he could not yet admit. The children were hurrying through their meal so they could go to get their riding clothes on.

"May we go get ready?" they asked excitedly. "We will ask Roszalia to help us."

Caitlin, sensing the desire in her brother to make the invitation to Roszalia himself, dabbed her napkin to her lips. Pushing her chair back,

"Aye, children, but I will be the one helping with your clothes, let Uncle Gavin finish his meal and ask Roszalia to accompany you on your outing." Caitlin gave Gavin a sly smile and shooed the children up the stairs.

Barrister O'Connor noticing the exchanges of looks between the siblings cleared his throat, "My boy, Roszalia has become quite a young lady has she not?"

Gavin did not quite know where this conversation would take him, "Aye, father that she has," he quickly added, "and the children love her."

William raised an eyebrow as he wiped his chin, "Ah, the

children. And what of you?"

The bluntness of his father's question made Gavin uneasy. He shifted in his chair. "Father, I merely thought it was a good idea to have Roszalia along for the children if they needed her. I know there are no planned lessons on this Saturday, and according to Caitlin she does not go out much, I merely thought..."

His unfinished sentence was cut short with the banging of the dining room doors. Devon strode in, emitting a foul mood, his brooding scowl a warning to all that his action and heavy drinking the prior evening left him ill tempered. Gavin looked his way, his brother, and his blood. A wave of revulsion passed over him, he thought of how as children they were always at odds, Devon resented being second born, always trying to win his parents' favor. As they grew older, Devon's animosity seemed to escalate with every accomplishment Gavin achieved. They now barely spoke to each other, a strained tolerance of one another at best. Devon looked at his father and greeted him with a nod, then at his brother. The favored son, her snorted to himself, he did not remember at what point he began loathing his brother, possibly after Gavin's announcement that he was leaving the estate for the sea. His mother, whose health at the time was not at all good, seemed to decline further, she had never been the same after that. Although Devon tried, he could never forgive his older brother for the pain it caused their mother. He was close to her, but he could never fill the empty place in her heart she kept for her eldest son. For this, he had a profound resentment for his sibling. Devon brushed by and sat down heavily in his chair.

"Good, Devon, you have awoken," William O'Connor said. "You will accompany me to Barrister Ausby this day." Devon never looked up, with his anger sparking he began devouring the meal that had been placed in front of him.

"And what of my brother, is he not so privileged as to ride to town?" He was barely able to hold the contempt in his voice for having to trek to town to meet with some stuffy lawyer while his brother is allowed to leisurely do as he pleases.

William finally lost his good humor at his son's last callous remark. "Devon, enough!" pushing his chair back with such force that the heavy wooden frame screeched against the smooth flagstone tiles sending it backwards. Only in a swift reflex did it recover from its fate of lying on the floor. Placing both palms on the table, he leaned in and glared at his youngest son. "You will be ready within the hour to leave, we have much to discuss!" The older man, never waiting for a reply, nor looking in Gavin's direction, headed for the main foyer and the library.

Gavin studied his brother, apparently not bothered by the event. He decided it would be to no avail to press the subject of respect for their father. Gavin rose, pushed in his chair, and left the room. Anxious to talk to Roszalia before her plans for the day were made. The thought of her made his step a bit lighter and he began to feel his jaw relax from the recent scene with his father and brother.

Roszalia had been in her room deciding which riding outfit was appropriate for the picnic. She did not want to seem like she had dressed for Gavin, but she also wanted to impress him, show this man that she had indeed become a woman. She brushed through her closet. Caitlin was always giving her clothing. She said that she would see it in one of the stores in town and just knew her friend would look stunning in it and could not resist. A burgundy velvet–riding coat and skirt had suddenly appeared one afternoon on her bed after her friend had been the city and the new boutiques. The material was exquisite and the cut was perfect for Roszalia's figure. Although she protested, Caitlin would not take it back, saying, "You will hurt my feelings if you do not accept this as a gift. I loved it, but the burgundy is just not my color, and winked." Roszalia knew she purchased it especially for her due to the fact that Caitlin was at least half a foot taller than she was.

Caitlin had become protective of her after the incident with Devon, and over the years the two women became close friends. Caitlin always marveled at Roszalia abundance of knowledge, from books, life, and some experiences that could never be explained.

Roszalia wondered if the outfit would be too much for their

outing, after all, it was a picnic. Perhaps the tweed would be more appropriate. Her thoughts were so intense she barely heard the knock. Her heart racing with anticipation, she hurried to open the door expecting to see Gavin. Samantha and Edward met her instead. They began to speak excitedly at the same time. Smiling at the children's enthusiasm, she told them to catch their breath as they entered her room.

"Now, tell me one at a time, what is all this about?" already knowing what they were going to ask but she did not want to dampen the excitement of telling her about the picnic.

Edward spoke up first, "Roszalia, we are going on a picnic with Uncle Gavin, and he is going to ask you too!" Elizabeth took her hand and said in her sweet young voice. "Please come with us."

Caitlin arrived, slightly winded from trying to catch up with the children. "I am so sorry, Gavin will be furious we spoiled his surprise for you, he is still with father and will be on his way to ask you himself." Caitlin shrugged her shoulder with a sheepish grin, "But there is no containing these two when they are excited!" Giving her friend a smile, she began to usher the youngsters out the door.

"Children let's leave so Uncle Gavin can pretend he was the one to invite Roszalia on your ride."

Samantha and Edward gave her a pleading look, "You will come with us?"

"Of course, but do not tell your uncle. We will let him think he asked first, all right you two?" She gave them each a quick hug, then looked at her friend, "I will be down momentarily to help get the children dressed for the outing...." Caitlin cut her sentence short, "My goodness! Take a moment for yourself, we will manage." Caitlin laughed then gave an exaggerated sigh looking as her children hurry down the hall.

"And off I go." She hesitated, "You really should wear the new riding outfit I gave you, the burgundy velvet one?" She winked at her friend, "No man, even my stuffy brother could resist you in that!"

"Caitlin, I am going on a picnic, not a rendezvous. You know

Gavin thinks no more of me than the children's governess," Roszalia objected, as a blush rose in her cheeks. Caitlin's smile widened at her friend's protest.

"We will see, but I do not think that is all he thinks when he sees you as of late." With that, she hugged her friend and hurried off in chase of the children.

Roszalia closed the door and began to unbutton her smock, when she heard a rap at the door. Thinking Caitlin had more suggestions on her attire for today, she did not ask who was there. Opening the door with her friend's name on her lips, she stood stunned for a moment as she looked at Gavin's handsome figure standing at the threshold.

"Roszalia, I am glad you are here, I want to ask you," he paused, "that is, if you do not have other arrangements today, to accompany me and the children on an outing, a picnic by the pond." Gavin could not believe he was actually nervous, his palms were sweating, and his words sounded rehearsed in his ears. He soaked in her hair and eyes and noticed the buttons on her blouse were undone, revealing soft skin. He shifted his weight as an uncomfortable feeling began, willing himself to think of the upcoming picnic.

Roszalia noticed his eyes travel to her bodice, feeling self–conscious she wanted to reach up and clutch the open cloth that was revealing a bit too much. Yet also feeling excited that he had noticed and wanted him to see her as a woman. Gaining a bit of composure, she moved from the door and said,

"I would love to accompany you and the children today." She smiled, hoping he would not notice the loud beating of her heart. Surely, he could hear it. Turning quickly she fastened her buttons, "I will be down to pack us lunch as soon as I am dressed."

Gavin, not ready to remove his gaze from her at this point, leaned against the door jam. "Not to worry, I have just come from the kitchen and asked the cook to fix a basket. As soon as you are ready, we will meet you at the stables. I will make sure the horses are saddled up." Roszalia turned, expecting to see him retreating from her doorway but was instead gazing into his magnificent eyes. They locked gazes for what seemed an eternity. Gavin cleared his throat to break the tension,

"Excellent, I will go now to let Caitlin and the children know you will be joining us."

With a sheepish grin, Roszalia confessed. "Gavin, please do not be cross with Edward and Samantha, but I am afraid they ruined your surprise." He looked at her with confusion. "They came to me only moments before you arrived at my door and told me of a plan for a picnic." She did not mention she had overheard him when he was in the dining room. "I am sorry, but they were so excited." Gavin gave a chuckle.

"I should have known, they put me on the spot for naught, rascals." He paused and with an earnest tone added, "But I am glad I had this time to see you alone." His eyes unconsciously traveled to her now covered neckline. Roszalia excited and wanting to hurry and get dressed said,

"Excuse me now, I must get dressed. I will meet you and the children in the stables." Gavin turned to leave as Roszalia touched his arm sending a warm, pleasant shock through him. "Thank you Gavin, for inviting me to join you." He nodded, not trusting his voice with the intense emotion he was feeling. After he left, she gently closed the door and leaned against it. *Oh yes, the velvet outfit it shall be today,* she thought with a smile.

CHAPTER THREE

It was a glorious fall morning as Roszalia headed out to the stables. The sounds of laughter as she approached the gate, told her the children were already inside. As she entered, Gavin was helping Samantha up onto her horse. She was a small gentle mare that Samantha had named Polka Dot. Edward was already mounted and fidgeting in his saddle as the groom held the reins so the boy did not take off without the others.

Gavin's gaze traveled towards Roszalia, he took in her beauty with appreciation. The deep color of the outfit she wore enhanced her hazel eyes and reflected mahogany highlights in her dark hair, which she had neatly tied back with a black ribbon. A few tendrils had escaped and framed her face in perfection.

Samantha was impatient to be on their way and brought him back in focus when she said, "Uncle Gavin are we ready to go?" Then as the child noticed Roszalia and she declared, "Oh, Roszalia you look so beautiful!" Gavin turned and faced her.

"Indeed she does," then added quietly looking directly in her eyes, "I would say breathtaking." Edward began to fidget again as his horse neighed in response. When Roszalia's horse was brought from her stall, she resisted and whinnied and stomped, then quieted down when she saw her rider. Reaching and stroking the mare's neck, Roszalia was glad to have a distraction from Gavin's gaze. "There is my beautiful Gypsy," she cooed, "ready for a ride girl?" The mare raised her head and whinnied her approval.

Barrister O'Connor gave Gypsy to Roszalia after the foal's mother had died giving birth. Roszalia insisted she could bottle nurse the animal and keep her alive. She would spend as much time with the foal as she could and even slept with her in the stall for the first few days of her existence. Her persistence and nurturing had worked, and soon the foal was able to stand and gain strength. Now two years old, the horse was a superb equestrian specimen. The mare was buff in color with a dark patch on her chest. Roszalia had named her Gypsy, for she felt a kindred bond that they both lost their parent and were survivors.

Roszalia was facing her horse, waiting for the groom to give her a boost, when she felt a strong arm lift her around the waist onto her mount. A small shock shot through her at Gavin's touch and she murmured,

"Thank you." Sounding flustered.

"Believe me, it is my pleasure," he said with a smile on his face, he thought how much he wanted to hold her. Turning abruptly and mounting his horse Samson, they exited the stable with Gavin in the lead.

When they passed the fenced area, Edward took off in a gallop with Samantha close behind. Both children had ridden since they could walk and were capable riders, their horses' gentle natures would not allow any trouble to befall them.

Gavin yelled to the children to stay in sight and then he turned his attention to Roszalia. She was smiling at him, and this made his heart leap. She rode astride as well as any man he knew, but today she sat sidesaddle in her riding outfit, her long legs outlined beneath her skirts. Her high black leather riding boots brought the vision to mind of earlier seeing her feet behind his curtain. The day was perfect for a ride, and the horses were content to enjoy the lazy pace. The children had circled back to them asking if they could go ahead to the pond.

"Of Course, we will follow shortly," Gavin replied with enthusiasm, and then adding as he turned his attention back to Roszalia, "that would be a perfect spot. We could spread a blanket under the oaks not far from the pond."

From the place that they chose for their picnic the water's surface glisten in the sun, reflecting the fall leaves that were turning red and gold. Gliding gracefully on top, were two snowy white swans. Gavin dismounted easily and reached for Gypsy's reins. At that same moment, a small fox darted out of its hole under the oak and spooked the mare. Rearing in fright, Roszalia grabbed her mane to try to regain her balance. The horse bolted forward heading towards the pond at lightning speed. Gavin reacted instantly. Remounting Samson, he took flight in chase of the frightened mare. Roszalia, unable to calm or stop her horse, held fast as she neared the edge of the pond. Gypsy suddenly came to a halt, bucking her rider off and landing her with a splash in the once serene water.

Gavin reached her, and the children, already playing near the pond rushed over. He told them to grab Gypsy's reins and take her and Sampson back to the tree. Roszalia sat in the shallow water soaked and muddy, her hair dripping, and her clothes wet. The look of surprise and shock on her features was too much for Gavin and unwillingly he burst into deep resonant laughter. Roszalia tried to get up only to slide on the murky bottom and splash once more, eliciting an angry yelp. Seeing the dismayed look on her face, he calmed his laughter. She looked helpless and so beautiful at the moment,

"Here, please, I am so sorry for my jovial behavior, but you do look quite a fetching damsel in distress." His broad smile warmed Roszalia until she too finally laughed.

"A gentleman would be helping a damsel in distress!" She was trying to look distressed, but the humor of the situation made her only smile. She extended her hand and Gavin reached towards it. He stepped to the edge of the pond to lift her out, when the slick mud under his own feet gave way, landing him upon Roszalia, both splashing back into the water. Samantha and Edward, witnessing this, burst in childish glee at the antics of the adults. Both Gavin and Roszalia were sputtering and laughing from the water they inhaled. Finally getting his footing, he lifted her in his arms, carrying her out of the water and setting her down on the grass.

Although the day was sunny, the autumn air was chilly enough to make her shiver. Shedding her wet riding jacket, she began the futile effort to wring the garment out, then laying it flat, in the hope that the sun would dry her clothes quickly. She looked up and a blush filled her face as she realized Gavin was staring at her. Her sheer blouse, now wet clung to her body and her chemise beneath did little to hide her exposed figure. Gavin, noticing her discomfort and glad to be distracted from her beauty, headed towards Samson to retrieve a blanket from his saddlebag. Somewhat reluctantly, he placed it over her shoulders. He removed his own jacket and also laid it out to dry, his white linen shirt had partially opened, and his tight riding pants, now wet seemed to mold to his skin. Roszalia could not help but marvel at his physique, and she had to pry her attention away. She was glad for the distraction as Edward and Samantha came running over to them. Both began speaking at once. Roszalia trying to make light of the embarrassing situation, retrieved the picnic lunch that had been prepared for them earlier.

"Well, now that your uncle and I have had our swim, let us see what we have in our basket." Roszalia busied herself spreading the picnic cloth on the ground under the tree and placing the food on the plates. The children once again ran off and Gavin untethered the horses to let them graze. The midday sun was still strong, and it began to dry their clothing. Gavin stood watching as she moved with grace, marveling how her attire accentuated her slender waist and curves to perfection.

He felt a bead of sweat run down his temple, he knew it was more from the emotions he felt looking at this beautiful woman than the sun. Suddenly feeling the need to be busy and put his mind on a task.

"Please, let me help," He unwrapped the cheese from its cloth and set it on the board next to the bread she had just set down.

"Gavin, perhaps you could gather the children while I put the meal out." He sensed she was uncomfortable that he was so close to her. He stood, and in an elaborate mock bow said, "As you wish milady, but I shall not go near the pond!" His grin widened as he heard her laughter and headed in the direction of the children.

Roszalia wiped her brow as she stared at Gavin retreating. She could see his broad shoulders, the heat rose in her cheeks as she remembered seeing him partially unclothed earlier and her heart racing as he fell upon her in the pond.

They sat on the ground and ate bread with cheese and meat slices. The children ate a morsel, and then they were off for more play. Gavin went to check on the horses, and Roszalia wrapped the remaining food and put it back in the basket. He returned to her with a bottle of wine he had put in his bag before they left along with two carefully wrapped glasses.

"To celebrate." He said as he filled them. He was pleased with her surprised reaction to his gesture.

"And just what are we celebrating?" she asked with an arched brow.

"We could celebrate that we did not drowned in the pond." He winked at her, and she frowned back. "Or perhaps..." he said softly as he took a step closer to her. She could feel the heat rise between their bodies. Touching her glass with his own, he looked deep into her eyes, "A perfect afternoon with a beautiful woman."

His hand reached to touch her hair, she felt the electric shock run through her. Could she be dreaming? She was here, soaking wet with the man she had always loved, and he just told her he thought she was beautiful. The world froze as Gavin bent to brush her lips with a kiss.

"Roszalia, Uncle Gavin!" a child's excited voice broke the moment. They quickly parted and Roszalia turned her attention to the children. Gavin's fingers still burned from where they touched her soft damp hair, he watched as they took Roszalia's hand and dragged her into their play. She gave him a glance and a timid smile, one that he returned.

The day had passed too quickly and the sky had begun to

cloud over. Samantha was sleepy, and Gavin decided that she would ride back with him on Samson. Roszalia kept hold of her horse while Edward took the lead on the return trip to the estate. They rode home slowly, all content with the wonderful outing they had, and as they reached the stables, Gavin saw his first mate Karl on the back steps. Karl did not often visit the estate unless something was amiss at the shipyard. Roszalia saw him also and sighed, she knew the man she loved would be leaving again soon.

CHAPTER FOUR

This year it seemed the autumn season had been brief and the briskness of winter was upon them. Today Truda and Roszalia were taking a trip to Dingle Harbor town to purchase supplies for the upcoming holidays. Donning a black wool skirt and a thick white cotton blouse, Roszalia quickly tied her long hair back in a bright blue scarf and headed down the steps to the children's quarters to ready them for the morning meal. She had been at the O'Connor Estate for almost five years. She cherished her days spent as the children's governess, and her friendship with Caitlin. However, this week, Andrew, Caitlin's husband was back from his work in Tralee, he had been gone exceptionally long this time. He loved his family and missed them while away, so the times they spent together were precious to them all. While Andrew was home at the estate, the family spent every moment possible together. Roszalia took these opportunities, when the children did not need her there, to help her aunt with errands and visit friends and family. The children were up, dressed, and ready to descend to the dining room for their morning meal when Caitlin came into their rooms.

"Come children, your father is waiting," she said with a smile. "Do try to have some fun this week my friend."

Edward took hold of Samantha's hand and walked ahead of their mother. Roszalia smiled and marveled at the love that Caitlin had for everyone, then went to her room to retrieve her wool cape, and sought out her aunt.

It had been a long time since Roszalia had been to town and today she would visit the apothecary on Strand Street and her Aunt Agnes. When her mother was young, she would spend as much time as she could with her aunt, learning the 'craft.' Agnes knew every herb combination to create any remedy or relief for illness. When Roszalia was a child, her mother would take her to visit. She remembered spending hours, sometimes even days, at her aunt's home. There, she learned to read and write. She learned the intricate art of healing medicines: the strengths that could cure, alleviate pain, or even kill if overdone. Her aunt had told her since she was a child she would need to have these skills throughout her life.

Agnes would tell Roszalia she had the gift of healing, and 'the sight' and would one day be an influential woman. She would shrug and say, "It is your destiny, as it is mine."

It had been far too long since her last visit, her aunt was what the people in the gypsy camps called a healer or a visionary. The town people called her a fortuneteller, but they all sought her out for her good luck charms and remedies. The apothecary was a thriving business with both commoners and aristocrats alike seeking her cures. The carriage approached the shops and stopped. Roszalia stepped from the buggy onto the cobblestones.

"I will meet you in the mercantile in a few hours, I am going to visit Agnes." Truda gave her niece a smile,

"Give Agnes my regrets, but there is so much to purchase for the holidays. A visit can be planned another day." Then Truda told the driver to continue to the livery stables.

Roszalia stood for a moment watching the retreating carriage, the intoxicating aroma of warm cinnamon buns enticed her from behind the door to the bakery. As she entered, two women chatting brushed past her. The shorter of the two gave her a contemptuous look, with her nose in the air remarked to her companion, just loud enough for her to hear.

"Isn't that the O'Connor gypsy? I don't see what the brothers see in her!" Both women laughed in her direction as they entered an extremely expensive boutique. She recognized the other blonde woman to be Vanessa Burke. She had been present at most of the parties that the O'Connor family hosted since the time she had been there. In year's past, Vanessa and her father, Barrister Burke, a dear friend and prior college roommate of William, had privately dined at the estate. She remembered Vanessa all but threw herself at Gavin. Caitlin brought the children in that evening to eat in the kitchen since they had guests. Roszalia smiled when her friend waved her hands saying she wished she could stay with them and she could barely tolerate that woman's offensive behavior. Gavin did not seem overly interested in this woman. Nevertheless, Roszalia knew the Vanessa was an excellent social match and her father would like nothing more than have his daughter wed one of the O'Connor brothers.

When Roszalia brought the children in to say goodnight to their mother and grandfather, Vanessa noticed Gavin watching her intensely. Furious that a servant could overshadow her, she moved closer to touch his arm, all the while keeping her eye on the dark haired woman. Gavin purposely stood up with the excuse to get another drink, dislodging her fingers. As he passed Roszalia, he smiled and said,

"I hope these two are not giving you any trouble this evening?" Playfully tussling his nephew's hair, yet never taking his eyes from Roszalia. As always when Gavin was near, she smiled and hoped he could not hear the loud beating of her heart.

"Of course not, these two are perfect angels." At this, Gavin laughed, and then returned to the table.

"Vanessa, Barrister Burke, It was my pleasure to dine with you this evening, but I must take my leave." He nodded to his father and sister. Vanessa looked as if struck that Gavin was leaving her. Caitlin seeing her face chimed in with a laugh to break the tension,

"Yes, you go do... whatever you men do. Vanessa and I shall

go into the parlor, and perhaps she can play father and I one of her wonderful rendition on the piano." At this, Vanessa's look changed, the attention was once again focused on her, and she all but forgot Gavin was still in the room.

The woman's laughter brought Roszalia's mind back from the past. She was used to sharp words from being from the camps. Deciding it was not worth ruining her outing, she shrugged it off and proceeded to enter the bakery to make her purchase and be on her way to her aunt's shop further down the street. The bell jangled on the door to the Apothecary shop as Roszalia opened it. Rich teak and mahogany gleamed all around, and her senses were overwhelmed with the familiar scents of comfrey, sandalwood, lavender soaps, and many other aromatic scents she knew so well. Large glass jars lined the isles containing crushed or powdered herbs and mixtures, the shelves housed different scented soaps, lotions, oils, and towards the back was Agnes's distinct selection for the wealthy patrons. Within a large glass case were an array of imported perfumes and glass atomizers to entice a woman of any class.

"Goodness," Agnes burst out in her native Hungarian tongue when she caught a glimpse of Roszalia. She was working with a new girl from the camp that had come to her asking to learn the art of the healing herbs. Her aunt quickly came forward from the back of the store. Roszalia admiring a bottle of lavender oil looked up and smiled broadly. The two women met each other with a warm hug. Roszalia as always marveled at how her aunt never seemed ageless, always full of energy and spirit. Agnes backed up scrutinizing the girl that stood in front of her.

"My, you are more beautiful every time I see you, it has been too long. An old woman misses her family." Roszalia was at least four inches taller than the woman in front of her.

"Yes, I am sorry to say, it has been months since I have been in town. I keep very busy at the estate with the children." The older woman took her niece's hand and led her back to the small sitting room where she had just brewed a pot of chamomile tea. As she passed, Helena, her new assistant, stood in the doorway,

Agnes introduced her to her niece.

The girl smiled, and then began speaking in Hungarian, "I have heard so much about you from Agnes and friends from camp... and finally we meet."

"Truda told me that Agnes had found an apprentice. I am so glad. I know you will love the craft." Roszalia replied. Helena's cold eyes gave Roszalia the feeling that she was anything but pleased to meet her. The bell sounded again and Helena excused herself saying in a cold tone, "I am sure we will meet again."

Agnes felt the tension between the two. She knew that Helena was very jealous of her niece, for this girl had wanted to be an apprentice for many years, but Agnes held many secrets that only family would ever know.

"Sit, sit, have some tea and baklava," she said, pointing to the pastry on the table. Roszalia placed the cinnamon rolls she had purchased at the bakery next to them, then sat in one of the stuffed chairs, as she had so many times before in her youth. Agnes had always hoped Roszalia would follow in her calling and come to be an apprentice at her shop. She had the gift of healing, premonition, and many others that her niece had not yet discovered. Soon after Roszalia's mother died, she had a vision that her niece's destiny was in another direction, and she worried that the end would not be good. As she set her china cup down she asked, "So how is your young man?"

Roszalia looked up quickly, knowing that she could not hide her emotions from Agnes she sighed, "I have no man in my life right now."

Agnes came to sit in the chair beside her and looked her in the eyes. "Ah, still denying your feelings to yourself, but you cannot fool me child. All right then, how is Gavin?"

Roszalia, in mock despair, threw up her hands but smiled at her aunt. "Agnes, does it ever get tiring of knowing people's thoughts? Gavin is doing well. He is out to sea again."

"And the troubled one, Devon?" Agnes gave a scowl, for she knew dark things about this man that no one else could, especially concerning her niece.

Roszalia averted her eyes, "He has been," she hesitated,

"civil lately. There was another incident a while back, luckily Gavin was at the residence and had intervened."

"Ah, perhaps these events happen because of two men…brothers with jealous hearts?"

Roszalia looked at Agnes, she had never even thought that way, and she said a bit too defensively,

"No, I am sure you are wrong, Gavin does not have those feelings for me, and he is a gentleman and would do the same for any maiden whom Devon disrespects."

Agnes took a sip of her tea and said off offhandedly, smiling in her cup, "Yes, you may be right, but you are not just any maiden. He does not admit he has these feelings for you, but he will." Taking Roszalia's hands, her aunt looked deep into her eyes. "Take heed child, follow your heart not what seems to be so, I see many disturbances ahead." Agnes just as quickly changed the subject to the upcoming holiday event. Roszalia was grateful that her aunt did not continue. It made her un–comfortable speaking of Gavin and her feelings for him.

The two women chatted for the better part of two hours when she realized Truda must be finished with her shopping. They bid their farewells and they promised not to be apart for so long. As she was leaving, Agnes wrapped a bottle of lavender oil she had seen her niece looking at, and told her to give her love to Truda. Roszalia left with a carefree feeling and thought of what her aunt had said; *Follow your heart*. If only she could.

Upon exiting the shop, she saw a commotion down the street. Crossing to the opposite side, she could not see what or who was involved, but knew it was in front of the Harbour Bay Inn, or the 'gentleman's hotel' as the regulars called it. Although she never judged the women whose plight led them there, she kept her distance, for she knew that if not for her lucky situation at the O'Connor Estate she too might have had the same fate. As she passed, she heard the name Devon mentioned and hurried her pace. Not wanting to hear any more of their conversation. Roszalia found her aunt at the fabric mercantile. She was unde-cided on which material to purchase for the holiday table.

Her aunt looked up when she walked over. She was speaking

to a pretty woman at a counter while holding two fabric bolts. The woman spoke with a French accent.

"Pardon, I do not mean to interfere but I mentioned to your aunt, for a holiday table I would choose the gold brocade and accent with the crimson." The girl held the two fabrics up.

"Yes, I agree, excellent combination." The girl who appeared to be about her own age held her slender hand out with a smile.

"I am Desiree; I am the seamstress at Madame Cooper's boutique."

"Of course, Lady Caitlin speaks so highly of your designs. I am Roszalia, I…" her sentence was cut off by Desiree.

"Ah, you are the governess at the O'Connor Estate." Roszalia looked at her in question. "I have heard Lady Caitlin speak of you when she visits our shop." Desiree sensing that she had perhaps said too much wished them both a pleasant holiday and abruptly left the shop. Roszalia stood perplexed, why would Caitlin be speaking of her to the shop owner? She was getting a strange vibration from this girl, as if she had been waiting to meet her and noted that she left without any parcels. Her aunt broke her thought.

"What a lovely woman, and I have heard of her creations for the boutique. Madame Cooper was very lucky to have obtained her talents; I heard she came from Paris, where she was working as a seamstress for a very wealthy patron until tragedy struck." Roszalia watched from the large front window of the store as the woman continued down the road towards the dress shop.

"That is the last item on my list for today." Bringing her attention back to her aunt who looked fatigued from the day's outing. They were glad the bulk supplies were already loaded and could be on their way quickly. It was early afternoon and they would have just enough time to return before dark. Roszalia took the small packages from her aunt and carried them to the stables where their carriage awaited. As she passed she saw her aunt's two small mares, and they whinnied to her, she took a moment to go to them stroking their shiny manes.

"There are the beautiful ladies." She said in Hungarian, and offered them each a cube of sugar that she obtained from her aunts home. The attendant made sure all their packages were secured in the outside carrier for their return trip, then helped each in turn enter the cushioned interior. When they passed the street that Roszalia had avoided earlier, she saw Devon casually resting against the wall, one arm around a tall blonde woman. As he stroked her face, she smiled. The woman turned a bit and Roszalia recognized the profile to be that of Vanessa Burke. This was an extraordinarily bold gesture, even for Devon to be making towards the daughter of a barrister. She quickly sat back from the window, hoping Devon did not see her.

Roszalia shivered, not knowing if it was from the cold or her near encounter with Devon. Wrapping the shawl tighter, she forced herself to think of the upcoming holiday. This seemed to calm her mind and the fact that Gavin was due home to spend time with the family gave her a different sensation, and soon her thoughts of Devon and Vanessa vanished.

Devon had spent the previous night at the Harbor Bay Inn. The establishment was a place for travelers to stay, but was also well known for its generous hospitality by the women who worked there. As Devon departed the building, he spotted Roszalia and Truda leaving the livery stables. During this time, Vanessa Burke had also seen Devon. She headed towards him just as Roszalia was passing. Devon, not wanting to make a scene, decided to use Vanessa as a distraction. As soon as he saw Roszalia's carriage round the corner and head down the path out of town, his grey eyes turned to cold steel. Abruptly, he bid Vanessa a brisk goodbye and left the girl open mouthed at the side of the street. Devon thought as he strode away, Vanessa was a spoiled woman, but at times she serves his purpose well.

CHAPTER FIVE

The winter months had arrived and with them the excitement of the holiday festivities and Caitlin's legendary gatherings. Gavin was home…for a while, as he always put it, and to make the holiday perfect, Caitlin's husband Andrew had decided he would not be working at the Tralee hospital this holiday. He was missing too much of his children's youth and he realized the toll his constant absence was taking on his wife. This was the time of year that Roszalia and Truda would meet with Agnes, and they would visit friends and family at the camp. These celebrations meant food, music, dancing, and festivities into the early morning. Although she was looking forward to seeing her old friends, she was not disappointed when her aunt had come down with an illness that she felt she should just rest. Truda wanted her niece to go without her, but she decided she would tell Agnes they would visit another time. Roszalia secretly rejoiced at the change in plans. For, in her heart, she did not want to stray far from the estate in the hope she had the opportunity to visit with Gavin. Before she closed her door, she saw Caitlin coming down the hall, holding her skirts up as she hurried towards her. Roszalia had to smile to herself. Her friend was always exuberant in anything she did. Caitlin finally reached her, a bit winded from her dash; she stood for a moment to catch her breath.

"Roszalia, I spoke with Truda. She said you were planning on staying in this evening?" She hesitated only a moment and then, with a panicked look in her emerald eyes continued, "I am so sorry, I know you were most likely looking forward to a quiet evening, but I cannot seem to get everything done on time." She waved her hands again this time in exasperation.

Roszalia smiled at her friend and said, "Caitlin, you never get everything done because you try to do too much. Now catch your breath and tell me how I can help." Taking her friend's arm in hers, they headed towards the hall.

"I do not have time to dress the children. I told them you were busy and Marie, God love the little thing, has tried to help, but Samantha is up there crying that she will not come down to the party, and she has set Marie to crying herself!"

"Is that all? I would love to." Roszalia raised an eyebrow and laughed. "I will go see what I can do now, and do try to calm down and enjoy your party for once," she said, patting Caitlin's hand and in return received a hug.

"Oh yes," Caitlin smiled broadly and with a glint in her green eyes said, "By the way, my brother is looking for you." She gave her friend a wink. Roszalia smiled but said nothing; she headed for the children's room. She had known Caitlin wanted nothing more than her and Gavin to become more than friends but Roszalia always insisted that it was not acceptable. That she did not have those feelings for him. Yet she knew her friend could see through to her real feelings.

When she entered the rooms, she found Edward and Samantha fussing over the clothes their personal maid had set out for them to wear. When Samantha saw Roszalia, she ran to her and hugged her tightly. The children loved her and were glad she was their governess and friend. They liked her stylish clothing, hair ribbons she wore, the stories she told, and even the lessons she taught them. Roszalia would allow Samantha to try on her bracelets and scarves. She told them stories of the gypsies and faraway places and taught them the festive Hungarian dances she knew. Seeing the dismayed looks on their faces, she asked,

"Now children what is all the fuss about?" Edward, now in his ninth year rolled his eyes as he stated,

"We do not want to dress up for a stuffy, boring party."

Scrutinizing the outfits, she held each up to the children and shook her head, "Let me see if we cannot find something a little more fun. Would that be all right?" She began searching the contents of Edward's armoire. After a short time, Roszalia pulled a black pair of velvet trousers with a white ruffled shirt and a black vest out for him, along with his black riding boots.

The boy's eyes widened as he peered at his new outfit. He went to his room to dress in the new clothing. As he returned, he was beaming. "How do I look? I believe I resemble Uncle Gavin." Roszalia agreed he did indeed. "But I shall set sail as a pirate! I shall scour the seven seas!" He grabbed a red scarf and tied it around his waist, then attempted to scare his sister.

Samantha shook her head and with her hands on her hips said adamantly, "Uncle Gavin would never do those things! Or try to scare me!" Edward just shrugged and went off to look in his full–length mirror at his attire. Samantha looked at her pale gown and made a grimace. "If Edward looks like Uncle Gavin, can you make me look like you?"

Roszalia looked at the child surprised. "Like me? I think you need to be dressed as a princess!"

Samantha said in her child's innocent way. "To me you are a princess, a beautiful gypsy princess," at this the child twirled around. "Like in the stories you tell us. Please, may I pretend to be you tonight?"

Roszalia was flattered. "Well, of course you can. In fact, we will make you the prettiest gypsy princess in all of Ireland!" She found a crimson velvet skirt and a pretty lace blouse that was both festive and appropriate for the party. "Now let us go to my room, I am sure we can find some jewelry you can wear."

She took the child's hand and led her up the backset of steps that adjoined the children's rooms to her quarters. After rummaging through her dresser, she found a black silk scarf threaded with gold strands and took the gold and ruby hair combs from her own hair, allowing it to fall about her shoulders. After tying the sash in a big bow around her waist, she swept the child's long bronze curls up in a twist and held them in place with the jeweled combs.

When they went back down to the children's rooms, Roszalia found a pair of black, soft, leather slippers in the bottom of the wardrobe and added them to Samantha's outfit. Edward had come over and Roszalia stood up, facing them both, she gave an exaggerated curtsy and said, "Roszalia and Master Gavin, your party guests are waiting!" This set Samantha to smile and giggle, and she skipped off towards the mirror. The young girl ran back to Roszalia, face beaming, and hugged her. They both startled as a deep voice behind them laughed aloud. The young pirate, Edward, drew his make believe sword on the intruder in the doorway.

"Well, you two will indeed be the talk of the party," Gavin raised an eyebrow.

Roszalia began picking up the other articles of clothing that the children rejected, placing them back in the armoire. She could feel Gavin's stare, feeling the familiar heat rise and flush her cheeks. When Roszalia turned, he was looking at her, and their eyes locked.

Samantha ran to her uncle with a giggle in her voice. "Am I a beautiful gypsy princess uncle Gavin, I want to look like Roszalia." Never shifting his gaze from Roszalia, he answered softly, "Yes, very beautiful."

Her hair had fallen down around her shoulders when she removed her combs and the fading evening light gave it an auburn cast, *like the sunset,* he thought, *a gorgeous sunset*. She was beautiful. He forced himself to tear his gaze away, shifting attention to his niece and nephew.

"I was sent to get the young lady and gentleman of the house to meet the guests."

Edward gave a groan, "I would rather stay here with Roszalia." Gavin laughed and said a bit too huskily,

"As a matter of fact, I would rather do that too, but we must not disappoint your parents or grandfather. So let's move out or I'll make you walk the plank!" Gently prodding the children out the door towards the staircase, Gavin turned before he followed, "What are you doing this holiday night Roszalia?"

She stood in silent surprise, for Gavin had never asked what she was doing. She replied with a slightly unsteady voice, "I was to celebrate with Truda and Agnes, we were to visit friends at the camp, but Truda has taken ill. I told Caitlin since she will be attending to the party; I will help the children with bedtime preparations and tell Elizabeth a bedtime story." Gavin took a step closer to her. He could smell the lavender in her hair, and so desperately wanted to run his fingers through it.

"No, I mean you, not the children," his husky voice was silk to her ears. Just then, Samantha burst back in the room,

"Uncle Gavin, please be my prince tonight...please, Edward wanted to be a pirate, and I don't like pirates." She declared with a frown on her face while pulling his hand in the direction of the stairs. Gavin gave Roszalia a mock bow, which made her smile,

"Well, alas, duty calls. My petite gypsy princess awaits." He turned and took Samantha's hand to guide her to the holiday party below. Just before he exited the door in tow of his niece, he looked back,

"Please find time for one dance with me." Then added, "I will come find you tonight." Roszalia closed the door and sat at the edge of Samantha's bed. With flushed cheeks, she finally exhaled and repeated Gavin's words, "Save time for a dance."

In a sudden burst of renewed energy, and smiling, she began tidying up the room. When the children came up to bed, she had a special story to tell them tonight, of a girl hopelessly in love with a prince. In this story, the girl would tell him her feelings and they would live happily ever after.

Gavin ushered his niece and nephew into the ballroom. Seeing their mother and father, the children quickly took off towards them, he easily caught up with them. Caitlin hugged her brother, thanking him for fetching her children, and then excused herself as she saw a new guest arrive. He spoke to his brother in law, smiling as he nodded in his niece's direction,

"Alas, I was her prince for five minutes."

The party was, as always, a tremendous success. Caitlin had a talent for entertaining and making all feel welcome at their home. Gavin watched as his younger sister glided across the room, greeting people she knew and making introductions to those who were perhaps new to the county. He noticed Andrew watching her also. Gavin thought of his brother in laws first meeting with his sister many years ago.

Andrew and Gavin had shared a room while they attended Cambridge University. Before the break for the holidays began, Gavin learned that Andrew did not intend to return to his home; instead, he planned to stay and study on campus. As was the O'Connor way, Gavin invited his new roommate to spend the holiday at their estate. Katherine and William O'Connor of course welcomed the young man into their home wholeheartedly. Caitlin had been on the upstairs landing when the men entered the foyer. Catching her breath at how handsome her brother's friend was. Unlike the ruddy boys she knew in her hometown, he was tall, with dark brown hair and mustache, chiseled features, and such a charming smile and laugh. Caitlin quickly tucked escaped copper locks into the hasty bun she had secured atop her head. As she came down the main staircase, Andrew stopped speaking in mid–sentence. His gaze froze on her. Gavin stifled a chuckle at his friend's reaction to his little sister's exuberant entrance, and a huge grin appeared on his face, "Ah and here is my sister Caitlin."

Andrew, immediately taken with Caitlin's confidence in her actions and by the end of the weekend, her love of life, kind heart, and beauty had overwhelmed him.

Now tonight, Gavin watched his sister with pride, and he mused on how she has grown into such a wonderful wife, mother, and woman.

"Andrew, I am glad of your decision to work in our community over the holidays. My sister puts on a good show, but there is no denying she misses you when you are gone, as do the children." Gavin picked up a glass of champagne as a waiter went by with a tray and took a healthy gulp.

"Yes, I did not realize the toll my absence made on my family." He was watching his wife. "Now I plan to make it up to my Caitlin. She truly is a gem isn't she?" He spoke with passion and love in his voice. Gavin was glad. He worried that Andrews, absence would lead to disaster when and if he returned. Andrew turned to Gavin and said, "So what of this woman Caitlin keeps telling me about? It seems she thinks she would be a perfect match for you."

Gavin swallowed the remaining liquid in his glass, offhandedly saying, "Aye, Caitlin always has some female she is throwing at me." Andrew noted the change in Gavin's demeanor, fully aware that the woman Caitlin would love to see her brother court is Roszalia; he changed the subject.

"Throwing at you… dear brother, I can't even get you to look at any of them. I do swear Andrew sometimes I believe my brother is married to his ships." Caitlin had come up to them at Gavin's last comment. She took Andrews's arm. "Come dear, time to mingle." It was now his turn to down his drink and with a shrug in Gavin's direction, the two headed off.

Gavin surveyed the room. It appeared his sister once again outdid herself and everyone in County Kerry was in attendance. His father was thronged by prominent men, and seemed to be enjoying himself. Across the room, he saw Devon, looking rather dashing this evening and not yet too belligerent. He wanted to go in search of Roszalia. He imagined the scent of lavender on her skin, the lights dancing in her hair. He wanted to bound up the stairs, bring her down with him to the dance floor, and give her the promised dance. Yet he knew she would never attend a party of this sort. Smart, he thought. He knew Caitlin had always tried to get her to attend. She was her friend, saying times have changed and that the family did not see her as the help, but a family member. Roszalia would say she was the children's governess, she knew her place. Gavin understood her conviction on this, and he knew some could be cruel with their high society's snobbery and did not want her hurt by their remarks. Right now thinking about her, Gavin could only think of one place he wanted her, in his arms. He walked out onto the veranda to escape the music and laughter and wondered when did he realize his true feelings for her? He was lost in thought when a silky voice said very near his ear,

"Mmmm, nice night isn't it?"

Gavin turned to see Vanessa Burke, a woman who would love to put the title of Lady O'Connor on her name. Gavin had accompanied her on a few outings in the past but never found her even mildly exciting. Soon after finding out she had been sleeping with his brother, his nominal interest disappeared entirely.

"Hello Vanessa," he said in an even tone. Her pouty face looked up at him.

"Oh, Gavin, you hurt me with your tone."

"Vanessa, I think you should sit down, you appear a bit unsteady." He could tell she was drinking heavily and wanted to get away from her without a scene. She took his arm and he resisted the urge to snatch it away.

"Yes, maybe you could help me find a place I could just rest a bit. Father will be furious that I am drinking. 'It is not lady like,' he would say." She held Gavin's arm tightly as to not let him slip away, seeing an opportunity to be alone with him.

"Perhaps he is right. I will get you to the parlor to lie down for a bit, I will have the kitchen prepare a cup of tea to help get yourself a bit more clear–headed." Gavin's expression softened a bit, she actually was not a terrible person, just insecure and trying to live up to her father's expectation to marry into a good family. Gavin led her to the parlor and over to a leather divan. He sat her down, and when he bent over to help her lie back, she wrapped her arms around his neck and pulled him to her. The sudden action was unexpected and he lost his footing and landed on top of her. Seeing this as her opportunity, she wrapped her arms tighter and began kissing him. Gavin extracted himself from her quickly. He straightened and looked down at her with contempt.

"Vanessa, I will order you your tea and have the maid bring it to you. Good evening." Vanessa screeched at his retreating back and it stopped him cold.

"Do not tell me you'd rather bed your little gypsy wench! You could have me!" He stood still, least he would raise his hand to her. She spat her next words at him, "Yes that is right…Devon told me all about your trysts with the gypsy." He faced her keeping a level voice, trying to contain his anger.

"I feel sorry for you Vanessa. I will send my brother in, I am sure he will oblige you."

"How Dare you speak to me that way! You will be sorry…" He walked out closing the door behind him, silencing her threats.

As one of the servants passed him, he nodded to the room he just left,

"Please find Barrister Burke and tell him his daughter is in the parlor not feeling well, that she wishes to go home immediately." The servant said he would right away. Gavin decided he had enough of the crowd and went to say his farewells. Caitlin was telling the children it was time to go upstairs to their beds and wait for Roszalia to help them undress. They were both whining that they did not want to leave yet. When Gavin offered to take the children up, she gave him a hug.

"You are the best brother a sister could ask for. Now children go with Uncle Gavin, Roszalia promised me to tell you a story tonight." With that and a kiss to Samantha and Edward, she whirled off in Andrews's direction.

He turned to find two exhausted faces looking at him. He walked them to the side stairs and prodded the two up to their rooms. Since Roszalia was not yet there, he took it upon himself to get the children ready for bed. He managed to find what he thought looked like nightclothes for each. Edward rinsed his hands and face with warm water that had been poured in the basin just moments before, then saying goodnight to his uncle, he headed for his bed in the adjoining room that opened onto the play area. Samantha handed her hairbrush to her uncle. For a moment, he looked perplexed at the brush until his niece's giggles brought his attention to her.

"You have to brush my hair before bed," then her voice turned very serious, "Roszalia always bushes it at least one hundred stokes. She says it will make my hair as shiny as mommas." Adding with a knitted brow, as she looked at the brush in her uncle's big hand, "Maybe tonight we could just do twenty brushes."

He smiled at his niece, "Well, that sounds good to me." after he finished, he placed the brush aside on the night table. "Now get into bed and I will tell a bedtime story." Samantha giggled at this, "What are all the giggles for?" he asked.

"Uncle Gavin, men cannot tell stories!" Gavin tickled her and she squirmed with delight.

"Well, let's find out, now under the cover." He tucked her in under the goose down cover, and then crossed the room to sit in the big chair that faced the foot of the bed. He noticed that Edward had come in and was in the big chair next to his sister's bed, also awaiting his tale. Gavin told them the story of a pirate in search of treasure. Although he scoured the seas all his life, he found it was not the jewels and trinkets. For love was the real treasure all along. He ended the tale with, "And after all of the pirate's travels he found that the love he searched for was right here in his own home."

Samantha turned over, snuggled deeper under her cover, and after a long yawn, whispered, "That was a nice story Uncle Gavin. I would like to be a pirate's love. He must have been very lonely all those years." Gavin looked lovingly at his niece and thought how wise she was, for she was right, he was very lonely. Edward was half-asleep in the big chair.

"Let's get you in your own bed." He followed his nephew into his room, pulled the quilt up and he said goodnight.

The hour was getting late and Roszalia knew the children would be tired. She had gone downstairs to the ballroom entrance to see if she could find Caitlin, and see if she needed her to take the children up to begin their bed preparations.

Andrew saw Roszalia at the archway, smiling as he approached her, "I you are looking for Edward and Samantha you are too late, I am afraid. Gavin brought them up. Of course they did not want to go." He noted the astonished look on her face.

"Oh I feel terrible that he left the party, I should have come down earlier." Andrew saw the concern cross her features, then added, "No need to worry, I actually think my brother–in–law used my children as an excuse to depart from the festivities, he really does despise these events."

Roszalia laughed, "Surely you jest, but I had better see if Gavin needs any help." Andrew smiled as he watched her head up the stairs and thought, *Yes, Gavin and Roszalia would make a perfect couple, ergo the cutting tongues of the gentry.*

As she neared the open door to the children's suite, she could hear Gavin's voice, he was telling them a story, and her heart swelled. She has never seen this side of him. As she listened to the story he told the children, she could only hope that the pirate he told about was himself. She stood in silence until he extinguished the lamp near Edwards's bed. As he came in the front room, she stepped in the doorway. Not wanting him to know she had heard she made the pretense that she had just come up from the party. Gavin put a finger to his lips and motioned her out the door, gently closing it behind them.

"Thank you Gavin, but I fear now for my position as governess!" she whispered with a smile. Gavin took her by the elbow and ushered her to the back stairs. She began to protest but he held up his finger to his lips again and she obeyed by not saying a word. They went down the west stairwell to an empty hallway near his father's library. He took her through a small sitting area out onto a patio, they could hear the music from the ballroom, yet only the moonlight fell upon them. Gavin took Roszalia's hand and finally breaking the silence

"May I have this dance?" He bowed deeply; Roszalia curtsied back and extended her delicate hand. He took her hands and they began to swirl on their own private dance floor. After a moment, Gavin pulled her closer and put his arm around her waist. She put her hand on his shoulder and they both moved to the music as one.

He could smell the scent of lavender in her hair, her skin aglow in the moonlight. She had changed her clothing. He wondered if it was for him. She had on a deep blue dress with a lower cut bodice than she usually wore, showing her creamy neckline. It was not expensive or fancy like so many of the women at the party wore trying to impress each other. Yet on Roszalia, it was perfection. Her feet clad in soft slippers, her waist so delicate, she felt like a precious doll in his arms. He wanted to tell her tonight his feelings for her. He wanted to touch her hair, kiss her lips, feel her warm body under his…yet for right now to be in perfect rhythm in the dance was enough.

Roszalia instinctively leaned in closer to Gavin, both her arms now around his neck, her breasts held tightly to his chest. She could feel the beat of their hearts as one and the dance seemed like magic. They drifted in their own world until the music ended. He bent down possessing her mouth with his. His deep kiss taking what little breath she had left from her lungs, she wanted more, she wanted him. She clung to him, not wanting to let go, lest he realizes he made a mistake.

The kiss ended as he looked down into her eyes, darkened with a passion, he huskily whispered as he kissed her neck,

"You are so beautiful, and the most vibrant woman I have ever known." He stroked her hair, she heard his words but only wanted to taste his kiss again, and she wanted to be his tonight.

A loud bellowing shattered the moment as it came from the hall outside near the library, a man's voice was yelling and soon others were all talking at once. One loud voice could be heard above the others,

"Where in hellfire is that scoundrel son of yours? No! Not Devon, the other one. The one who attempted to dishonored my daughter. Gavin!"

Roszalia head jerked in the direction of this comment looking confused, "What is going on Gavin?"

"Stay here. I will find out." Gavin exited the room to find a group of men, including his father, trying to calm down Barrister Burke. Upon seeing Gavin, he made a lunge for him. Gavin sidestepped him but caught the end of his fist on his chin.

Barrister O'Connor quickly stepped between them holding the older man away before he could render a second blow at his son. His own voice now boomed with anger, "Victor, what is all this about, you cannot go throwing punches at my son."

"Your son," Victor snorted with disgust, and the veins in his neck protruded with his anger making him appear much like a bull ready to charge. "He has disgraced my Vanessa! She is hysterical in the parlor."

There was silence in the hall, and then they all turned to where Gavin stood rubbing his chin. He looked at Vanessa's father and said behind clenched teeth trying to remain calm and show respect to the older man, who had just lunged at him. "Sir, I do not know what your daughter told you, but let me assure you I did not accost your daughter or attempt to do so in any manner."

"She told me you forced her to drink, and then you told her you would treat her as your gypsy wench!" He turned and spoke to William O'Connor, the veins in his thick neck still bulging, "And he would have his way with her! She is still so upset I cannot get her to stop crying!" Vanessa's father spat.

"Victor, you have known Gavin for many years and you should know he would cause your daughter no disrespect. I am sorry but if Gavin claims he did not make any such advances, I believe him. Is it possible Vanessa had a bit too much to drink on her own and is mixing up the facts?" William said trying to suppress his own anger at the outrageous allegations made of his eldest son.

Pulsating with anger, shock was on the barrister's face. "We will take our leave now but never let me see your son near my daughter again!" He turned abruptly and withdrew to the parlor where Vanessa's sobs continued.

"All right, let us all call it a night shall we?" Wearily, Barrister O'Connor looked at the open door Gavin had just come out of and saw Roszalia standing there. He looked back at his eldest son and said, "I need to discuss some business with you and your brother in the library." He then turned and headed the others back to the ballroom.

Before Gavin reentered the room, Vanessa was coming out of the parlor door. Through tears and puffy eyes, she looked right at Gavin and gave a small smirk, then began her tears again.

Gavin closed the door and turned to see Roszalia's face. It was ashen, looking at him, the warmth and passion he saw moments ago was gone.

"Roszalia, please, I did not touch that woman, she was angry because she had been drinking. I told her I was sending for her father to escort her home. I presume she thought this would make her father angry enough so he would not notice her inebriated condition." He chose to leave out the fact that Vanessa attempted to seduce him, but his words sounded unconvincing to his own ears, and he feared what Roszalia was thinking.

"It does not matter what I think," Roszalia's voice was quiet, expressionless. She was fighting to keep the tears back. Her mind could not erase the words Vanessa had said about *Gavin's gypsy wench*. He went to move towards her, but she withdrew.

"Good night Gavin, thank you for the dance." She turned before she left and said, "I believe you when you say you did not touch her, for I do believe for a few moments I had your heart." Tears were in her eyes. She turned and quickly headed towards the back stairs, not wanting him to see them fall.

Gavin stood in the spot just moments before he had held Roszalia in his arms, her soft curves against his hard chest. He did not enjoy this feeling of helplessness, yet he did not know if he should go after her and take her in his arms. Would she refuse him entirely? He ran his fingers through his hair.

"Damn, Vanessa," not even realizing he had spoken his thought out loud. He then remembered his father waiting in the library for him. He decided he would talk to Roszalia in the morning, and invites her to ride with him, alone if she would allow it. With that thought, Gavin angrily strode to meet his father. The Library was empty when Gavin arrived. He decided he needed a whiskey after the altercation that had taken place. The dance with Roszalia had been magical, it had given him a few moments of pleasure he had never felt before, he knew she was confused, hell, he didn't know what happened. He downed the amber liquid, hoping it would dull the throbbing in his temples. The door opened and Devon came in the room with a smirk on his face.

"Tisk, tisk, brother. I hear you have angered out lovely Vanessa tonight." He headed towards the bar and poured an ample amount. Swirling the liquid he gulped deeply, then sat down on the divan. "So you made Vanessa mad and now she has accused you of tarnishing her virtue." With the thought of his brother in trouble with the barrister, Devon could not restrain a sadistic smile. Gavin barely able to contain his anger at his brother's obvious pleasure with the whole misunderstanding, countered with,

"I am sure you could straighten her father out about his daughter's virtue…or lack of."

"Touché brother, but it seems you are the one she is bent on destroying right now." At this comment, Devon raised his glass as in a toast, his grin never wavering. Gavin drained his glass and wished his father would make haste; he had no desire to converse with his brother on the subject further. He wanted to seek out Roszalia, let her know his feelings were sincere for her. Remembering the way Vanessa had called her a gypsy wench. Anger welled in him. Pouring himself another drink, he tried to control it. Their father came into the room as Gavin capped the decanter, both men stood.

He motioned, "Sit, sit." William closed the door silencing the sounds of the party in the background. "I do not know what led to the recent event in the hall, however Victor is very upset." He looked not at Gavin but directly at Devon, noticing his smirk and guessing he somehow had something to do with the whole misunderstanding. Then continued, "It seems that my sons have been less than courteous to his daughter this evening. She is claiming you took advantage of her, tarnishing her reputation."

Gavin put his glass down with a bit too much force, showing his anger, cutting off his father's sentence. "Father, if the girl has plans to lie and trick her way into marriage with an O'Connor, then let it be Devon. He seems to have taken a fancy to her. But I will have no part in her games." Gavin moved towards the leather high back chair and sat down heavily.

"Calm yourself. Vanessa is his only child, and he only wants to protect her."

"Then he had best lock her in her room." Devon said as he took another gulp, smiled. His father gave him an angry glare.

"Enough of this, I will speak with him in the morning. We need to discuss a venture I am contemplating with a colleague I spoke with earlier. Even with our guests present, this issue needs our immediate attention. I do believe I have had enough festivities for one night." William O'Connor moved to the window side of the room and sat down in his large leather chair. With a tired look on his aging face, he looked at his feuding sons. Many family discussions had taken place in this room, and he could not help but think that he would not be a party to many more. He knew he had a health condition, but he would not let his family know, or worry... not yet. Clearing his thoughts, he began.

"Gavin, There is a fleet of ships over in America that I want you to negotiate the merger of O'Connor Shipping Company with. An old acquaintance has developed quite a large shipping business. It seems he lost most of his capital during the war. He has overextended himself and is looking for a partner to help financially or he must liquidate. Gavin came over and took the seat adjacent from his father. Devon refilled his glass and remained standing by the bar. The elder O'Connor continued,

"They are docked at Boston Harbor in America. I think that this would be an excellent addition to our fleet, and this would open up our shipping relations with America. Devon, I would like you to go also to set up the accounts with the mills there. You will need to take Karl, he is the man I would like to head up the American side of this merger and protect our interests abroad. I have been corresponding with a large millhouse there that wants to discuss purchasing raw materials such as wool. I believe it would be wise that we broadened our resources in America. You will take two ships from our fleet. We will export nonperishable goods and transport passengers. Then, after the negotiations are closed and all documents are signed, Gavin, you will escort two additions to our current fleet back to our docks, four ships will remain in American under Karl's guidance to serve the eastern seaboard."

Putting the Vanessa business and their differences aside for a moment, both men gave their approval. Gavin believed this would be a financially sound venture. America was a place he had visited many times. This was a country growing. Trade and industry were rapidly expanding and involvement at the early stages would be an advantage for their company. Devon had never been on such a long voyage, his territory of operation extended to the borders of Ireland and England, but he was eager to see what America had to offer. He had heard stories of considerable wealth and prosperity for any man willing to stake a claim. He would take care of the scheduled business and then see what he could manage to invest in himself.

Business taken care of, William O'Connor concluded with a heavy sigh, "Now gentlemen, can we try not to produce any more problems tonight, enjoy what is left of the party and we will discuss this further tomorrow. I would like you both to be ready to set sail within a week." Devon put his empty glass on the bar and headed for the door. Gavin watched his brother exit the library before he spoke,

"Father, I never touched the girl."

"I know son, Vanessa Burke has a lot of growing up to do, and perhaps this trip will give Victor time to calm down in your absence." William O'Connor put his hand on his son's shoulder as the two men walked from the room and out to the hall, where the laughter and dancing continued. Gavin did not feel like merriment, he wanted to see Roszalia. However, the hour was late, and he had a lot to arrange before he shipped out. He made a mental note that before he set sail, he would speak with her and clear this misunderstanding up.

After Roszalia had left Gavin she made sure the children were tucked snug in their beds. The dance had been magical, her love for Gavin was so overwhelming, and then Vanessa's accusations, was he with her before he came to see her? She shook her head, "You know Gavin better than that." She realized she had spoken aloud. Still, her perfect night had been shattered. Resisting the urge to go to his room and confront him with her feelings, she thought once again aloud, "That, you foolish girl, would only drive him away." She decided the best thing to do was to avoid Gavin as much as possible. He would be gone again soon. Her heart felt heavy at the thought of not seeing him, but she knew it was best. Lying down, she drifted off to sleep. Soon the music was lifting her in a dance, her gypsy skirts swirled around her bare feet, one more turn and she was in the embrace of her love.

CHAPTER SIX

The next few days were hectic. Gavin had tried to talk to Roszalia but when he sought her out before breakfast in the kitchen, the cook told him that she had eaten early. When he did approach her, the children were always present and he could not speak freely of the other night and of his feelings. It seemed she was avoiding him. He would be gone for a long time on this trip and he needed her to believe the kiss that night was real and his feelings were true for her. He made a vow when he returned this time that he would start settling down at the estate, taking on his first–born duties and that would include winning the heart of Roszalia. Gavin smiled to himself, yes, he would do everything in his power to sweep her off her feet.

The docks were bustling with activity. Karl Moore had worked with Gavin for over ten years on the docks and crossed the seas with him. Karl was indeed a man Gavin could trust. His stocky build and strong sea legs told of many hard years at sea. The man had a full head of red hair, biceps the size of timbers. He was quick with a smile and one of the most likeable fellows he knew. His father, as he always did, made the best choice appointing him to oversee the American fleet. Karl signed on with Gavin's crew when misfortune destroyed his farm and family years ago. The O'Connor's had opened their hearts and home to him, and in return, he was a devoted, dedicated worker and foremost, a trusted friend.

The two men stood near the plank of the Lizzy Wind. The powerful thousand–ton clipper ship's cargo bay could easily carry enough supplies for their long voyage.

"She certainly is an impressive ship" he said as he watched the loading.

"That she is. So Cap," Karl said with a wink, "now we will be in the people shipping business also, eh?"

"Seems so, but people, wool, or any other cargo we haul, you are the best man for the job." Gavin grinned at his first mate.

A burly man with a large wooden crate pushed past the two men and up the entry. The loading was going smoothly, and Gavin decided he would head into town before setting sail. The streets were crowded with carriages and townsfolk going to the general store, the pubs or the bakery or any of the shops in town. Rowdy laughter drifted from the Harbour Bay Inn. On this beautiful day, many of the shops had carts out in front of their doors to entice the customers to enter. Gavin, passed by the coffee house, the smell of fresh ground beans and roasting coffee filled the air, and next the bakery, where the smell of bread overwhelmed his senses, a bit further down he stopped as he came to the apothecary shop owned by Roszalia's aunt Agnes. He would pick something out and have it delivered to Roszalia. Gavin had met Agnes many times in the past, both here in Dingle and at the estate, when she would come to visit her niece or Truda. Many of the men that sailed on his ships would go to Agnes for potions to ward off illness and charms or amulets that they felt kept them safe at sea. Agnes was a slight woman, who seemed never to age since he first met her. The woman wore her stark white hair braided down her back, neatly tied with a ribbon. Agnes had the same array of colors in her hazel eyes as Roszalia. Just thinking of her drew a smile to his lips.

The bell announced a patron's entrance with its jingle. She smiled as she recognized the handsome man that entered the store.

Gavin walked over to a beveled case that held several elegant containers, next to this there was another similar case but with a single crystal atomizer. It had a half moon stopper and was filled with an opaque purple liquid that seemed to glow from the light reflecting on it, but there was no light source near. He knew Roszalia's aunt was well known and respected for her medicinal mixtures, and her exquisite collection of fragrances. He also heard that many people feared this gypsy woman and thought her strange and mystical. As Agnes came to greet Gavin, she could see a disturbance in his aura. She could feel Roszalia in his thoughts. Her bright skirt and bangle bracelets swished and chinked as she headed towards him, pulling his attention away from the cabinet and its contents.

He had to smile at the site of her. The woman's flamboyant dress and attitude fit the part of every story he ever heard of a gypsy.

"Ah, Gavin," she said, extending her hand to the man, never a woman to bother with titles.

He took it with a mock bow, "Agnes, it has been a long time. I need your services in finding a gift." Agnes's eyes widened.

"A gift you say, perhaps for or a young woman?"

"Yes, I think you can help me, it is for Roszalia," he smiled broadly. "I will be gone quite some time, and I will not get to see her before I sail. I would like her to know she will be in my thoughts."

Agnes could sense the bond and love as he spoke of her, even if he did not admit it to himself, yet. She also felt a disturbance, because of her strong spiritual bond with her niece, the visions concerning her were never clear. "Follow me over here I have her favorite lavender soaps and oils."

Gavin followed Agnes to the back of the store where she kept the scents. Now he knew why Roszalia loved to visit her aunt, they were very much alike, he thought as he passed the shelves of herbs and jars. Agnes took a bottle of lavender fragrance and cake soap from the shelves. Gavin remembered the display of crystal atomizers in the case. "Please choose one of the crystals and place the perfume in it. I believe that would make the gift special."

Agnes laughed, "Well, there is hope for men after all!" She took an elegant teardrop crystal atomizer out and emptied the pungent liquid into it. She then wrapped the gift in red tissue and handed it to Gavin.

He looked at the wrapped item with dismay. "I will need you to have this delivered, my ship departs soon." He hesitated a moment and added, "Agnes, please send a dozen long stem red roses along with it." Agnes raised an eyebrow,

"My, my quite the romantic aren't you?" Gavin laughed.

"Agnes, you are the only woman who has ever accused me of that! Nevertheless, after this voyage, I intend to try," giving the woman a knowing wink.

"That is what this old woman lives for, to see young love bloom."

As he headed back to the ship, he had lightness in his stride. This trip he would have Roszalia on his mind, and he hoped his gift would open her heart to him, and when he returned, she would be waiting.

The trip to Boston Harbor was planned to take six weeks, the late fall weather this year was mild and given they did not run into any unforeseen elements, all should proceed as planned. The last of the provisions and cargo loaded, they were ready to set sail.

Devon was sailing on the Elizabeth, a passenger schooner with a bit more comfort but still not to his liking. No trip out to the sea set well with him, he much preferred land. The seafarer's life was one thing he would never envy his brother. On this voyage, he decided the majority of his time would be in his cabin, knowing it held an abundance of fine whiskey. He would be glad to be in American and get to dry land business.

Gavin stood in the middle of the bridge of the Lizzy Wind and gave the orders to set sail. Appearing from nowhere, a cool breeze caressed his check, sending an ominous chill down his spine. Not a superstitious man, he tried to shake it off, but the feeling remained. The Elizabeth set out immediately afterward.

The ships had been out to sea for fifteen days, they had separated when the Elizabeth made a stop on the coast of Iceland to pick up more passengers bound for America. The Lizzy Wind continued on, she would remain docked in Boston Harbor until the Elizabeth arrived. The seas were calm and all seemed to be going as scheduled.

While docked at Iceland, the captain of the Elizabeth received news of a formidable winter storm front directly in their path. Given the passengers the ship carried, he made the decision to stay in port at least forty–eight hours until the worst of the storm moved south. Knowing the Lizzy Wind was days ahead in the open waters, they could only hope their sister ship had gained enough knots to put the storm behind her.

Gavin stood on the deck taking notice of the change in the air, dark, ominous clouds loomed overhead, and the waters becoming rougher as they proceeded. Karl walked up to the rail beside him.

"Cap, seas not looking too good is she?"

"We've seen worse my friend…" he hesitated, "But I do not have a good feeling for this one. I think we may want to look at options." Karl followed Gavin to the room where the charts were set out. The two men looked at a possible alternate course. It would take them days further south but away from the artic undercurrents. The two men conferred their current course was heading them directly into the eye of the storm. Turning back was not an option at this point either. They plotted the alternate course southwards and the seasoned crew prepared and braced themselves for the imminent onslaught of weather.

Karl took the first watch. The skies were black and the men's nerves were taut with anticipation. Twelve hours later, both Gavin and Karl realized they had seriously underestimated the power of the North Atlantic and the undercurrent of the Arctic Ocean in the winter. The storm had begun to change and had taken on much greater speed than expected. The seas swelled and the winds were reaching gale force. Karl came into the room his face stoic, so as not to let his boss see his concern.

"Cap, it's looking like there is no getting around this storm, should we change course?" Gavin looked at the charts spread on his table. Very rarely did Karl ever see his captain and friend look so distressed.

"Karl, we are too far into it. We could head towards this cluster of islands, we may be able to reach one and wait the worst of it out." Karl nodded his approval.

"We will meet back up when the Elizabeth docks in Boston." Both men felt the ominous chill as they listened to the roar of the icy north wind outside. Thinking of the passengers aboard their sister ship, they prayed they stayed in port.

"Get to the bridge and get us on the new course, I will tell the crew to secure what they can. This is only the beginning; it will get a lot rougher." He followed His first mate out.

"Aye, to that." Karl gave a somber but knowing nod and then made haste heading to the wheelhouse. Gavin made the announcement, and the crew jumped into action. It was not the first time they had seen storms in the Atlantic, and his crew were some of the finest sailors he had ever known. Never less, every man on board could sense, this storm was going to be devastating. The winds were gusting up to eighty knots and the sea had turned white with foam. Below the crew tried to stay positive. Gavin was topside, making his way to the wheelhouse. He was drenched by the cold sleeting rain. Pulling himself along the rope that was taut with gusts of icy wind, he lost his footing and slammed into the rail. The impact would have swept a slighter man over board. Entering the wheelhouse just as a wave surged up and slammed the side of the ship causing her to list to her left, the timbers groaned.

Gavin yelled to Karl over the ocean sounds, "Where the hell are we, how far off course?"

In vain, Karl wiped the water from his brow, His voice strained, "The storm set us at least twenty knots from the island cluster, and keep pushing us further out. Cap, we are not going to make it to them."

Another wave crashed against her hull, this time a snapping sound accompanied. Through the porthole, Gavin saw the first of the masts ripped away from her deck.

"We are going to have to ride it out," Karl yelled. Gavin nodded and said a silent prayer, he had never encountered a storm this fierce in all his years sailing, and he was not sure the Lizzy Wind could hold up. The door burst open and banged on its hinges from the force of the storm outside, a panicked young crewmember stumbled into the room.

"We're taking on water captain. The last wave knocked us into an ice mass. She has a hole in her hull, do not know how badly, but cargo is flooding." Gavin headed for the door, he yelled back to Karl.

"Just try to keep her steady." However, both men knew it was a futile attempt. The icy blasts cut through him, as he made his way down to the midsection of the ship. He saw the massive hole ripped into her. It was still above water level, but with every wave blast, she took on more water. Barely heard over the roar outside,

"Get everything you can find to patch the hole, keep her from filling farther." The cargo hold was already waist deep and filling up fast, the pump was not able to get the water out as fast as it was entering. The situation was dire. One of the crew yelled above the rushing water entering,

"Cap, a few more big ones, and we will be under the line." Gavin knew the man was right. Gavin knew all efforts to save his ship were futile, the storm and her rage were winning, and the only thing to do now was to save the lives of his crew. At that moment, he bellowed, "Get to the bridge. Tell Karl to get the men to the boats."

"Aye captain," the man took flight with his orders. Gavin stood for a moment watching the icy water enter the gaping hole and rise rapidly. His mind racing, *how could this be happening*? Yelling to be heard above the rushing water,

"Get topside, everyone out, now!" Making sure all the men were ahead of him, he headed for the ladder and shut the heavy wooden hatch. A thunderous roar sounded as the side of the Lizzy Wind ripped open, filling her hull. Gavin fought his way back through the stinging rain and salty water to the foredeck where Karl stood trying to secure the wheel.

"Karl, go now!" nature's chaos outside muffling his voice, "make sure all the men are with you." Gavin grabbed the wheel, in a vain attempt to keep her steady until the jollyboats could be cast off.

Karl nodded his head, he began to speak, but he knew better than to argue the point that Gavin should go too. He would not. He would stay until the end and try to maintain the wheel. Karl embraced his friend, and then left leaving the howling wind screeching through the door.

Gavin barely heard Karl yelling orders and saw the first boat crowded with men hit the stormy sea below. It seemed to disappear beneath the waves, and then bobbed to the surface again. Gavin knew his crew may not have a better chance in the boats, but soon they would have no chance on the Lizzy Wind. Her bow was rapidly sinking.

The sound came first, a deafening roar. He looked up just as a massive wall of water was engulfing the ship. His last thought was of a beautiful dark haired girl that he never told he loved.

As the clouds dissipated, two small jollyboats bobbed in the water. Karl was in the front of one with five crewmembers, the other held ten men huddled under a tarp. They had tied the boats together after they collided during the storm. Six boats cast off last night with the crew in them. Today after the storm, only two were afloat. In the far distance, the ship listed half under water, like a broken toy. Supplies and wood were everywhere, amongst them the unfortunate bodies of the crew that did not make it. No one said a word. They took the stored oars and began rowing to see if they were any survivors in the water. They all knew the answer. The sea was an icy tomb.

The Elizabeth had stayed in port until the storm passed. When the harbor master cleared them for departure, they set sail with their passengers and cargo to continue the trip to Boston. On their fifth day out, a small fishing boat, hailed them. It had encountered two jollyboats and rescued the men that were badly beaten by the storm, but alive. Karl told the captain and Devon of the Lizzy Wind's fate.

"I feel it is my duty to return home and relay the devastating news to my family." The captain agreed. After arriving back at the Iceland port, all sixteen men secured passage on a ship returning to Ireland. When the surviving men arrived at the docks, word of the wreck spread rapidly. The Harbor Master prepared the messages for the families and gave them to the men who immediately set out to personally deliver the messages to the families of their fellow crewmembers that had perished. Twenty–four sons, husbands, and fathers met an icy death or were unaccounted for in the storm, including their captain, Gavin O'Connor.

Karl sought out Devon before they left the ship, thinking he would perhaps like some company while delivering the tragic news to his family. The two had never been friends, but Caitlin and her father considered Karl as family, and he felt the situation warranted camaraderie.

"Devon, I could accompany you to relay the tragic news, I know this is difficult for us all."

Devon faced Karl with his cold grey stare and responded,

"Karl, you were such a good friend of my brother, and my family thinks more a son of you than myself," he paused and narrowed his eyes, "so be my guest, the news is yours to deliver, I for one am going to spend the evening at the Inn." With this, Devon left the ship and headed in the direction of the Harbor Inn.

Karl stood for a moment, then shook his head in disgust at Devon's retreating and decided he would ride with haste to the O'Connor Estate lest the family hear the news elsewhere. When he arrived, the door attendant opened the massive front doors upon his first knock. As Roszalia passed the entrance hall and recognized the visitor's voice. She came towards him with an ominous feeling, as she knew he was bearing ill news. He should be on his ship, with Gavin right now, and weeks into their voyage.

Approaching the door attendant Roszalia said, "I will bring our guest to Barrister O'Conner." She made a feeble attempt at a smile, but the knot in her stomach grew stronger with every step she took. Roszalia had known Karl for years and in all that time never had she seen him without a smile, however today his face only held sadness.

"Ah, lass..." He began to speak, but she held her hand up. It was not her place, but she had already known. As Karl walked in the parlor, all conversation ceased, and all looked confused at his presence. Not able to say a word he handed the note to Barrister O'Connor, who opened the seal with trembling hands and read the words written within,

To the family of Captain Gavin O'Connor,
We regret to inform you there has been an accident of nature out to sea. The Lizzy Wind has gone down. Twenty–four members of her crew are missing or have perished. Your son, Captain Gavin O'Connor is among those missing.

Our deepest sympathy,
Dingle Harbor Master

"Father, what it is?" Caitlin noticed her father's face turn pale, he crumpled the note and it fell from his fingers. She quickly came to his side. He did not say a word. Retrieving the note, she smoothed it and as she read her slender hand flew to her mouth, she looked at Roszalia, "Gavin," is all she said. Roszalia looked at her friend and felt the panic rise. Caitlin's eyes welled with tears as she said, "His ship went down, and he is lost at sea."

Roszalia felt her heart stop, she did not hear correctly. She reached for the note and read for herself. Caitlin had gone to her father and was crying unashamedly in his arms, the children looked on with wide eyes. Roszalia was stunned, and acting purely on instinct, called to the children.

"Samantha, Edward, let us go outside for a while," trying to sound like there was nothing wrong.

They obeyed, not used to seeing their mother cry and a bit confused. The sun was shining, but the breeze had an ominous chill to it. Roszalia told the children their mother just had gotten some distressing news and would be fine. As children do, they accepted this and ran off in the direction of the barn. Roszalia walked over to the garden bench and sat, she stared into the field for a long time. How could he be lost? She could still feel him, see his face, she imagined his kiss. Then she felt the hot sting of tears running down her face.

"I love you Gavin." Roszalia said to the wind. She let her tears flow freely.

Agnes was at the stables when a vision flashed in her mind and she knew of the disaster. Hurrying to her store, she set her tealeaves out. She did not sense nor read in her leaves Gavin's death. He was alive, somewhere...but alive. She only hoped her niece's intuitive feelings would tell her the same.

CHAPTER SEVEN

Gavin fell in and out of consciousness as the waves crashed against his body. He felt a sharp pain as the bone in his leg broke through the skin. The deep laceration near his eye stung from the cold salt water. He knew his only hope to not freeze in the icy waters was to stay alert and stay atop the planks he had pulled together. Darkness began to invade his thoughts again, and in his mind she whispered his name softly saying, *Gavin, come home to me.* Numbness and delirium were pulling him in deeper, he could smell her lavender, and see a shimmer of mahogany hair. Then the blackness engulfed him and there was only silence.

The sound of a woman's voice, a real voice, reached his ears. He tried to open his eyes, but bandages prevented it. His head was pounding and his limbs felt week. What had happened? Where was he?

"Easy now boy. You have had a rough time of it. Let us look at that gash." He felt gentle hands unwrap the bandage that was covering his left eye, bright light assaulted him and he winced and then grimaced from the pain it caused. "Lie still now, let the light adjust." It was the woman's voice again.

Slowly, Gavin opened his eyes, everything was a hazy blur,

and he closed them. The woman spoke in a dialect of Icelandic and Danish. Although Gavin was no stranger to these languages from years with shipmates from other lands, but his state of mind did not allow him to process her words.

"What happened, and where am I?" he said in English, hoping the woman also spoke this language. His throat was dry and burning. The woman said something, and a younger female voice responded,

"My mother does not speak English well; I will ask your questions to her." The two women conversed for a moment, and then the younger woman spoke again. "You have been very ill, the fever wracked you. My brothers plucked you from the ocean's wrath. They were fishing and did not make it back when the storm came.

"Was anyone else found?" Gavin winced in pain as he spoke. The young women spoke softly,

"No, not alive, and we feared we would lose you, you have been in an out of consciousness for over seven days." He needed to think, but could not remember. Yes, the storm, but then?

"You have many broken bones and your head has many deep wounds." The older woman was speaking to her daughter. "My mother asks your name? You were rambling with fever in Gaelic when we first brought you in; you spoke of Karl, Devon, and a woman."

"I can't…" he began but hesitated and tried to clear his mind, "Gavin. My name is Gavin O'Connor, I cannot remember much right now." Again, the pain from his injuries caused him to close his eyes and breathe deeply.

"Mother says you are lucky to be alive. Rest now. Tomorrow she will take off the bandages and see how your wounds are healing." Gavin tried to sit up, but a sharp, excruciating pain shot through his chest. "Lie still, some of those bones you broke were ribs, you must lie still to heal. I will bring in some broth for you." The older woman was rapidly speaking, and then left the room.

"Mother made you a sleeping tonic. It will help you heal." The girl held the cup so Gavin could drink. After taking a painful swallow of the bitter liquid, he asked,

"What is your name lass?"

"I am Annalisa, now rest." Taking the oil lamp as she left the room, Gavin appreciated the darkness. Soon sleep won over the pain, and he fell into a dream. *The waves were crashing and the ship was going under, he looked up and a beautiful dark haired girl was next to him. She trembled with fear from the impending doom the final wave would cause, but she clung to him. "Kiss me," she whispered.* With her kiss, the ocean swallowed him into a deep sleep.

Gavin was the perfect patient he stayed in the bed, letting his injuries heal. Not a man to be idle he soon began to feel restless. He learned that he received a severe gash on his thigh and seemed to have broken the bone also. His caregivers had set it and sewn closed the deep wounds while he was still unconscious. As the days went on, he began gaining his strength back and was soon able to move about. His right leg did not function as before. He knew he would need to exercise if he were to regain full mobility.

Annalisa watched over Gavin day and night, and when she saw his unsteady gate, she brought him a cane that her father had carved before he passed away.

"Now it will do you good to sit in the sun in the gardens." She helped him out to the lawn and on a bench.

"Dear lass, you do spoil me." Gavin winked at her.

"I am only trying to nurse you back to health," she said as she turned to hide her blush.

"So where did you learn to sew a man up and tend to wounds so well?" Gavin asked as Annalisa sat next to him.

"A man is not that different from the sheep or horse when it comes to tending wounds, I have always helped on the farm."

"Well, I cannot thank you and your family enough for their care."

They sat and talked as the afternoon sun began to wane, and she had been right, the fresh air and sun did make him feel much better. As they sat, he noted the way she looked at him. The young girl was comely. She wore her pale blond hair tightly pinned back. He thought if she let her hair down and smiled, she could be attractive.

Gavin still could not seem to remember much before he woke up here on the island. Fragments of memory seemed to be just out of his reach. Annalisa was talking about the pastures and her brothers, but Gavin's mind kept glimpsing an image of a dark haired girl.

"Gavin, we should be going back in now, mother will be making the evening meal, and you do not want to get chilled when the sun sets." Annalisa's brother, Jorgen, came round the corner of the barn and saw the two. Jorgen had been the one who pulled Gavin from his makeshift raft. He was cut, bloody and battered, and he and his brother, Josh, at first thought he was dead, but as they pulled him up, they saw life. Bringing him on their own battered boat, they made haste for home. The man was almost as tall as Gavin and built like an ox. His shoulders were wide and his smile wider.

"Ah, my friend," Jorgen said as he approached them, his English was laden heavily with his native accent. "Bit of air and sun do ye wonders, get ye strong, and we be taking ye up to the valley to help tend the herds. Or back to the sea to fish, if ye could stomach it."

"Aye that I would enjoy!" Gavin had immediately liked Jorgen, and he guessed him to be around his age, good humored and a hard worker. He noted the look of disapproval on Annalisa's face at their conversation, and added,

"As much as I enjoy your sister's company, a man does get a bit restless without a good day's work, and it would be good to smell the salty ocean air again."

Grimacing as he stood, Jorgen extended his strong hand, grasping his arm. Leaning heavily on the cane, thankful for its support, they headed towards the house as Annalisa skirted ahead to help prepare the meal and let the men talk.

"I do believe our little lass is smitten with ye friend," Jorgen said as he watched her leave. Gavin, uncomfortable with the silence, knew he should say something, yet he did not know how to respond. The other man put his hand on his shoulder. "My sister has not seen many men, but I do suspect that ye have a lass of yer own back home?"

Gavin shook his head and sighed, "That is the trouble my friend, I feel I do. I catch glimpses of a woman but cannot get my mind focused. I must get word to my family that I am alive." Jorgen nodded.

"We can pass the information out on the fishing boats to the larger vessels they encounter. They will spread the news that you are indeed alive."

"Yes, when I am a bit stronger we will go to the docks."

The pain in Gavin's leg was throbbing from overexertion, and he sought out Annalisa to see if she had some of her herbal tea to ease the pain. As he watched her begin to grind herbs, the memory of the dark haired girl who was waiting for him to come home became clear… Roszalia.

As the weeks went by, memories and flashes of images came back to Gavin, the ship, the storm, and Roszalia. The deep gash over his eye was healing fine, and although a scar would remain, he had his full sight back. Annalisa's mother had removed the last of the dressings yesterday from his leg and felt pleased with his progress.

The tiny island he came to be on was indeed remote. He found it had very little communication with the outside world, and to his dismay, only a handful of ships ever stopped there. The people were very self–sufficient, fishing and farming. Jorgen had told Gavin to feel free to ride whenever he felt the strength. A chestnut stallion took a liking to him as they were in the barn, his walking had improved, but he had a slight limp. He knew the bone had not set right and probably did not heal correctly, but was grateful for the attention and care this kind family had given him. He owed them his life, and was feeling stronger every day.

"Jorgen my friend, I feel it is time I begin to pay back to the family. I would like to go out on the next fishing trip if you could use another hand?"

"We can always use another mate, we will be heading out in a days' time. We will spread the word on the docks too."

Gavin also felt he needed to avoid Annalisa's constant watch. He realized that she looked to him for more than friendship, but he was careful not to give her any reason to think otherwise. She had not seen or known many men in her young life, and when she saw Gavin and tended his wounds, she had fallen for him deeply. He felt the less he was around her; the better things would be when he finally left for home.

The days were spent herding, planting, tending crops for the season, and alternatively taking the fishing trawler out. As Gavin's health improved, he realized that he had to find a way back to the estate, for all there must think him dead. Moreover, he agonized over the woman back home, and the memory of her sweet kiss at their dance. His heart ached that he could not even tell her he is alive. This family had done more than just tend his wounds. They welcomed him as a part of their family. It was unspoken, but they all knew that eventually the day would come when he would be leaving.

The winter months took their toll on the village, the men had set up ice fishing huts, but Gavin was feeling the cold in his injured leg and could not stay out for days on end. He would have to stay at the farm and help tend the animals. He finished bedding the horses and the hour was late, Gavin went to the room that the family had given him for as long as he needed it, turning the lamp down low, he removed his shirt and pants and climbed into the down bed. A soft click came from the direction of the closed door then the soft sound of footsteps crossing the floor. Gavin felt a slender body get into his bed, he was awkwardly aware he was naked and realized it was Annalisa. She reached over to touch him and he grasped her wrist gently.

"Annalisa, I do not think this is a good idea." She recoiled like a snake. "You are a lovely person, but you need to keep yourself and heart for the one who will always be there for you. I cannot be that man. My heart belongs to another far away."

The young girl, humiliated by his rejection, got up and fled his room. Gavin sighed, he did not want to hurt her, but he could not lead her to think there were more feelings than friendship. He tossed, turned, and finally fell to sleep with the vision of Roszalia on his mind.

After that night, Annalisa did everything she could to avoid Gavin. He tried to talk to her but she ran off every time they were alone. The afternoon sun was warm on the mountain and Gavin was enjoying the fresh air. He had gone out on the troller the past week with Josh and Jorgen. Gavin had spread the news to all the fishing vessels that they should be on the lookout for any cargo ships, they had a telegraph massage drafted telling that Gavin O'Connor was alive, and on the island, and to pass it on to these ships that were heading to Ireland. The fisherman were more than happy to oblige, there was camaraderie among sailors no matter what their nationality. Although the men all concurred that not many ships passed close to their bay, he felt this was his only way to get back to Ireland on the chance a ship did come to port.

His efforts paid off in the spring, Jorgen rode to see Gavin on the mountainside one afternoon. "Gavin, good news from the port my friend."

"Aye, what news have you?"

"Annalisa and Mother have just returned from the markets, there is word of a ship out in the harbor, one of a fleet from yer family in Ireland. One of the fishermen told them of yer rescue and they are heading this way. They should drop anchor and the jollyboats should be at the dock within the hour."

The two men made haste and rode back to the farm. Annalisa was there and her face showed her sadness,

"I knew this day would come, you are leaving."

Gavin took her small hands in his. "Yes, I have to go. You know I belong at my home land, but I will always appreciate and be grateful to you." He kissed her head and he saw a tear roll down her cheek for the love she could never have.

The ship was familiar. It was one Gavin and Karl had sailed together many times. As the plank lowered, the stout red haired man bounded towards where Gavin stood.

"Cap, you're the finest ghost a man has ever laid eyes on!" Gavin clapped Karl on the back. "Aye and you are a wondrous sight, yourself!" The men walked over to Jorgen, Josh, and their mother.

"Karl these are my friends, they plucked me from the sea's grip and nursed me back." His eyes scanned for Annalisa, and then he saw her, hanging back, he went to her and gently took her arm. "And this is the angel that tended my wounds. Karl took Annalisa hand, bowed, and gave it a kiss.

"An angel indeed. Miss, thank you for healing our Captain."

Gavin noticed Karl took a bit longer letting her hand go and did not seem to want to look away. Inwardly he smiled. Perhaps fate had a plan. The boys and their mother made the men say they would allow them to cook a farewell dinner for Gavin and the Karl would join them. Gavin began to protest but at Karl's sudden acceptance, he agreed. On the way to the farmhouse, Karl's mood was somber as he told Gavin of the events after the wreck.

"We were only fifteen survived, well now sixteen with you 'Cap. The Elizabeth stayed in port 'till after the storm, then she headed back out to deliver her cargo and passengers. Your brother decided to return home with us, and not go on with the Elizabeth to America." Karl decided to leave out the detail that Devon chose not to accompany him to the estate with the news.

"And my father, how did he take it?" Gavin felt tightness in his throat.

"As well as you can imagine, he didn't believe you dead, he sent two more ships out looking, for months, but then," Karl trailed off. Gavin placed his hand on his shoulder.

"It is all right. Karl, I would have done the same." He wanted to ask of Roszalia but thought better, he would see her in a few weeks. The evening went well, Karl had taken to Annalisa, and she seemed to enjoy the attention. She smiled at him coyly and then danced after the meal with him. Reluctantly Karl said they would have to be on their way for they sailed at first light.

Gavin bid his farewells to the people who had been his family for all these months. When he came to Annalisa, he gave her a hug and kiss on the cheek,

"Perhaps we will meet again," he looked towards Karl and winked. She smiled and hugged him tightly whispering,

"Your girl is a very lucky woman. I shall never forget you."

Gavin overheard Karl ask Annalisa as they were leaving if he could stop back at port and see her again on his next trip to Iceland. He did not wait to hear the response, but entered the wagon that Jorgen was taking them back to the docks. His mind was on home and a beautiful dark haired woman waiting there.

Every person at the O'Connor home felt the deep sadness, all mourned the absence of the eldest son, though no one admitted he was gone, many felt it. Roszalia refused to believe he was dead. After the news, she had gone to be alone, but she could not grieve. She could still feel Gavin's presence, this she knew in her heart was the sign he was still with them, somewhere, and he would return. Roszalia sought out Caitlin,

"I feel Gavin is alive, I know he is." The conviction in Roszalia's voice gave Caitlin hope.

"I have always trusted your intuition, and I pray that it is not your heart that is telling you this. But we will not give up hope." Caitlin squeezed her friend's hand.

Devon arrived two days after Karl had delivered the ill–fated news of the Lizzy Wind and Gavin. Roszalia and Caitlin were with the children in the parlor, and heard as he entered the adjoining library. His father was at his desk, and as she went to close the door, she heard him speaking to his son in a strained tone. Moments later, Devon came barreling through the parlor as he left the library. He did not speak to Caitlin or Roszalia but headed for his quarters. Roszalia was glad, for she had planned to avoid any conversation with Devon about the disaster.

The weeks and months that followed the terrible news of Gavin's disappearance seemed endless. Although Gavin was often gone on a trip for months or even a year at a time, the thought that he would return had always kept Roszalia's spirits up. She looked forward to the day she could look upon his handsome face again. Now as each month past, even her optimism began to fade. Devon was not a problem, she knew he was waiting for the time when his father would give up the search for Gavin, and declares him the new heir. Until that time, he stayed absent from the estate. She presumed he was at the Inn on the wharf. She had heard he had a favorite there that he paid the owner a large sum to keep for his pleasure.

Roszalia spent her days trying to keep busy with the children's lessons and other chores, but her spark was gone. The man she loved was missing, and she never told him her feelings. Since the news of the wreck, every night she would lie in her bed and relive the dance and their kiss.

Tonight, just before sleep overcame her, she started, as a clear deep voice sounded in her head. 'Do not give up my love, I am almost home.' Sitting upright, she looked around but knowing no one else was there. He had said it. Gavin's voice was clear in her head. He was coming home! Putting on her robe, she hurried to Caitlin's room, rapping on the door.

"Caitlin, Caitlin," she was too excited to worry about the time, or waking Andrew.

Caitlin recognizing Roszalia's voice came to unlock the door, holding a night wrap around her, "What is it, is it the children?" Caitlin blinked her eyes as she looked at her friend.

"He's on his way, Gavin is coming home."

"How do you know?" Caitlin, now fully alert, questioned.

"He just came to me, he told me to not give up, and he's coming home."

Without question the two women embraced, Caitlin had known Roszalia had the gift of sight, and this time she wanted to believe her more than ever. Both women were weeping with the renewed hope and joy that the man they both loved was alive and coming home.

The news arrived late in the afternoon. The family was just sitting down for a late dinner when the messenger knocked. The butler brought the note, Barrister O'Connor stood up and a huge smile broke onto his face as he bellowed, "Gavin is alive! They have received word from the port captain. He is on a remote island in the Greenland Sea, north of Iceland. Karl got word from a ship that encountered a small fishing boat. He sent the message on to the estate and set out to retrieve Gavin and bring him home." Devon spat his wine,

"What? Gavin is alive!" His look was one of total shock. He poured another glass of wine and downed it in one gulp. He was too disturbed even to speak his thoughts. *How? Where was he all these months? Damn him again!* He stood, pushing his chair back, and stormed from the room.

Caitlin jumped up and went to tell Roszalia, but she had heard through the kitchen door, Caitlin came in exclaiming,

"You were right, he is alive and on his way back to us!"

The next few weeks were joyous, yet the time seemed to stand still for Roszalia. When the news came that the clipper was due in port that day, William O'Connor summoned the family to accompany him to the docks. Caitlin came to find Roszalia to have her come with them.

"No Caitlin, you must go with your father, I will stay with the children so they can see their uncle when he arrives home."

Caitlin nodded, knowing she could not sway her friend's decision, and went to fetch her cape and meet her father, waiting in the carriage. Devon decided he would go to the pier, but not to meet his not–so–dead brother. He needed solace at the Inn, and whiskey.

The ship came into port and Gavin made his way down the plank, the sea journey home was rough on his injured leg and he leaned heavily on the cane Annalisa had given him. He saw Caitlin's face beaming up at him, then his father's look of joy and relief. Quickly scanning the crowd, but Roszalia was not with them. Friends had come to greet the ship, the men were slapping him on the back, and the women were hugging him and crying tears of joy. It was slow making it past the row of well-wishers, and to his family.

He picked up Caitlin, and kissed her cheek, "Ah, you never looked so beautiful little sister," she giggled.

"Son!" William embraced his son tightly. Gavin noticed his father looked frail and not well, but considering the recent events he had to endure it was understandable. Returning the embrace, they all walked towards their awaiting carriage.

"Oh, Gavin, you are limping?" Caitlin's worried look creased her pretty features. He kissed her head and smiled.

"It is nothing, a broken bone set wrong, I will not win any leg races for sure but I can still walk, I will tell you all about it after I get home and have a hot bath and a good meal."

He followed his father into the carriage, sitting next to his sister. She wrapped her arm through his and rested her head on his shoulder.

"You did give us all a scare, you know," she sighed.

"Aye, it was a bit frightening for me also for a while." The ride home was wonderful for Gavin, he realized how much he loved his family and his home, and knew he would be settling down now. Unable to resist any longer, Gavin asked, "Caitlin, is Roszalia watching the children? I thought they may have been with you at the dock," he tried not to sound anxious. His sister gave a giggle and squeezed his arm.

"Yes, dear brother, she is looking forward to seeing you too, although I think she should run off with someone who will stay on land for a while!"

He smiled at his sister. His father was talking of events while he was gone but his mind was thinking only of the woman who was waiting for him.

It was dark when they arrived at the estate. The servants were all anticipating Gavin's arrival. They had the hall lights ablaze and greeted him with warm heart felt happiness for his safe return home. He saw the children coming down the stairs and they rushed over to hug their long absent uncle.

"We missed you uncle Gavin!" Samantha chirped and gave him a huge hug and kiss,

Edward, who seemed to have grown a foot put his hand out to shake then embraced his uncle. "I am older now, but it is still alright to hug you?" Gavin laughed and hugged the boy tight.

"We are never too big or old to hug the people we love." Released from the boys clasp, Gavin looked up to see Roszalia standing back with her hands wrung in her skirt. He noticed she wore the same dress as the night they danced so many months ago. Did she choose this for him? He wanted to rush to her, kiss her, tell her he loved her, and make love to her this moment. She walked slowly forward to the family group.

"Gavin, we are so glad you are home safely." Roszalia's own voice sounded alien to her ears, she wanted to hug him and have him take her, but instead she spoke as if he was a stranger. Gavin stepped towards her and she noticed the cane and his limp. Her heart full of love went out to him.

He took her hands and then pulled her towards him and embraced her tenderly. His warm breath in her hair as he whispered, "I have missed you." They both felt their hearts racing, and he let her go abruptly, lest he would never be able to. She stumbled a bit back and quickly gained her composure by turning her attention to the children and telling them to let their uncle come into the room. Caitlin was bustling about and the staff dispersed back to prepare the welcome home dinner.

"I really wish to have a hot bath, a good shave, and fresh clothing." The elder O'Connor put his arm around his son.

"Yes, yes, then get some rest, there is time to talk later, you are home and that is what matters." The older man's joy that his first born son was home, safe, could be seen in his aging eyes.

"Aye father, it is wonderful to be home to the ones I love." His comment directed at the beautiful woman who stood in front of him. The passion and desire apparent in his eyes. She felt a flush of heat rise from her heart. Gavin was home.

CHAPTER EIGHT

Gavin had been home for only two days, and he spent most of his time resting in his chambers. This morning the sun was glorious. He decided to take his stallion for a ride through the countryside. He rode hard through the fields, pushing him along the paths, his horse knew the area, and he could feel the excitement in his flanks at having his master back to ride with him. The smell of wildflowers and mimosa was in the air. Gavin was exhilarated. He had ridden in the fields and pastures while he was gone, but not on his property and not with the camaraderie of Samson. His shirt was unbuttoned to let the sun and the breeze press against his chest. Reluctantly, he turned Samson towards home. They had ridden hard for almost two hours. Knowing he needed to allow his horse to rest and cool down, he gently tugged the reins to slow him to a trot. They had just arrived back at the stables when the groom greeted him with a message from his father. All family members were to be present at a meeting set for midmorning. He had planned to groom his own horse today, however, with his father's request, he handed the reins over to the stable attendant that was waiting next to Samson's stall.

Samson nudged at his shoulder. "Sorry boy, not today, duty

calls. We will ride tomorrow." He turned and headed for the house. As he entered through the side door into the kitchen, he smiled as he heard Roszalia softly humming. He walked softly, not wanting to disturb her, it seemed since he was back she was avoiding him. Had he been too forward when he saw her after being gone for so long? If she only knew how he truly wanted to greet her, how seeing she made his loins ache. Thoughts of Roszalia had been invading his dreams during his absence. Since he had been home he could not wait to rise with the morning sun in hopes of seeing her, or hearing her angelic voice and laughter as she would tend to the children.

He stood in the doorframe watching. She was beautiful, he had thought this since the first time he saw her so many years ago hiding in the shadows. Since his return, he could not deny his feelings, too much had happened, and he had almost lost her. Her sleeves were pushed up revealing creamy forearms and delicate wrists, her fingers worked dexterously, grinding herbs together and did not hear him enter. Gavin knew that Roszalia had a unique gift and learned the art of the healing herbs from her mother and Agnes. Yet the care and compassion she added in everything she did, he was sure, helped heal far better than any of the mixtures.

Roszalia wiped at her forehead with the back of her hand where a strand of hair had escaped its confines. As she looked up, she saw Gavin, a half smile on his handsome lips. As always, when she was in his presence, a blush rushed to her cheeks, and she quickly turned to hide her nervousness and delight at his proximity and the memory of the closeness they shared the night on the balcony. Although it was over a year ago, the emotions and memories were as if time had not passed at all. During Gavin's absence, Roszalia's thoughts of him were constant, always believing he would come back. After the night of their dance, knowing he would go back out to sea, she felt it was easier to avoid him as much as possible. No good could come of them being so close and alone. Yet as the months passed by, the uncertainty of where he was or if he would return, she often thought of her foolishness of pushing him away after the incident with Vanessa. So many times in the solitude of her rooms, fantasies of what she would do and say when she was alone with him. Now, when the moment is available, she could only blush and hide her true feelings. His masculine scent so close behind her, his arms folded as he leaned relaxing against the wall, he was so confident, so handsome.

He noticed her discomfort, and the silence between them only added to it. To break the tension he said, his voice huskier than usual, "May I ask what remedy are you preparing today?"

Roszalia did not trust her voice, but said, "I am mixing a tea for the headaches Caitlin has been having of late." His eyes were warm and shining as he looked at her, she felt a wave of want and need flow through her and thought of his words to her as they met upon his arrival, 'I have missed you.' Could this be true? How she wished it so.

Seeing his opportunity to come close without her running from him, he seized it. As he reached to look at one of the bottles of herbs his arm brushed her shoulder, the touch sent emotions for them both, and for a moment, neither moved.

Needing to defuse the moment and with genuine interest, Gavin asked, "Tell me what all these ingredients are for." He wanted to keep her close, to hear her sweet voice.

Now feeling a bit more confident in her element of knowledge, and glad to have something to ease her mind from his nearness, with a raised eyebrow Roszalia smiled his way.

"Gavin, an enlightened man such as you does not have an interest in my herbs."

"But I do, I have seen how your teas have helped Caitlin's attacks and the children have had far fewer illnesses with your remedies," Gavin said in a truthful tone.

"All right then, these two herbs," she held up each glass container of herbs as she spoke, "White willow bark and Valerian root combined, create a powerful pain killer, include Chamomile and this gives a soothing effect. Every herb has a purpose, when combined with each other they can produce powerful results." She grew serious and looked directly at Gavin as she spoke, "There is a legend among the gypsy camps, of an extremely powerful potion that would join true lovers' souls together through lifetimes. Only a few true healers have known the secrets. But it is said that if it were their destiny to be together, then neither time nor death could separate them." Roszalia could not look away, mesmerized by his closeness and eyes looking into her own.

An awkward silence followed. Gavin cleared his throat and asked, although he already knew her answer, "You believe in two people having souls destined to be together?"

He was very near her and she was beginning to feel uncomfortable speaking of love to him. If her heart could be read, he would know how she ached for his love. Afraid her eyes, if they met his, would betray her, she turned towards the cupboard and said without conviction,

"As I said, it is a gypsy legend." She turned her head so he did not see her eyes, "But I have never had someone love me to know this personally."

Her words cut through him, he wanted to take her right here and now and tell her that he loved her, he would be there for her always, yet he stood rooted, unable to say the words. Roszalia went to the cupboard that held the dried herbs she used in her compounds and opened it. She rummaged through the glass jars near her, and then found what she needed on the upper shelf. She moved the stool over and lifted the hem of her skirt. Taking a step up, Gavin watched as her slender ankle was exposed. He began feeling an emotion he had to contain.

As Roszalia stretched to reach the jar, she lost her footing and began to fall back, releasing a sharp cry as she prepared to hit the floor. Gavin instantly reached out, and she fell into his in his arms. She seemed weightless and the smell of lavender and rose invaded his senses. Holding her a bit longer than needed before setting her on her feet, he knew he had to leave now or god help him. The electrifying effect she had on him shook his composure. The feel of her soft body in his arms, even for that moment, tormented him. He did not want to let her go. He wanted to bury his face in her fragrant hair, kiss her velvet skin, and stroke her body.

"I must go now," he declared as he turned abruptly and strode off towards the stables, needing to ride off his frustration. Father's meeting would have to wait, he thought. Why did he not have more self–control whenever he saw Roszalia? He knew the answer but refused to accept it to even himself. Why could he not he just tell her his feelings?

Staring blankly after Gavin as he dashed out the door, she had barely touched her feet on the ground before he abruptly left. Her heart sank. She was a fool to think he could ever feel for her. She put her pestle down and hung her head. She had not seen him for months, they had magic at the party with their dance, and now she had run him off with her silly chatter. Roszalia went to the door but he was nowhere. Assuming he went back to the stables, sighing heavily, she placed her herbs back on the shelves and went upstairs.

She headed towards the children's room to tidy it before they returned. As she approached the master bedchambers, she heard female laughter coming from the slightly open door to Devon's room. At this, she hastened her pace; not wanting to imagine what was going on inside, and continued down the hall. As she passed by Gavin's room she saw that the maid had not placed the clean towels out for him, they sat at his door front, probably sidetracked by Devon, she thought with distaste. She would leave them in Gavin's room for his return. Sighing again as she thought, this was as close as she would get to him. Opening the heavy wooden door, she quickly entered, and before she realized what she was doing, she closed it behind her, like so many years ago. There in the center of his room she stood, taking in a deep breath, Roszalia could smell a combination of his cologne and leather. Absently wandering to his dresser, she picked up his brush, pulling the hairs out that had collected in it and put them in her pocket, a habit she had since she was young. Gently putting the brush back, she stroked the tortoise handle of his shave blade, thinking of a time years ago when Gavin had caught her in his room. She had loved him since she first saw him. Now no longer a child, her foolish heart only grew stronger.

Roszalia thought how in the past Gavin had come to her rescue from Devon's amorous attempts more than once. A sad smile crossed her face. Many times when he was gone, she would wonder if this would be when he would return with news of taking a wife. When he kissed her at their dance, she had a moment of fantasy of being his, but she knew it could never be. Their social status was too different. Was it just the music and moonlight, and maybe a bit too much wine that possessed him?

Here, now in his room, with his masculine scent all around her, she hugged her arms together. Glancing at the high four–poster bed, she envisioned Gavin's strong hard body lying atop her, and she blushed with the thought of making love with him. So deep was her fantasy, she did not hear the oak door open behind her. As it closed the lock clicked, she spun around and stood only inches from Gavin. He reached out his hand and took hold of hers. Roszalia looked confused and began to turn, but Gavin held her firm,

"Roszalia, I was leaving you again, foolishly, and I realized... I had to come back and tell you…" His voice trailed off as he looked deep in her eyes and fell silent. Their eyes locked and the love he felt at this moment shook him.

Roszalia felt her heart would stop, realizing she had been holding her breath. As she looked into Gavin's handsome face, she felt she could drown in his gaze.

"Yes, Gavin, what do you need to tell me?" she asked in a whisper almost too quiet to hear. Still not breaking his gaze from her, he pulled her closer afraid she would run away from him.

"When I was in the ocean, and felt life slipping from me, you were the only thought I could imagine. When you are near, I feel happy, you brighten me, and I look forward to returning to the estate only to see you. You are beautiful, and I have been a fool to deny my feelings for so long. I now know I need you in my life to make me complete."

In a small voice, almost a whisper Roszalia said, "Gavin, I feel this is a dream, please, my heart cannot take such a jest. My feelings for you are the same."

Gavin brought her close and cupped her chin to upturn her

face to his. Her eyes showed her love in them as well as her fear. Slowly he bent his head and brushed her cheek with his lips, moving slowly to her lips he gently kissed them, her soft skin responding to his touch with a warm glow. Moving closer to his body, her breasts pushed against his chest. She ran her fingers through his hair. His kisses became more demanding. Parting her lips with his own, he drank her sweetness in an intoxicating kiss. Both of their bodies were shaking as Roszalia returned his kisses with equal passion. She had dreamed of this moment, her head was spinning and her body melted further into his, wanting more, wanting to be one. He withdrew his lips slightly to murmur softly in her ear,

"This is real, and we are here, together." Stroking her face as he lifted her up to carry her over to his massive poster bed, he watched her eyes for any sign of refusal, but none was there. How often she had fantasized of this moment, her anticipation of his body on hers. He whispered in her ear, "I will be gentle, please tell me if you do not want this."

Roszalia answered by deeply kissing him and reached up to remove his shirt over his head, his bare chest inches above her. He slowly unbuttoned her blouse, all the while caressing her arms, face, and hair. He marveled at her beautiful body as it strained against the chemise she wore. Roszalia watched as his eyes turned dark amber with lust as he looked at her beneath him. He wanted to relish in her beauty, her body was perfect, skin, soft and glowing. Very slowly, he moved his hands down her shoulders and traced the outline of her body, hesitating only a moment to make sure she did not object, he wasn't sure he could stop if he wanted to. The deep look in her eyes, the quick intake of her breath as his fingers brushed her told him he did not need to. His caresses were searing hot and delicious on her soft flesh. Roszalia arched her back, a soft moan escaped her parted lips with the pleasure he was giving her, and she was feeling a passion she could have never imagined. She pulled him closer to her, wanting him. When Gavin stood up, she felt abandoned. He bent quickly to taste the sweetness of her lips her lips. In one swift motion, he removed his boots and trousers.

Now standing naked in front of Roszalia, she had of course seen naked men before but none as beautiful as the man before her.

Gavin's hands moved with skill as he gently removed her skirts, this only adding to his already aching state. He held back the urge to take her immediately instead he caressed her now rigid naked body. Roszalia had never been with a man and resisted the impulse to hide herself, but as Gavin's expert hands and lips began caressing every inch of her, she began to feel a warm sensation, and the waves of desire that were building gave way to hot passion. She responded with a lust she never knew existed within her. Gavin fell atop her, hungrily kissing her, probing her dark sweetness with desire. She cried out as she dug her nails in his back. "Gavin take me, make me yours."

Gavin giving in to her wants slowly entered her warm womanhood. Roszalia gave a startled cry and he held still, then he gently began again. He felt her body quiver as a moan escaped her lips. No longer able to control their emotions, they reached their ultimate pleasure and clasped each other tightly. She had never felt anything as wonderful. Feeling a warmth rush through her body, causing her to feel wave after wave of unimaginable sensations with the man she loved. The two fell together their bodies and emotions in perfect harmony, neither daring to speak, afraid to beak the blissful moment.

Finally Gavin looked into Roszalia's eyes and brushed her damp hair from her face, gently stroking it, "Are you all right, I did not hurt you?" Roszalia smiled and licked her lips,

"You are the man of my dreams and the only man I have ever wanted."

Gavin lay back, cradling Roszalia in his arms. He pulled the coverlet up over them and stroked her hair. She was so happy, she could stay forever in his arms, and barley heard him say,

"Roszalia, I do fear I have fallen in love with you." The softness in his voice told of his honesty. Roszalia hugged him closer and replied,

"Gavin I have always loved you with all my heart. Gently rolling over she looked into her lover's eyes. She touched the scar over his right eye and put a gentle kiss on it. "I really must go now. I need to get the children ready for their meal." Roszalia got up, a bit self–conscious of her vulnerable state, feeling Gavin's eyes penetrating her. She grabbed her under-garments, hastily putting them on and then donned her skirt, blouse, and apron. She hastily tied her hair up and only then did she turn to face him.

Gavin was propped on one elbow, staring at her with lusty eyes. "Roszalia, you are so beautiful, come stay with me to-night, here in my arms." Roszalia bit her lower lip, wanting to declare that she would stay anywhere with him, but her guilt would not let her.

"Gavin that would not be right, besides if the children should need me, or Caitlin, how would it appear?"

Gavin grabbed her wrist and pulled her onto the bed he rose up and kissed her deeply until she had to push away for breath.

"Damn if I care how it appears, I love you and want the whole world to know!" he then looked earnestly into her eyes, waiting her response.

"Of course I wish to be with you, but how would it look for the future heir of the O'Connor Estate to be declaring his love for a gypsy servant."

Gavin hushed her sentence with his mouth on hers. Roszalia felt her will slipping away in the sweet warmth of his kiss, yet she resisted and pushed herself away and said a bit breathless, "I must go."

If she did not go now, she would not be able to resist him at all. Once again, she tidied her hair, knowing he was watching her as she slipped out the big oak door. Roszalia had never felt so happy, giddy. She was in love, of course, she had been in love with Gavin for years, but now he had said he was falling in love with her, their lovemaking was far beyond any of her fantasies. She was indeed a woman now, Gavin's woman. Roszalia floated down the hall towards the stairs, up to her room. Even if this was a once in a life experience with him, she did not care, his scent and image was in her heart forever.

Devon had finished with the maid and sent her on her way.

He needed to get ready to go downstairs to the meeting his father called. As he closed his door, he heard Roszalia's voice coming from Gavin's room. His father forbade him to go near her, and unwilling to be disinherited if he went against his wishes, he had obliged. His anger boiled inside of him. Once again, his brother had gotten the prize! His drunkenness compounded his lack of good judgment and, and not caring of the consequences he intended to also have his way with her.

Ahead in the dim hall, Roszalia saw a figure blocking her passage up the stairs. A feeling of dread began to grow in her stomach. Giving him a curt hello as she attempted to pass. Devon had been keeping his distance as of late, but she felt his demeanor was different tonight, dangerous. He extended his arm up in front of her to prevent her escape.

"Well, well, the prim and proper governess." Devon said in a light cajoling voice that Roszalia knew was insincere. "Seems my brother has finally had you?" the last words Devon spat at her and they sounded so dirty and sinful. Her perfect moment was shattered with reality.

"And what now, will you marry him, be mistress of the estate?" He added in a cruel tone, "Or perhaps you can socialize with the other ladies of society?" The look on his face and the darkening in his grey eyes scared her. Devon had come much too close for Roszalia's liking, and she could smell the foul whiskey lingering on his breath.

In an instant before she could retreat, he lashed out, grabbed her wrist much too hard, swinging her around he pushed his body close to hers, and said in her ear,

"Now I will show you what a real man is like and how a servant is to be treated." Devon clasped a strong hand over Roszalia's mouth so she could not make a sound as she struggled for her breath. She was wedged between his hard body and the stairwell wall. His other hand reached around to her bodice tearing the material. Roszalia, fighting back tears, tried to struggle, but he held her tight against him. She could feel him harden and the revulsion she felt for him welled up inside her. *How could this be happening?* She did not know if she spoke these words aloud thinking how just moments before she was in her lover's arms, so warm, so safe. She knew she was no match for Devon, and Gavin was at the other end of the hall with his heavy oak door closed.

Devon still with his hand over her mouth, reached beneath her skirt, pinning her against the wall with his body. Roszalia closed her eyes and shut out the tears. She tried to make her mind a blank.

Devon said in her ear, "So wench, let's see what you have left for me," Devon began to run his fingers up her thigh, at this Roszalia desperately fought to escape, but he was too strong. Suddenly the weight of his body was gone. Devon stumbled back as a strong arm pulled him away. It took her a moment for Roszalia to realize Devon was no longer on top of her and she could breathe without his hands on her. She instinctively covered the torn bodice and peered in the dark to see who her rescuer was.

"Devon, if you ever try to touch Roszalia again, make no mistake, I will make it so no woman would ever come near you," Gavin's voice was steady and menacing.

Devon roared with an angry drunken laugh. "Oh good god brother, please tell me you are not seriously going to protect this gypsy wench's reputation."

Before he could finish his offensive remark, Devon felt the sharp pain of Gavin's fist as it shattered into his jaw, sending him sprawling on the stairs. In one swift movement, Gavin positioned himself between Devon and Roszalia, in case his brother decided to take his wrath on her. Slowly Devon erected himself rubbing his jaw.

"Damn you both!" he looked directly at Gavin and the venom in his voice sent a chill through Roszalia. "Mark my words brother, you will not always be around to protect her, and I will have her, this I promise."

Gavin, not waiting for more words, took Roszalia by the arm and led her up the stairs away from his brother. Roszalia was shaking and as they went into her room she collapsed into Gavin's arms sobbing deeply. He held her close, stroked her hair, and just let her cry.

"You are safe now. I will make sure this never happens again." Gavin murmured into her sweet smelling hair. He led her to her bed and lie next to her, holding her small figure. He cursed his brother and himself for allowing him the opportunity to humiliate her. Roszalia nuzzled her head into his arm and finally stopped shivering. Gavin gently stroked her hair and her back. He felt such a deep love for this woman and wanted to protect her and make her feel safe, and he now knew exactly how he would do this. After some time, Roszalia's body began to soften against his and her breath came in slow shallow rhythm. Gavin knew she had fallen asleep and as much as he hated to leave her, he knew he had to go to talk to his father. Slowly and tenderly, he unwound his body from hers and kissed her on the forehead whispering, "I love you Roszalia, we will soon be together always."

Gavin slipped from Roszalia and headed towards her door. He took one last loving look at his gypsy princess and closed the door, making sure the lock had caught.

CHAPTER NINE

Devon was lounging on the leather divan when Gavin walked into the massive library. William O'Connor was a scholarly man and his collection of literature was his passion. Gavin noted that his father was not in the room, but thought better than to discuss what had just occurred on the stairs between them. The love making with Roszalia and the thought of her beauty as she finally slept peacefully above was too sweet to taint with the memory of his brother's attempted violation. He walked over to the bar, his limp more pronounced with his anger, and uncapped the brandy decanter, then decided on a straight whiskey, pouring a sizable amount in a glass. Having a feeling to get through this meeting without a major battle with his brother present, he would need it.

Devon was watching his brother from narrowed eyes, and he could not resist baiting him, knowing well that Gavin was purposely avoiding the subject of the little gypsy wench.

"So, I presume our little, um, lady is upstairs all snug in her bed?" Devon noticed Gavin's grip on his glass tightened and his jaw set rigid at his comment. "Oh dear brother," A laugh escaped Devon's lips to further antagonize his brother. "Please do not tell me you really are taken with the wench? Why I am sure she has bedded half the staff here by now, and is only interested in what baubles you can give her." Still taunting him Devon continued, "No matter, once you take off on another one of your ocean adventures, I plan on making sure she will never want the likes of you again. After all, I can be very persuasive."

Gavin, unable to tolerate one more word concerning the woman he loved, slammed the glass down and took three steps to reach his brother. Grabbing Devon by the neck and with his face only inches from his, said in a low guttural voice,

"Never go near Roszalia, and never speak ill of her, and never be mistaken that I will kill you if I hear otherwise." Gavin shoved Devon back on the divan and stood glaring, legs planted and fists clenched, ready for retaliation.

Devon instead only stood up and gave a mock bow and applause. With a sick and malicious smile his grey eyes darkened showing his true meaning, countered.

"Then perhaps you should never leave her alone."

Both men glared into the other's eyes and there with an unspoken hatred too deep for words. The sound of their father's voice approaching broke the deadly thick silence in the air.

William and Andrew strode in the library followed by his lawyer and lifelong friend, Barrister Ausby, noting Gavin's stance in front of his brother and the antagonistic look on their faces, broke the tension ,

"Good, I see you two have managed not to kill each other before our meeting, Where is Caitlin? This concerns all three of you." As if on cue, Caitlin floated in the room on a whirlwind, hair pulled back with strands escaping everywhere, her cheeks flushed but a smile as always on her face. "Here I am father, sorry, the kids are such a handful sometimes. I went to find Roszalia to help watch them but poor girl was sound asleep. Father, she really does work too hard around here, why she takes care of my children, helps cook, gardens, cleans and I swear she is the very heart of this place! We need to do something special for her." Caitlin, in her usual manner continued without letting speaking and seemed not to take a breath. Only when Devon suddenly burst out with laughter did she pause and look his way.

"Oh yes, the poor girl is working so very hard, I am sure you agree brother?" He said looking at Gavin, his mirth tinged with sarcasm that did not escape any of them in the room, yet only held meaning for the two brothers.

"Enough!" William O'Connor bellowed, more than a bit agitated with his son's childish behavior. "Caitlin, please come sit. We have things to discuss concerning the future of O'Connor Estate. I will ask you two to be civil towards each other. This meeting concerns all of us and all of the people who live here at the estate."

Gavin retrieved his whiskey and came over to sit in a high backed leather chair across from his brother, not trusting him without seeing him head on. Caitlin sat next to her husband on the other divan, next to where her father stood, and Devon stretched out again to show his utter boredom with family affairs. William went to pour himself a brandy, and then facing his family, he began,

"As you know, I have been in poor health these last few months. Caitlin's face took on her worried look and she began to speak, but her father put up his hand. "I did not say I am going anywhere soon, but to face life's eventuality is to prepare for the future. I have tried to make a decent life for my family here at the estate as my father and his did. Your mother, God rest her soul, loved this place like no other on earth, and it would do my soul good to know that our home and all who Call it that, will continue to thrive after I am with her."

Gavin noticed that Caitlin was visibly pale and he went to sit next to her as Andrew held her hand. Devon, in his usual callous manner, was now sitting up with more attention, he felt that he might be handed the reins to the estate since his brother was so often absent. William, taking in different reactions of his three children continued,

"Today you will hear what will become of the estate and all who reside here. Your mother and I had discussed these matters, but since she is no longer with us I have made some changes in my personal will and the estate. I will give you each a copy; I have made this as simple and fair as possible. Now, Barrister

Ausby will read it aloud, and please hold any comments until he is finished." William was looking directly at Devon.

Barrister Ausby handed each a set of documents. Clearing his throat, he began in his dull droning voice, "I Lord William Edward O'Connor the second, being of sound mind and body, decree this as my last will and testament. In the matter of my death, I convey that O'Connor Estate and the measured acreage that encompasses the property in the legal real estate records shall be split in equal shares amongst my three children: Caitlin Katherine O'Connor Anders, Gavin Edward O'Connor, and Devon William O'Connor. And thereafter, the future generations of their offspring shall have equal rights in the running of the property. The livestock and stockyard shall become the property of Devon William O'Connor, to be managed under Gavin Edward O'Connor's advice. The Shipyard and ships shall become the property of Gavin Edward O'Connor. All Stocks, jewels, and household possessions, along with the country manor on the Dingle Peninsula, shall be the property of Caitlin Katherine O'Connor Anders and her husband Andrew Anders. No portion of the estate, its tenant holdings or the Big House shall be sold, traded, or given away for as long as a family member is residing on the premise. The immediate management and ruling of the estate, the stockyard, shipyard, and the staff shall be bestowed upon the eldest son, Gavin Edward O'Connor. If he so declines, or upon his death, the appointment shall be passed to the next in line, Devon William O'Connor, if he so declines, or upon his death, the appointment shall be passed to Caitlin Katherine O'Connor Anders. All hired help is to be treated fairly and each hired hand is to receive two years wages upon my demise." Barrister Ausby was still talking, but Devon was no longer listening, he was now sitting rigid on the edge of his seat. He was furious! Yes, he wanted the stockyards and livestock but to have his brother manage what he did – he could not, and *would not* tolerate that insult! He heard his father's voice,

"These are my wishes, now do any of you have any comments?" Devon was about to speak when he noticed his father was looking directly at Gavin apprehensively. Gavin also noticed that his father was focused on him. This was no surprise to him; he had known he would have to make a decision on what he would do when the estate was passed to the family. His father had consulted him on a prior draft when his mother was alive. Gavin swirled his drink and watched the amber liquid for a moment, gathering his thoughts before speaking. A few years ago, he might have considered giving it to Devon and head back out to sea, but things had changed during his long absence from the land he loved. He saw Roszalia's eyes in the fiery amber liquid in the bottom of the glass. He loved her and would never leave her again. To let Devon run the estate would be a mistake. Devon would put the estate in ruins. Gavin looked up at their faces. Caitlin's, concerned, his father's, tired and worried, Barrister Ausby's, solemn and waiting, and Devon's, cold and calculating. As he stood, a moment of pain shot through his injured thigh from sitting.

Still holding his glass, he faced the group, "First... I know this all depends on my decision, but there is one announcement that I want to make right now." Devon's eyes narrowed and Caitlin looked bewildered. "I have decided to take a wife."

His father's look of astonishment might have made Gavin laugh if not for the seriousness of the subject. Devon's lips curled in a half smile, snarl, as he thought this some kind of ploy to get out of the responsibility of running the estate, and began to feel a premature confidence.

"Father, I will invite the lady to be my guest to dinner tonight." Gavin lifted his brandy, "With that said, I accept the position of running the estate, but let's hope there are many years before that comes to be," and raised his glass and drained it in a toast to his father.

William O'Connor seemed to take his first breath since he walked in the room. He walked over to Gavin and embraced him. Caitlin beamed and gave Gavin a hug and announced that she had to go to the kitchen to prepare a special meal for her mystery soon to be sister–in–law, and scurried out the door, secretly hoping it was to be Roszalia.

"So my boy, tell me have we ever met this lady?" His father

asked. Devon came up beside the two men and with noticeably clenched teeth added, "Yes, do tell us brother have we ever met this lady? I have never even known you to be vaguely interested in any particular female."

Gavin, not about to let his brother ruin his moment, just shrugged his shoulders. "You will all meet her at dinner." He shot his brother a narrowed look.

Devon turned to leave and under his breath Gavin heard him mutter, "Things will change!" and he stormed out of the room.

William O'Connor looked at his son and said in a father's proud tone, "Thank you for accepting this Gavin, you know that this is the only way I can be sure that your sister and her family are taken care of, and well your brother too, he will need to be advised."

"Father, I have indeed had a change of heart lately, but Devon is a grown man and in no way will he listen or take advice from me! But let us not talk of these things now. I need to go ask the woman I love to be my bride!" Gavin seemed to just remember that he had not even considered Roszalia's response.

His father chuckled, "Well lad, usually the girl is the first to know, so get to it!" Gavin began to leave the room and hesitated. He turned and looked at his father.

"What is it son?" concern apparent on his aging face. Gavin took a step and embraced his father, a response quite unexpected by the older man and he awkwardly returned the hug. Gavin backed up, "Father I never tell you of my respect for you, and I truly hope you can accept my decision on my choice of a bride and not be disappointed or …"

William O'Connor put up his hand and looked at his eldest son and said seriously, "Gavin, I have never known you to make a bad decision, even when you left after your mother's passing, I knew that you would one day take your place and the responsibility that is your birthright," he paused and a smile lightened his face, "I think I have an idea who will be dining with us. I may be old, but I can recognize a man's look of love at a woman, and I do approve." The older man clasped his sons hand and said, "Now, please go tell Roszalia so we can celebrate with our new daughter!" Gavin smiled widely and practically sprinted from the room and took the steps, three at a time, to reach the third floor where he had left Roszalia sleeping.

Devon was furious. How had the situation turned against him so fast? Not just the slap in the face that his brother was to be his watch dog, but the announcement that Gavin would be taking a wife! Devon had never known Gavin to be serious about any women; he had never brought one to the estate. Could it be Vanessa? He shook his head and mumbled, "No, Gavin cannot tolerate her." He suddenly stopped short in his stride, as if a flash of light hit him, the gypsy wench! Gavin would not do such a thing, then he had to hold back a laugh, father would never allow it, he would be angry for him marrying out of his class. He would disinherit Gavin and the estate would become his to run. Caitlin received the country home where their mother had grown up, and where his father and mother lived when they were first married. He experienced a moment of grief as he thought about his mother. She had understood him, his moods, and his desire to always be the best. He knew her background but loved her dearly, if Katherine was alive, things would be different. But, he was sure his father would not approve of Gavin's choice. Devon felt a new sense of security, and then he mused aloud, "The first order of business will be to banish my brother from the premise."

Devon now strode with an easy gate towards the stables, he felt like riding, he would take Fury, his horse out for a long ride, clear his head and make his future plans. Yes, he thought, and made a promise, things would work out just fine, he would see to it, no matter what he had to do to accomplish it.

Roszalia had fallen asleep resting in Gavin's arms, but now she found herself alone in her room. And thought, *I am a fool, my love for Gavin can only lead him to trouble.* She had no misconceptions that she could never gain the title as his wife. But to not have him in her heart was too hard to bear the thought of. She got up and washed her face and donned a new dress and smock to get ready to prepare the children for dinner. A knock on her door startled her and she spun. "Who is it?" Gavin had locked the door and Roszalia was glad, lest it be Devon.

"Roszalia," Gavin's voice was soft and caring, "May I talk with you before you go to the children?"

Roszalia opened the door and let Gavin in to the sitting area. She held her breath, for she thought he would tell her of the mistake he had made bedding her earlier. Looking into his eyes, she would face whatever he had to say.

Gavin reached to hold her hands in his, *so petite and perfect*, he thought. "Roszalia, I love you, I want you to be with me and take care of you, always." Roszalia was not sure she what he was trying to say to her.

"Gavin, I know that you cannot let it be known what we did and that you will take a wife of class someday soon, so if you need to tell me you cannot ever make love to me again, I will accept it. I had your love once and my heart will remain yours."

Gavin looked at her with a blank expression for a moment then burst into laughter and hugged her to him. "Oh dear love, you are too sweet, but I came here to ask you to be my wife, to marry me." He let her go to see her reaction.

She was sobbing but smiling. "Gavin, please do not tease me, I thought I lost you and now I have your love."

He cut her off with a kiss. "Yes or no, those are the only two answers. Will you have me?"

Roszalia stared at his face for only a moment and said, "Yes, but…" She was still not sure if she had not really woken from her dream yet, but when he lifted her up and kissed her deeply to assuage her doubt, she hugged his neck and kissed him back.

Gavin set her down and with a smack to her back side said, "Now get on your dinner dress, my betrothed is having dinner with the family tonight."

"Oh no! Please do not make me sit at the table with Devon, and what if your father hates the idea? I am a servant, and you the heir."

Gavin kissed her again, sitting her on the edge of the bed, he sat beside her. "Has Caitlin never told you the story of how my father and mother met?" Perplexed, Roszalia shook her head, she really did not see how this story pertained to their situation, but she listened. Gavin sighed,

"You see, my mother, Katherine Callaghan O'Connor, grew up at the country manor, in Dingle." Roszalia knew this, but listened as he spoke again, "Her mother had passed away when she was very young. Rupert, her father, never a healthy man, took to drinking heavily to ease his sorrow of losing his wife, leaving his daughter to the care of the servants. When she was twelve, her father's drink and gambling had put them in financial ruin. He had dismissed all of the staff except two would not leave, Addie, who was my mother's nanny, and Grieg, who was Rupert's butler and friend. They stayed with the two even though there was no money to pay wages. They were family and they loved Katherine as their own." He stood and went over to the window, pulled the drape back and looked absently out.

"The creditors were trying to take their home for payment. Katherine, then fifteen, went alone into Tralee to seek legal advice and help. Being a female and so young, she was turned away by ever firm…but one. The day she entered the office, there was a new young partner who had just received his barrister's license. He was willing to take her case."

Dropping the drape, he faced Roszalia. "The young barrister was my father." Roszalia sat in silence. She now knew why the family always treated all their staff, especially her, almost as family. Gavin's mood changed back to jovial, "Now, no more talk of not being accepted! If you do no hurry I shall have to dress you myself and throw you over my shoulder and take you to dinner, then what will they say?"

'Oh you would not!" Gavin raised an eyebrow and grinned. "I will change and meet you on the stairs." She began to turn when he gently took her hand.

"I have something for you to wear tonight, it was my mother's. It was given to her by my father after my birth. She left it to me in the hopes I would someday marry and that my wife would love it as much as she did. I think you will." Gavin withdrew an object from his pocket. It was a wooden box and in it, lying atop a silk lining was a delicate strand of gold chains with the most exquisite pendent, a gold teardrop, embedded with a multi–faceted emerald gemstone. Roszalia stared at the necklace mesmerized.

"Gavin, I could not, it was your mother's."

"Yes, and now it is yours, to bind us together always. Please, read the inscription." He took it from the box and turned it over for her to examine. On the back of the delicate gold that held the stone, it read, *binding our love forever.*

"That is how long my love will be for you – endless." He clasped the sparkling jewel around her slender neck. It fell perfectly and looked as if it was crafted specifically for her. Roszalia looked in her mirror, she touched the glistening gold strands and felt a warmth spread from it. She looked back at Gavin and saw only pure love in his handsome face. And as the tears threatened to fall once more, she gave Gavin one last hug and pushed him out the door so she could dress.

Roszalia was happy, happier than she ever could imagine. Dropping down on her bed and hugged her pillow. The man that she has loved for most of her life has just asked her to be his wife. Truly, this is a dream. Through her joy she heard the rap on her door. Gavin had returned to give her another kiss she thought. Roszalia quickly stepped to the door, and as she opened it, she flung her arms out and just as quickly, she recoiled. There stood Devon, a huge smirk on his face. He stood resting against the opposite wall with his arms folded.

"Well, well, that was quite a welcome I did not expect."

The remembrance of the event on the stairs only a few short hours before was still too fresh in her mind. Trying to not show her fear in her voice she said, "Devon, I thought you were someone else"

"Obviously." He gave a chortled grunt. "So it is true, my dear brother does intend on marring you. Well, I guess the best man won, eh, Roszalia"?

She did not understand why Devon was at her door, he seemed to almost be giving up, but after years of knowing his devious ways, she knew better than to trust him. Devon unfolded his arms and came close. He put one arm on the door to stop her from closing it until he had his say.

There was a dangerous glint in his steel grey eyes. He began with slow deliverance, "But keep in mind what you are doing to your beloved and this family Roszalia. Gavin is to be father's successor, heir to the title and all you see, and with it goes a very high responsibility as well as the expectations of his station. He will need a wife of impeccable virtue and status. Someone who can present herself and her husband at social and political functions." Devon leaned much too close and in a deep almost seductive yet malicious voice whispered, "Someone of pure blood, not a gypsy wench." As he spoke these words, he took a lock of her mahogany hair and wound it in his fingers pulling her close to his face. "I however, do not care. For if he marries you, father will disinherit him and I get it all, including you, my sweet." Devon's hot breath spread across her cheek and his lips brushed her hair. He breathed in her scent, intoxicating.

"So by all means, be my guest and ruin his life. He will not stay with you for long, be assured of this." And in his mind he thought, *and I will finally possess you.*

Roszalia, stunned by his words, flung herself back and pushed his arm away. She slammed the door and turned just as the tears began to fall on her cheeks, for she knew in her heart, Devon was right. Even now, knowing the story of Katherine O'Connor, it made little difference. Katherine had not been a child of an unwed gypsy.

Gavin was surprised that he found himself shaking, sweat was on his brow, walking with a quick gate, barely noticing his limp, down the narrow steps and towards his chambers. His normal composure was shattered as he sought her out to ask Roszalia to be his bride, at the last moment he allowed himself the thought that she would possibly refuse and this thought terrified him. He had traveled the world, engaged in countless dangers along the way, and the thought of not having the woman he loved by his side terrified him. But alas, he grinned, she said yes, and she loved him, of this he was sure. He saw it in her beautiful eyes when she looked at him.

Gavin reached his heavy door to his room and entered, closing it behind, he decided to lock it, not wanting Devon to enter and dampen his elation. As Gavin disrobed to dress for dinner tonight, he allowed himself the luxury of remembering her soft skin as he held her right here on his bed, he could still smell her lavender hair, he could still taste he red lips, and feel her open to him like a rose in the early morning. A groan escape with these sweet thoughts of the woman he loved. The thought of her in his strong arms from now on was almost too much and he knew he would have to have her again, if he did not calm his mind. He went to the wash stand and splashed the cool water over his face and grabbed for a clean shirt, as he did, he heard a knock on his door, 'Damn,' he thought, what a time for one of the maids to choose to come and tidy his room. He donned his breaches quickly.

"Gavin" a small familiar voice said behind the solid oak door, "may I speak with you?" Gavin's ached for Roszalia's sweet voice. It sounded like music to his heart. He reached the door in two strides and swung it open.

Roszalia stood there in the same dress he had seen her in only minutes before, a look of anguish on her beautiful face. Gavin took her hand and lead her in the room. He began to close the door when she held her hand up in protest.

"Please, this will only take a moment Gavin," Roszalia bit at her lower lip and wrung her slender fingers. "I cannot come to dinner with you, I…" she paused and could not meet his gaze but knew it was one of worry and anguish. "Please believe that I love you, I always have and will, but please understand, after you left my room I was about to dress and I realized that to think of being your wife was a foolish dream." Gavin reached for her hands but Roszalia turned and went to his window.

"Please hear me, I appreciate you telling me your family's story, but I am not a lady, I am a gypsy servant. I could never live up to the family's expectations of lady of the estate." Roszalia suddenly turned and looked into Gavin's face. Tears were brimming in her hazel eyes, making them almost emerald in color. "I will be your mistress if you will allow that, and love you for eternity, this is my place."

Roszalia then waited for his reply, wringing her hands further. She had been so elated when Gavin asked for her hand, she was not thinking straight, but she would still love him and take care of him until a time he would wed a woman of his class, and then only her memories would remain.

Gavin looked into her eyes, he marveled at their depth and emotions they caused in him, and in them, he saw the love and pain she held inside. He simply said,

"No, Roszalia, I do not accept that."

"I am truly sorry, if you do not wish me as your mistress I understand. But, you must wed a lady, and I do not wish any heart to be broken..." Gavin cut her sentence off and with determined sternness and finality in his voice said,

"But to only break your heart, and mine? You misunderstood me Roszalia; I said no I will not take you as my mistress, because you will be my wife." He took both her trembling hands in his own, slightly shaking on his own, he would not lose her, he thought, and he would prove his love and devotion. "I will not lose you again, Roszalia, I have loved you for longer than I could admit. I believe one reason I would leave again so soon after coming home was due to the fact I was afraid of these feelings I have for you, afraid you would reject me, my love and what I can offer you. When I was in the ocean, my last thought before I lost consciousness was of you, and the entire time I was away, I only meant to come home to you. Please do not break my heart, for after today I am a different man, but only half without you by my side." Gavin felt a hot tears burning in his eyes, but did not care.

Falling to his chest she sobbed, dampening his crisp linen shirt, but could not stop. He held her close, stroked her hair, loving her, wanting her, realizing how much he needed her. After a moment, Gavin pushed her back, and kissed her eyes and cheeks where the tears had fallen moments earlier.

"Roszalia, please tell me you will be my bride, there will never be another, and noble blood or gypsy, you will be my only

love and lady of this estate I will ever have in my life time."
Gavin spoke in a soft, velvety tone to calm her fears.

Roszalia composed a bit now nodded, "I will try to believe
that, but please do not make me go to dinner tonight with you. I
could not bear what your father will say and Devon's sarcasm,
or worse." Gavin kissed her on the lips and made a promise that
he would tell them and she could be absent.

"I will come to see you tonight my love, and we will discuss
our future further." Roszalia reached to button his shirt and he
covered her hand," I would rather you unbutton these" he
teased. She gave him a scowl, still not fully convinced she was
doing the right thing, but her love for him was so strong she
would do anything he wished.

"Go to dinner Gavin, I must attend the children and then I
will wait for you tonight."

Roszalia turned and almost ran out the door, she was still
shaking and still so unsure. She thought of her mother and her
love affair that gave reason to Roszalia's being, and how bitterly
it ended. Was she doing the same? She told herself it was not the
same. Gavin truly loved her, she knew that, but would that love
withstand society's distain? Roszalia climbed the stairs to her
own room, this time not noticing the shadow that stood just out
of sight from Gavin's chambers, but close enough to hear every
word that had just been said.

After Roszalia entered the stairwell, Devon emerged from
the shadows and with a sinister smile, entered his own room. He
closed his door and said out loud, "So now all I need to do is
keep this little couple apart, and dear brother with his broken
heart will be heading out to sea as soon as he can. Then the estate will be mine. Now for this special occasion of dinner, oh
what fun this would be," and Devon's usual sour mood gave
way to elation.

Gavin wanted to be happy, he wanted to rejoice with
Roszalia over the knowledge that they would be together as
husband and wife, but her reaction made him wary. He felt
heavy hearted at the likelihood that people in certain circles

would look down upon her, and he winced. He was sickened at the thought that anyone would hurt her by being so bold as to say as much, but aristocrats are snobs. This he knew, always despising the boring events and parties and ceremonies required of him to attend as a young man. However, as heir, he would have to accept these social responsibilities. Gavin let a long sigh escape and then thought of Roszalia's soft skin, tear stained as she stood so proud in front of him, attempting to protect him from the sharp tongues that others would have of their union.

"Damn them all," Gavin said, a bit louder than even he expected. He finished dressing for dinner, brushed his hair and flung the brush on the dressing table. Somehow, he would make sure no one hurt her.

As Gavin left his chambers, Devon was closing his own door. The two brothers eyed each other warily, Gavin with suspicion, Devon with a devious humor.

"So will the little, ah, lady be joining us?"

Gavin continued to walk towards the staircase without turning his head and said, "No Devon, I would not give you the satisfaction of ruining anyone's evening." Gavin, not stopping, reached the landing and descended the stairs two at a time to get as far from his brother as possible.

Caitlin and Andrew were already in the dining room after checking on the children, Edward and Samantha usually ate their evening meals with Roszalia in the kitchen, but tonight another staff member was with them. Caitlin hoped that the reason for Roszalia not being with them was that she would be the one dining next to her brother as his intended bride. Then Gavin entered–alone.

"So, where is she?" Caitlin asked anxiously. Gavin stepped to his sister and told her that he would explain when all were seated. Devon swung around behind his brother and said in a low mumble that only Gavin heard, "And what a story this shall be." Devon sat in his usual chair at the left side of the table towards the middle. Caitlin in her usual hurried way, went to the mirror on the wall, pinned her escaping curls back in place, and returned to her seat next to her father and Andrew. William

O'Connor finally entered the room. Usually Caitlin would be fussing to her father of this or that, but tonight all eyes were fixed on Gavin and the empty seat beside to him

"Well, son have we scared the poor girl off even before meeting her," his father gave Gavin a wink.

"No father," up until now Gavin had been resting near the china buffet. He now came over to his seat and leaned on the back of it. "I do regret that my intended bride will not be here to dine with us. She felt that this may be a situation that the family needs to accept her in their hearts before she can feel comfortable in their presence."

Caitlin stared at Gavin for a moment then waved her hand as if to dispel the notion. "Why in the world wouldn't we accept and love any woman you would wish to marry?" At this Devon could no longer keep silent and let out a half snicker, half laugh,

"Oh dear brother, just tell us the woman's name, we are all so anxious to welcome the newest *member of society* into our hearts and home!" The malice in his voice was even noticed by Caitlin. William O'Connor abruptly held up his hand to stop Devon from further comments. Then to Gavin,

"Son, we can respect the girls wishes, so do tell us and let all here be their own judge. I know we will all love our new daughter." A kind understanding and encouraging smile was on the older man's face.

"Very well," Gavin had never wanted his family to be more accepting of anything in his life, and continued. "The woman to be my bride is already one we know and love, it is Roszalia." Gavin paused to study Caitlin's face, then Andrew and last, he looked at Devon. Unaware that Devon had already known it was Roszalia and was plotting his scheme by using their love to gain his place in the hierarchy.

Not a word was spoken. Gavin was about to speak when Devon burst out with laughter, "Bravo, I applaud you, leave it to you brother, first you run off to sea and break mother's heart, and now you will put father to shame with this insult by marrying a member of our *staff!*" He said this last word with distain.

Gavin's fists balled in anger, as he took a step around the table, William raised his arm in front of him to hold him at bay. He then snapped in Devon's direction,

"Be silent!" Looking back at Gavin's angry face, he nodded for him to sit. Too angry and having too much respect for his father to do otherwise, he heeded him. The elder man smiled broadly and declared,

"I for one think this is a wonderful union!"

Devon's mouth dropped and his jovial demeanor turned to dismay. He was seething. Father accepted this foolish union like it was a match made in heaven. Now he would have to find a way to separate them, as he looked at his brother with contempt, he thought, *you two will not be together*. He tried to hide his anger as he went to the bar and poured another whisky.

"I have known Roszalia since she was but a child, and there is not one society lady or royal that could be any more of a pure, loving, good hearted and spirited woman than she. And I will be proud to announce Roszalia as my heir's wife and a member of our family." William held up his glass in a toast and paused as he noticed Caitlin's broad grin.

"Caitlin, do you have a comment?"

With the speed of a gazelle, she sprang from her chair, ran to Gavin and threw her arms around him hugging him tightly. After a moment she released,

"You brother, are truly a devil. To have Roszalia as my sister would be an honor. Now, go get her and tell her not to be foolish. We all love her already and think her a family member, and this just makes it...well, official!"

Gavin gave Caitlin another hug, and whispered, "Thank you Caitlin, this will mean everything to Roszalia knowing you will accept her." Caitlin floated back to her seat saying,

"I just wondered why it has taken you so long to realize what I already knew!" Andrew got up and went to clasp his brother–in–law on the back.

"Finally I will not have to hear any more of the matchmaking!' Then Caitlin began chattering on about preparations for the wedding.

"Let us not go too fast, Roszalia is still a little unsure of how her standing in society will be greeted, and I have not even begun to talk of a wedding."

Gavin suddenly felt he had already lost this battle with his sister. He looked to his father and Andrew for support, but both men just smiled. He thought maybe it was just what Roszalia needed to feel she fit in, to plan their wedding with Caitlin at her side. He sat back, and for the first time since leaving his room, he smiled. Immediately after the meal, Caitlin took her leave from the men and bounded up the stairs to find her friend and soon to be sister–in–law.

Roszalia was still unable to accept what had taken place just a few hours ago. Everything she had ever dreamed of with Gavin, the man she has always loved was becoming reality. He wanted her to be his wife, Lady of the estate. The thought terrified her, yet her love for Gavin was far more powerful than her fears. Hearing the knock Roszalia answered,

"Coming, one moment," she was more cautious, remembering her mistake of opening the door to Devon. When she unlatched the lock Caitlin came bursting in,

"Oh Roszalia, this is the happiest day! We will truly be sisters!" She took her hand and began dragging her out of the room. "You must come down stairs and celebrate, Father is so pleased." She hugged her friend until Roszalia felt the breath leaving her lungs.

"Caitlin, slow down, please I told Gavin to make his announcement, I want the family to approve"

"Oh posh, you have always been family to us, now it will be official and you will be not only my friend but my sister also!" Still being pulled along, Roszalia saw Gavin's familiar, handsome figure entering onto the stair landing, she looked pleadingly for his help to extract her from his sister's grip.

"Ah, I see I cannot even tell my intended bride myself that the family approves! What is the heir to the estate good for around here?"

Caitlin waved him off. "Oh Gavin, we have so very much to plan for the engagement party and the wedding." At this, Roszalia planted her feet and Caitlin jerked to a halt. Turning, she saw the look on her friend's face and gave her a sheepish grin. "Oh, perhaps I am jumping the gun." As Gavin gave a sigh, Caitlin pouted, "Alright, I will just go see the children now, I see you two need to be alone for a while." Before she left, she once again gave Roszalia a huge hug. Even in her whirlwind she could not help but give a laugh at her friend's enthusiasm. Gavin watched his sister seem to bounce with her enthusiasm down the stairs.

"Well, I guess I need not tell you everyone's reaction," Gavin said with a boyish smile. He took Roszalia's arm and led her down the stairs to the parlor. When they entered, he closed the door and kissed her hungrily, she returned his kiss with equal passion. Looking down in her eyes, but not letting go he asked,

"So will the future Lady of the estate allow her soon to be sister–in–law the pleasure of helping plan our wedding day?" Gavin still held her close as if he let her go he would lose her.

"Of course, it seems strange though, still like a dream. I am still a bit uneasy, you said it to me once that society can be cruel. What if they shun you and do not accept me?

Gavin hushed her qualms with a kiss. "You will be accepted as your own loving, beautiful self." A sound outside the door made them both turn as William entered the room.

"Ah, there you two are!" He was beaming. The older man came over to Roszalia and embraced her, "Welcome to our family, you know I have always cared deeply for you as one of the family, now you just have to put up with this man!"

Roszalia gave him a quick kiss on the cheek, "I do not think you have to worry about that, I will cherish the opportunity to be a part of your family." The love in both of their eyes told him this would be true for both.

CHAPTER TEN

The final meeting pertaining to the merger with the American shipping company was arranged and then Gavin vowed he would settle down at the estate, only traveling to Dingle when needed for business, and finally begin his new life with Roszalia. The trip made Roszalia apprehensive, but she knew that he must go. The final merger meeting would take place on the west coast of Iceland. Gavin expected to be gone no longer than one month. Caitlin promised to keep her soon to be sister–in–law busy with wedding preparations. This time when he left, the spring air was warm and he would not let anything delay his return to his love.

Five days before he was due to sail, William O'Connor suffered a massive heart attack. Gavin insisted he would send Karl in his place but his father would not hear of it. He said it was his last wish that his eldest son ensure the company he had built would continue and prosper through this merger.

Gavin agreed out of respect for his father. William knew he was far worse than he let anyone know. The weakness he had battled for years, finally won. With the help of his friend, Barrister Ausby, he was satisfied that he had his affairs in order, and now only hoped he could stay in this life until his eldest son's return. Caitlin and Roszalia kept vigil at his bedside, but his health was declining daily. Andrew did all he could to keep his father–in–law comfortable.

Gavin attended the overdue merger negotiations under duress. When all was signed and completed, he headed back home with an ominous feeling that he would not be hearing his father's voice again.

Roszalia sat gazing out the window, the wind was howling and the rain beat upon its sills. A thin layer of fog had begun to appear, as an intricate lace spun on glass. The fire crackled as it struggled to keep the chill out of the room, and began to dwindle. Roszalia pulled the cotton throw that was on her lap up tightly to her chest. Even though the hour was late, she decided she would wait for the opportunity to see her love. The message said he would arrive tonight. As she sat in the parlor in a large leather high back chair, she inhaled the scent of the room, the sweet combination of leather and pipe tobacco. This was a favorite room of Barrister O'Connor and Gavin. She breathed in deeply as if she could summon him with her thoughts. Roszalia had been feeling ill as of late, and as she placed her hand on her abdomen she sighed, yes, she could sense the life within her, and she hoped Gavin would be happy with this knowledge. Her thoughts went back to the sadness that William O'Connor the Second passed on today.

Roszalia felt hot tears sting her eyes He was a kind man who always treated her with respect. When Gavin announced that they would wed, Barrister O'Connor was ever gracious and accepting of his son's wishes, even to wed one in their employ. Wiping her now damp cheeks, she decided she must get up to replenish the fire or it certainly would burn out. As she unwound her legs and touched the cold floor, she glanced towards the window, the wind was blowing, yet the thought of Gavin made a tingle run down her spine as she remembered the warmth and comfort of being in his arms, his strong body pressed hard against hers in a passionate deep kiss. He was on his way home, after finishing his father's last request on this voyage.

William wanted Caitlin and Roszalia to promise him that when he took to his bed, the wedding plans would continue. He did not want his illness to cause any delay for his son's happiness. They both promised to honor his request, yet Roszalia did not feel like planning or celebrating, even her own future.

The wind gave another angry howl and a tree branch scratched at the windowpane. Gavin had been gone for over a month and her heart ached every moment he was gone. She had no word from him in this time. She knew how much he loved the ocean even after it tried to take his life. She tried to picture him on the deck, shouting orders to the crew, leather breeches and his boots, his shirt open to allow the cool breeze and sun darken his skin. She was drifting off to sleep when she thought she heard a woman's soft voice and a lower male voice, but the darkness enveloped her and she could fight the sleep that overcame her no more.

Caitlin's voice awoke Roszalia as she pulled the drapes open, letting the sunshine through the library's windows.

"Gavin came in extremely late, the livery boy told me, and he was drenched and needed to sleep. You may want to go wake him. I am sure you are the one person that would comfort him upon waking." Caitlin was fussing with her friend's hair. "Go on now. I will take care of the children this morning."

Arranging her skirts, she pinched her cheeks to add some color. She was excited to see Gavin but sad at the same time under such circumstances. She wondered if her own news would make him happy. She had a moment's thought of her mother and then shook her head to clear it. Her current situation was different. They were different. They were to be wed within the month. She reached the main stairs and headed towards his familiar door. Roszalia was about to knock when she decided she would just enter quietly and give him a light kiss to wake him.

Turning the knob, she slowly opened the door. The curtains pulled from the night before left the room cast in shadows. Roszalia knew his room well, she made her way to his bedside and saw his long form under the warm down cover, she was about to bend over when she caught another sight, a movement from the other side of the bed. Roszalia straightened up in surprise. A woman sat up, the covers falling from her chest exposing bare breasts. She looked at Roszalia with fire in her eyes yet did not speak. As if in a bad dream, Roszalia stood horrified as she watched this woman slip from Gavin's bed exposing her naked body, Vanessa Burke stood there displayed for Roszalia. With no modesty or hurry, she reached for her dress that thrown over the bed, pulled it on, pinned her long blonde hair up and turned to leave the room. As she stood in the open door, she blew a kiss in the direction of the still sleeping figure of Gavin. Roszalia, still dumbstruck and rooted to the spot, felt her legs go weak, her stomach churned, she felt she would vomit right where she stood. Gavin as if on cue, rolled over, opened his eyes, and saw her above him.

"Roszalia? Ah, god my head, I feel like I have been drugged." He sat up, sheets falling to his waist and revealing his naked torso. Gavin reached out for her hand and she recoiled. "What is it?" he asked, becoming more alert at her reaction.

He began to get up when suddenly her legs took motion. Turning, she fled from his room, leaving his door open. The tears now streamed down her cheeks as she reached the landing to the third floor. She stopped to catch her breath. Her heart was pounding, breaking. He was with another woman. Vanessa was in his bed, and he did not even care that she saw them! She made it to her room and shut the door behind her. Flinging herself on her bed, she wept in her pillow, and all the time cursed herself for the fool she had been and was. Yes, she was her mother's daughter.

Devon stood in his doorway, oh, this was too easy, he thought, the breakup was inevitable now. Vanessa Burke had come home with him last night. Knowing she despised his brother ever since the incident at the holiday party years ago, when he asked if she would be his ally in the breakup of Gavin and Roszalia, she was more than happy to oblige. She had always resented Roszalia for having Gavin's love, a common gypsy, preferred over her. Vanessa was now lying in Devon's bed.

He had told her the simple plan. Gavin would be drugged. All she would need to do was lie in his brother's bed until Roszalia came in the morning, then get up and leave just before Gavin awoke. As an added bonus, Devon let her languish in his chambers, and told her with Roszalia out of the way, Gavin would have to look for a wife soon. He knew this pleased the stupid girl, for she grinned and took his bait.

Right now, he was giddy that the plan had worked so well, he watched as Roszalia left Gavin's room, tears in her eyes. Late last night before Gavin got home, he had slipped the mixture that Roszalia always gave their father when his pain had gotten unbearable, which allowed him to sleep, into the brandy bottle. Knowing Gavin always had a brandy before he retired, he had stowed Vanessa in his room and waited until the mixture of brandy and the drug had taken effect. Gavin had fallen into a deep sleep quickly. Vanessa then slipped out of her dress and under his cover and waited for Roszalia to enter.

Vanessa was never a woman of honor or scruples, in her twisted mind she thought perhaps by helping Devon, if she did not marry Gavin, and then Devon would be looking for a wife. Either O'Connor would do, she decided to make this morning extra memorable for him. As she saw him watching Roszalia leave the other room she said in her sultry voice,

"Devon, come to me and let's have some fun now," patting the bed. Devon closed his door and looked at her, she was attractive, but not a beauty like Roszalia, her pale skin and hair, a sad contrast to Roszalia's dark perfection. He began to get aroused thinking of the gypsy he could not have.

Instead, Vanessa was here, lying naked in his bed and she was perfect for his intent, she did her part well. His excitement began to build. Not for the pathetic wench that lie naked under his bed sheets, but that his plan to drive Roszalia and Gavin apart and him back out to sea had gone so smoothly. With Roszalia alone at the estate, and with Gavin and his father gone, there was no one to protect her. His plan was coming together. A menacing grin appeared on his face as he began undressing, he picked up his belt as he came towards Vanessa.

"Yes, let's have some fun, my special kind." He sat on the bed and tied a blind fold on her eyes.

She began to feel nervous. "We have never done this. I can make you really happy without this."

Devon looked at her and decided he did not want her to speak to annoy him and his thoughts. He took a cloth and tied it around her mouth so she could not scream, she attempted to get off the bed but he had his knee pinned against her legs. He stroked her arm and said in a smooth voice,

"Now love, I am going to make you feel things you have never felt before, so relax." His thoughts were of Roszalia beneath him. If Vanessa could have seen his face at that moment, a contortion of sheer sadistic pleasure, she would have been terribly afraid, but his words belied his intentions, and she became still. Knowing the solid oak door was virtually sound proof. He stepped towards the poor girl, belt raised and stripped the covers off her, flipping her over, he let the belt down sharply, and no one heard her screams.

Roszalia cried what seemed for hours, she heard Gavin's knock on her door, pleading for her to open it, yet could not face him. What lie would he tell her? How many other women had she not caught in his bed? She felt such a fool. Today were the funeral services. She would have to pull herself together, but after William's funeral, she would make plans to work at the apothecary with Agnes. She could not stay so near to Gavin, where her heart would break with every breath she took.

He knew that she was in her room he could hear her sobbing. He had no idea what was going on. The news of his father's passing was disturbing enough, and now the woman he loves refuses to speak to him! He tried knocking and calling to her again to no avail. He would have to go see Truda or Caitlin and try to make sense of things. As Gavin descended the stairs by the children's wing, he heard Barrister Ausby's voice below. Raking his fingers through his hair, he tried to focus on the next few days. He would have to speak with Caitlin about Roszalia. Damn, his life seemed to be taking a downward turn, and the pain in his head was pounding mercifully. He so wished Roszalia would be here by his side. Barrister Ausby saw Gavin approach and extended his hand, a strong grip for such a frail looking man, Gavin thought.

"My deepest sympathy, your father was my dearest friend," Barrister Ausby began.

"Thank you. Can I get you something?" Gavin responded a bit impatiently. He wanted desperately to go to the kitchen on any pretense, in hopes Truda would be there.

"No, no, I have come to discuss the proceedings before the services today with the family." Barrister Ausby noticed Gavin holding his temple.

"My boy, by all means, go get something strong, you do look like hell." Gavin looked at the concern on the older man's face.

Not wanting to create more grief, he straightened up and said, "I am fine, should we call the family in?

"Well, yes, in a moment, but this concerns only you, and as I am to understand your new bride to be?"

Gavin looked up sharply. "What concerns Roszalia?"

"May we call her down here please?" Gavin shook his head and thought, *well this is one way to see her. And find out what is going on.* Gavin rang the bell in the parlor and Marie, one of the maids appeared.

"Please go tell Roszalia that Barrister Ausby is requesting her presence in the parlor, I believe you can find her locked in her rooms." Gavin's tone had a harsher edge than he meant it to as he addressed the girl, causing her to widen her eyes and glance towards the door. Gavin waved his hand for the girl to go and raked his hand through his already tasseled hair.

The maid hurried off in search of Roszalia. Barrister Ausby raised an eyebrow and said with concern, "Locked in her room?" Ignoring Barrister Ausby question, Gavin needed a brandy to clear his head. The empty glass was where he left it the previous evening, but the decanter was missing, "Damnedest thing." Gavin muttered not for anyone to hear.

"What is?" Barrister Ausby asked, peering over the rim of his glasses.

"I had a brandy when I returned home late last evening. Here is the glass, but the decanter of brandy is missing." Gavin began to feel something was amiss, and he intended to find out what. Interrupting his thought as the door opened and Roszalia entered the room, wearing a modest black dress, subtle and muted. She was beautiful, long silken brown hair pulled back off her face, tendrils escaping. Gavin so wanted to brush them aside, her red lips so inviting, he thought how, even in time of sadness, his heart lifted at just seeing her.

Roszalia was shaking as she entered the room. Why did she have to see Barrister Ausby this morning? She knew Gavin was there, Marie the maid had said Master Gavin and Barrister Ausby were in the library, and she was to join them immediately. Roszalia decided she would show no emotion, she had cried all her tears for him. She would take care of this situation and then leave without further discussion. There was nothing Gavin could say. He betrayed her heart. Barrister Ausby was speaking again.

"Now Gavin, before your father took gravely ill, he engaged my services to find Roszalia's paternal parent." Roszalia, taken aback by this news, looked stricken.

"My father?" she muttered.

"Yes, your aunt Truda thought it may help you to know, given your wedding and Barrister O'Connor's imminent demise. He said this would be his wedding gift to you, to know who your father was," Barrister Ausby continued in his monotone voice. Gavin reached over to Roszalia and took her hand, for a moment she let him. Then, as the image of the naked woman getting out of his bed appeared in her mind, she snatched it away and folded them in her lap.

"Roszalia, your father was Joseph Danyovok. He came from a highly influential and wealthy family in Debrecen, a northern town in Hungary. He passed away five years ago in a riding accident. Now what I will tell you came from his sister Anna. When Joseph was with your mother he loved her very much, yet family pressures of him being heir to the family business and wealth were great. Then your mother found she was with child, they were young, and foolishly, they thought love could make them both happy. She decided not to tell Joseph until he told his father and mother of their plans to marry. They were together when they told his parents that they would marry. His father's anger was unleashed, expelling your mother from the estate. Joseph went after your mother knowing he would be denounced. The family business along with his inheritance would go to the younger brother. Joseph loved your mother and was willing to give it all. But your mother would not let him. She said they would find a way to be together and he could not let the fortune go to his brother, who was foolish and unjust. Your mother swore she would leave and he would never find her if he denounced his position, for she knew she could never be accepted into high society. Your mother told Joseph of her condition only after he promised he would not do anything foolish and that he would never tell anyone in the family. Joseph promised to respect your mother's wishes. He loved her.

After your birth, your mother could not stand being so close to the only man she ever loved, nor did she wish to complicate his life, so she moved on with a band of gypsies, only telling Joseph she would love him throughout all time. He searched for her, but when his father became seriously ill, the pressures of running the family business took over. Joseph took a wife, an arranged marriage by his family. He never stopped looking for your mother or you, his heart always belonged to Marguerite. Joseph found your whereabouts a few years before he passed; He decided that it was better for you if he stayed away." Barrister Ausby finally took a deep breath.

Roszalia sat ashen faced. What does this all mean? Now she knew who her father was, but her mother always told her he broke her heart, why? More deceptions. She looked at the thin man in front of her.

"And," she began slowly, "why is this important now, it was so long ago." Roszalia wrung her hands, desperately wanting Gavin's arms around her. Instead she sat still, she had too much grief right now to add more.

Barrister Ausby looked at her. "Roszalia child, you are of prominent lineage, you are the eldest daughter of Joseph

Danyovok. Your father declared you his legitimate child."

Gavin stood now. "Ausby, is all this true, documented?"

"Yes, he did not let it be known until someone came looking for the truth. He kept his promise to your mother of never letting your birthright be known, but he always acknowledged you are his legitimate daughter." He looked at Gavin. "After Joseph passed away the brother took over, and as expected, ruined the family business and lost everything of value."

Here is the sealed letter to you, he wrote it shortly after he learned of his illness. Anna said her brother placed this in a safe box for you." Roszalia sat rigid, looking at the letter.

"Roszalia," Gavin's voice broke her trance.

"Yes, yes, but you must understand how this all sounds, my mother always told me my father left her, betrayed her, now to know he wanted to find me all this time." Barrister Ausby handed her the letter and the box. Roszalia stared at the handwriting on the outside and with the crest seal, she ran her fingers over it, and then stood. "Please excuse me, I need to be alone." Turning, she left the room. Gavin took a step towards her, but Barrister Ausby detained him.

"Son, this is a lot for the lass to hear, she needs some time to come to terms with it all. Let her read the letter from her father she never knew." Barrister Ausby looked at where Roszalia had just exited. "That young woman has always acted and seemed of superb lineage, now we have the legal evidence."

Gavin now sitting was as taken aback as Roszalia. He had never known the story of her mother and father. He had always assumed her father was a wandering gypsy from the camps that left when she was young. No wonder she has so many emotions about coming into a prominent family and trusting him, after hearing what happened to her own mother. Gavin no longer felt the pain in his temples, only love for Roszalia in his heart. He wanted to hold her, kiss her, and give her his strength, yet still she pulled away. Not knowing what changed her feelings for him he was determined to win her back, no matter how long or what it took. Caitlin arrived just then, approaching Gavin with a look of concern.

"Gavin, what happened to Roszalia? I passed her on the stairs, and she looked up with tears in her eyes. I said we would meet after all is settled, on the wedding plans, but she looked at me and said there would be no wedding."

Now Gavin looked stricken, had she found another? Was this news so disturbing that she did not plan to marry him? His mind raced, he needed a drink! Pushing his fingers through his hair,

"Excuse me for a moment." He needed a whisky, and a moment to think. He made his way to the kitchen and saw the now empty decanter on the drying rack. He did not know why this concerned him. The butler was in the galley and asked to be of service. He noticed the disarray and pallor of Gavin and was concerned. "Carlson, why is the brandy decanter in the sink empty? It was full last night when I arrived home." Gavin said, waving in the direction of the empty container.

"Begging your pardon, Master Gavin, I was told you asked that the brandy decanter be emptied and refilled by this morning," Carlson said. "Marie said that you requested this, I took it upon myself to make sure this was done." Carlson had also thought it strange, he had made sure it was full just this afternoon and wondered why it emptied so fast.

"Thank you Carlson, but I do not recall speaking to Marie last night." The butler made a mental note to watch this young girl for she had been acting very skittish as of late.

"I will refill it immediately," he paused then continued. As the butler began to leave, Gavin stopped him.

"Carlson, could you have one of the grounds men cut a large bouquet of fresh roses and send them up to Roszalia, tell her they are from her new family that loves her."

"Yes, sir." Carlson smiled at this request.

This would let her know he was thinking of her. Filling his glass, he headed back into the library to see what else Ausby required of him.

Marie had been hiding in the shadows of the pantry, now panic seized her body. Gavin was asking questions, he knew he had not spoken to her and was questioning the brandy. The girl quietly fled the area to find Devon. He would know what to do. Devon scared her terribly, he could be severe, and he sometimes hurt her, yet he also gave her nice things, jewelry, clothing, and sometimes they would drink wine in his quarters if he were in an amiable mood.

She was not an especially bright girl, so the baubles that Devon provided her were enough to keep her loyal to him and have her do as he told without question. The fear and pain he would inflict on her also kept her silent.

Marie saw Devon out the back door, just off the stoop. He was removing a pair of black gloves, which he stuffed into a barrel before he entered the back foyer. As he closed the door, he was startled to notice Marie beside him.

"Damn Marie, you gave me a start, what is it?" Devon sounded annoyed and a bit winded. His eyes had the piercing look to them today, like a wild animal trying to confuse its enemies. Marie put her hand up to him for comfort, but he shook her off. "Marie get a hold of yourself, now what is it?"

"Devon, yer brother…well," Marie stammered, making Devon all the more agitated and anxious for her to move aside. He reached out to her and took her by the shoulders, "Now calm down and tell me," he said.

"Gavin was questioning, you know, the brandy, what I told Carlson." Marie had the look of a frightened doe. "Oh Devon, I cain't do this, I cain't lie, I…" Her words cut off mid–sentence, with a swift movement. Devon had his large hand encircled around Marie's delicate neck, squeezing just enough to let her know his wrath. His face was only inches from her now frightened and wide eyes.

"Now Marie," Devon began in a low menacing voice, "you will say exactly what I told you to anyone who asks. I give you lovely things, do I not?" She shook her head a small bit, "and I want to remain close to you, I like you, I do." Devon moved his thumb over the front of her throat and gave a bit more pressure, her eyes now wide with terror. "But make no mistake I could snap your lovely neck in two at any moment if you do not do what I tell you, do you understand?"

Devon loosed his grip and Marie reached up to protect her neck, she knew better than to whimper, or even move. Devon smoothed her hair down and gave her a quick kiss on her head then walking off without a backward glance. Marie waited until she could no longer hear his footsteps then she collapsed against the wall, covering her face with her hands, and wept.

Gavin, Caitlin, Andrew, and Barrister Ausby all sat in wait for Devon, Gavin had a fresh whisky, he swirled it and once more thought of Roszalia's eyes in its depths. Some minutes later, Devon strode into the room, clothing disheveled, with sweat beads on his brow. Gavin took notice of this and the mud on his boots, very unlike him. "Out riding this morning brother?" Gavin said casually. Devon gave his brother a venomous look. "When did the favorite son get in?" The sarcasm dripped from his lips.

"Late." Gavin did not trust any other answer, he did not know what Devon had planned, but he would find out. He downed the liquid in his glass and sat down in the chair he had been in before. He kept his eye on Devon. He seemed nervous this morning. Barrister Ausby began to drone on about the upcoming funeral arrangements. Gavin had stopped listening and was trying to put the pieces together. Something was not right.

Roszalia entered her quarters, from the outside door on the servants' floor, not wishing to encounter the children. She thought of the children and Caitlin, she was her dearest friend, and Roszalia would love to have her as her sister–in–law, but after Gavin's betrayal, how could she marry him? Now her entire childhood beliefs of her father, was a lie. She turned the letter repeatedly in her hands. The neat handwriting only had her name on it. Roszalia Danyovoc. With shaking fingers broke the wax seal. The parchment slid out with ease.

My dearest Roszalia,

I have missed my first–born child's life. I can only hope you had a good, happy one, your mother was and is my one true love, and if you are, as I know you will be as beautiful and talented as my Marguerite, then your life shall be blessed. I can only tell you the wisdom that I did not heed, follow your heart, others will put you astray, but in the end, the heart and love will be all you have. I do not feel anger for what she had to do, for she and I will be together one day again where no one will judge us. Be happy.

Joseph

Barrister Ausby had finally concluded his formal business at the estate and afterwards took his place as a family friend. Andrew invited him to stay the evening. He agreed and the family went into the dining room, none hungry but for the consolation of friendship in time of sorrow.

Gavin, knowing he had much to begin to arrange, decided to take his leave with this pretense. He could not wait a moment longer to see Roszalia and console her. Was this why she would not give her love to him, did she fear her destiny to be that of her mother? Given her now known bloodline, he felt she should be happy, yet she seemed to reject him further. He would confront her. Making his way to the back staircase, he passed his brother's room, as he looked in, he saw Marie in side straightening up.

"Marie," the young maid jumped with nerves, the look of fright on her face bewildered him. "Sorry to startle you, but I needed to ask you a question." Gavin noticed she held a yellow dress in her hands, he briefly thought this should have some significance but at the moment could not think why. "Marie, why did you tell Carlson you spoke to me last night? I do not remember a conversation."

The girl visibly paled and began shaking. She started to stutter a reply, "Beg, yer pardon, Master Gavin, but we did speak, you told me to refresh your brandy, and, er..."

At that moment, Devon's voice coming up the stairs broke her trembling and she curtsied and darted out the door towards the servants' steps, yellow dress still in hand. Gavin decided to avoid his brother and went to find Roszalia.

The events of the last few days were too traumatic for

Roszalia to handle. Her entire safe, secure existence had crumbled, the man her every waking moment revolved around had betrayed her. Now to find out, after twenty-four years to find out her father never sent her mother away. She needed to get away. She would wait until after the funeral ceremony and then go live with Agnes in town. She could not be under the same roof as Gavin. She could not stop loving him, but her heart could not let her forgive him. She was drafting her letter to Caitlin explaining her termination of employment, when a knock came at her door. She creased the letter and put it in her drawer, "Enter."

Gavin gently opened her door, she turned and wanted to run to him, to cry to him, to hit his chest for betraying her, and beg for him to make love to her all at the same time, instead she sat rigid in her chair,

"Yes, Gavin, how can I be of service?"

"Yes, Gavin? Roszalia, I thought of you every moment since I left, I dreamt of seeing you, holding you, loving you, and I return and you reject my very touch, you will not look me in the eye, what have I done to lose your love?" He stood with palms open as if to plead his case.

Roszalia did not move, she just sat silently for a moment and then she looked at him, "You have betrayed my heart." Gavin stepped back as if struck.

"I really do not understand, how? When? Roszalia I love you, I have never loved another as I love you. Please for god's sake, tell me how I have betrayed the heart I love?" His voice was on the edge of desperation and anger; trying to make sense of this. Roszalia got up, walked towards the door where he stood and with her hand on the knob said,

"Perhaps, Vanessa can help you understand." With that, she closed the door only inches from Gavin's face and he heard the lock catch.

Standing there bewildered. *Vanessa*? What has she been saying to Roszalia? He would find out and make her tell the truth, there is nothing between them. He did not try to confront Roszalia again. He would have to speak to Vanessa and straighten this out. Right now, he would ask Caitlin try to convince

Roszalia that she is the only woman he wishes in his life.

Marie had run up to her room, she was packing what small belongings she possessed. She had to leave O'Connor Estate. She had lied to Master Gavin, she liked him, he was kind, and she liked Roszalia. The thing that Devon had done with that wench Vanessa to them was a terrible thing, yet she was too frightened of what Devon would do to her if she told. She decided to go to the alehouse near the harbor she could cook and serve and she could maybe work for a place to stay until she could figure something else out. She only knew she had to leave. The last thing Marie did was scribble a note to Roszalia, her writing was bad, and her grammar worse, but she managed to write out,

Roszalia,
Please do not blame or distrust Master Gavin, he did no wrong. It was the other one, and that devil woman, Vanessa plan to break you apart.
There was no name just… *A friend.*

Marie slipped it under her pillow. She thought when the head housekeeper realized she was no longer at the estate she would find the note and deliver it to Roszalia. Marie took her small satchel and left unnoticed, out the backdoor.

The staff was busy with all the funeral preparations and no one noticed Marie's absence for days. When they finally did, the note was cast aside to a table in the library, where it lie unread.

CHAPTER ELEVEN

The next few days were a blur of events, so many people came to pay their respects, and even Devon seemed sober and contrite. The legal affairs of the estate, and the preparations for the funeral consumed Gavin's time, but the situation with Roszalia was never far from his thought. He did not have the chance to ask Caitlin to help him discover what had happened in his short absence concerning Roszalia, nor did he think she would be up to it. He would have to take care of the immediate concerns and then he would resolve this.

Caitlin was trying to hold herself together, but emotions were high and she would burst into tears easily. Roszalia kept the children as occupied as she could, keeping their minds off the absence of their beloved grandfather. In this way, she was able to avoid Gavin as much as possible. Her heart and soul missed him terribly, but she was too sad over the loss of Barrister O'Connor and the betrayal of the man she loved to chance any confrontation with him.

Agnes had come to the estate before the memorial service to deliver the family a spiritual healing prayer. After, she sought out her niece. Agnes found her in the pantry area. She could feel pain and sadness veiling her aura. Of course given the recent passing of William these emotions were to be expected, but there was something deeper. Yet with her niece having the same gifts, she had never been able to read her completely.

"Your heart is sad child," she began. Roszalia avoided the older woman's eyes for she would see through to her soul if she let her. Agnes took her hands. "What is it child, there is more that the barristers passing that saddens you."

Roszalia shook her head, "Agnes, Gavin has betrayed me, and I witnessed this with my own eyes." She now hung her head to veil her tears. Agnes did not feel any betrayal, but she felt there was trickery involved.

"You must follow your heart, listen to what you feel is right." Roszalia shook her head,

"It is not that simple, my heart has been betrayed. My mother tried so hard for me not to befall her fate, I will never forget my love for him. That is why I cannot stay here; I have acted foolishly, as my mother had."

Her aunt sighed and reluctantly dropped the girl's hands. "I am saying that you know the truth is in your heart. You are not your mother, nor is Gavin your father, just listen." Agnes tapped her own heart, and then placed her hand on Roszalia's belly, "for all of you." Roszalia did not question that he aunt knew she was with child, she had not told her, but there were things her aunt always knew. She told her niece she would not be going to the cemetery for she had to go back to Dingle before nightfall. They embraced and Agnes told her she was always welcome at her home, but to try to listen to the signs of truth.

The Memorial services were at the family church in Tralee. The same church where William and Kathrine had declared their wedding vows so many years prior. It seemed everyone in County Kerry came to pay his or her respects to Barrister O'Connor and his family. Both the elite and common class stood side by side to mourn the loss of this exceptional man. The last few days had taken their toll on the family. Caitlin, Andrew, and Devon sat in the front pew of the opulent church, the tall colored glass windows looking down on them all. Roszalia sat with the children behind their parents. She listened and watched as Gavin gave the eulogy, thinking this was possibly the last time she would look into his eyes. He looked at her the whole time, as he spoke of love, family, and forgiveness. If only she could. When her tears flowed, they flowed for more than one reason this day. Gavin tried to ask Roszalia to ride with him to the cemetery in his carriage, but she avoided his eyes and entered the door held for her and the children by Barrister Ausby and his wife.

Carriages lined the dirt road into the cemetery along with people paying their respects one last time to the man and family they knew, respected, and loved. Caitlin trying to be strong, now let the tears flow freely as William O'Connor the Second was laid to rest in the family mausoleum alongside his wife. As the cemetery began to empty, Roszalia noticed that there were four armed guards near the family's carriages. Barrister Burke stood looking at them, a dour look on the older man's face. She also took notice that Vanessa was nowhere in sight. Devon seemed very nervous today, when he saw the barrister he began fidgeting uncomfortably. After talking with the last few remaining people, Gavin, who had been watching the four guards, walked over to Barrister Burke. As he extended his hand in a gesture of friendship, one of the guards took a pair of handcuffs and snapped them on his extended wrist, grabbing the other and clasping them before he had time to resist.

Gavin's loud voice brought attention from everyone still present. "What sir is the meaning of this?" The older man never moved, but the look of hatred in his eyes was unmistakable. One of the offices stated,

"Gavin Edward O'Connor, you are under arrest for the attempted murder of Vanessa Burke."

At hearing this, Andrew reached them in four strides. "What is this, this is a funeral. Have you no respect? There certainly is some mistake!" Devon looked on with astonishment, yet never moved. Caitlin burst into tears and Roszalia went to her.

Through clenched teeth, Gavin managed, "Sir, I hope you are prepared to back up your accusations, for they are entirely false. I have not seen Vanessa for over a year!" Roszalia turned to look at Gavin, she saw no hint of falseness in his statement, but she had seen Vanessa leaving his bed just the other night. What is happening? Suddenly she felt sick. She looked over to where Devon stood rooted, looking pale but not saying a word. Roszalia had a terrible feeling that there was something deceitful going on and Devon was involved somehow. Unable to stand seeing Gavin like this, even with her confusion, she quickly went over to where the officer now held him. She looked at Gavin.

"Roszalia, I do not know what the hell is happening." She touched his brow,

"I believe you, my love. We will have Barrister Ausby clear this up."

At some point in the confusion, Devon had made his way over to where they all stood. He seemed nervous, yet almost pleased at the situation.

"My brother and I do not always get along, but I can assure you he would not murder anyone." The officer corrected Devon in a monotone voice, "He is not accused of murder Sir, the victim is alive, barely, but the sentence can change if she does not regain consciousness."

Roszalia noticed Devon take a small unsteady step back and an ashen look briefly passed over his features. Yes, he was involved, somehow. The younger guard knew the family well and spoke to Andrew sympathetically.

"Gavin would be detained in Cork until a trial can be arranged. Everyone should pray to God the girl wakes up. Barrister Burke wants justice." As they ushered Gavin towards the carriage, Roszalia came up to him, kissed him, and whispered,

"I am sorry Gavin, I know now something is terribly wrong. I do love you and we will get you out as soon as we can."

Gavin closed his eyes. He was too angry to trust his voice, but he opened them and looked at Roszalia's small figure, "I will be home soon and then we will straighten everything out." He gave a sharp look over to Devon before saying to Andrew,

"Take care of Roszalia, I do not trust Devon."

Andrew nodded. They all stood incredulous, as they took Gavin away, at that moment, her mind heard her aunt's voice say, *follow your heart and listen...* She would save the man she loved, no matter what it required her to do.

By the time they returned to the estate, what started as a very sullen and sad day had now turned into a nightmare of events.

Roszalia helped the children to change into their daily clothes and sent them off with one of the young maids, so she could try to make sense out of what was happening. Had she jumped to conclusions? She had seen Vanessa only three mornings earlier getting out of Gavin's bed, naked, and yet she believed him as he said that he had not seen her in over a year. Had Vanessa been playing a cruel joke on them? She could not tell anyone what she saw that morn, or it would make Gavin look guilty. Roszalia had decided she would announce that she had been with Gavin all night and every night since he had been home. She did not care if she would perjure herself, she would not let the man she loved stay in prison.

Roszalia was about to enter the room, when Carlson came over to her and handed her an envelope.

"We do not know who left this, but it was on the table in the library with your name." Roszalia looked at the note front with her name scrawled in terrible penmanship. Thinking one of the other maids had sent her sympathy, knowing how close she was to Barrister O'Connor, she folded it again and put it in the pocket of her black dress and entered the library. Barrister Ausby came back to the estate after speaking with the authorities and needed to meet with the family. Caitlin and Andrew were already present. She sat in one of the large leather chairs, the same one she fell asleep in when waiting for Gavin to return only three nights previous.

Devon made his appearance finally, looking pale and having too much drink in him noticeably. He sat on the opposite side of the room from her. She was glad. She did not like the bad feelings she was getting about this whole situation, and she felt that Devon was involved.

Barrister Ausby cleared his throat, "The situation is not good, I must say. Vanessa took a turn for the worse. When they found her, she was severely beaten with lacerations on her back." The older man paused and looked over to Roszalia and Caitlin, "I fear this may be too much for you ladies to hear." Roszalia shook her head and braced herself.

"No go on, we need to know the facts."

He cleared his throat, "Very well, the poor girl was found bound and gagged, wrapped only in a dirty bed sheet. When the men who found her brought her to town, she was barely conscious, her throat was constricted, but she managed to say *O'Connor*." Andrew stood up. He poured a brandy from the decanter and took a deep swallow,

"That does not prove her condition had anything to do with Gavin!" He slammed his glass down and returned to Caitlin, and she said softly,

"That poor girl, I know it was not my brother, but what beast could do such a thing." Andrew put his arm around her.

Devon poured himself a whiskey and downed it in a single gulp. "So you say Vanessa most likely will not pull through? What will that mean for Gavin?"

Roszalia could not read Devon, what was he concerned with, his brother's life or his place in line for the estate? In addition, the callous way he spoke of Vanessa's situation made her cringe. She thought of the day she saw them in town, him whispering in her ear and her laughter.

"I am afraid if the woman does not make it, then Gavin will go to trial for murder, and Barrister Burke is a very powerful man. I understand there was an event between Gavin and Vanessa a few years prior at a party?"

Roszalia stood up, "Yes, but it was also false. You see I was with Gavin at the time Vanessa said he had, well, taken advantage of her, so he was innocent then just as he is now."

Caitlin looked at her friend, not knowing whether to believe her but knowing she would back her up. Roszalia continued,

"Barrister Ausby, I believe I can also clear this misunderstanding up. The truth is, I have been with Gavin every night since he has returned, in his chambers."

Devon slammed his glass down. Even in his drunken state, he knew better than to say anything to the contrary, lest they know his part in setting Vanessa up with Gavin that night.

Barrister Ausby looked at her and said, "Now lass, this is a solemn thing you are saying. If you were with him, this might be his alibi, but do not perjure yourself in the eyes of the court or the Lord, even for love."

Roszalia never flinched. "I know what I am doing." At that moment, Caitlin stood up and went to Roszalia.

"And I can vouch for her for these past nights I have taken care of the children myself so Roszalia and my brother could have private time together." Caitlin locked arms with her friend and squeezed her hand in a knowing kinship. Devon sat back in his chair, no longer paying attention, thinking that Vanessa must not pull through. He would make sure of this. He would need to go out this evening to make an arrangement. Perhaps Gavin would escape the noose. However, he did not want to feel the rope around his neck for this crime he committed. He should have made sure she was dead before he left her.

"Well, I see, then I can assume I am to go to the court tomorrow and present my alibi witnesses?" Barrister Ausby smiled, "And no doubt I will find a dozen others in this household to confirm?" Roszalia smiled back,

"I would say at least that many."

"Alright then, let's get some rest, tomorrow we will have to set out to the court early, we need to get that boy home as soon as we can. Prison is no place for him." With that, Barrister Ausby opened his book and began making notes for his presentation to the magistrate. Caitlin and Andrew walked with Roszalia up to their rooms. When they were out of earshot Caitlin said, very seriously to the other two,

"I feel terrible even saying or thinking this, but I think Devon is hiding something. Do you think he had something to do with Vanessa?" The drained look on her friends face and after all that has transpired these last few days made Roszalia hug her friend and lie,

"No Caitlin, I am sure Devon has nothing to do with this, he is under a lot of grief too." Deep inside, she felt just the opposite. She did not trust Devon and felt he was capable of anything to keep his brother and her apart. She shivered at her own thoughts as she bade goodnight to her friends. Entering her room, she made sure the bolt was on the door. Roszalia was removing her dress when she felt the note in her pocket. The writing was poor and she had trouble making out the words, but after a moment her eyes widened and her hands trembled. Dropping the note to her bed as she sat down, her legs weak. Devon and Vanessa had set them up, Gavin did not know anything about Vanessa in his bed, and she had been missing since that night. Roszalia knew Devon was somehow involved. She had not trusted her own heart or Gavin to believe he would not betray her. She wanted to run to him, and her soul felt heavy. He was alone in the prison cell right now, accused of a crime he did not commit.

"Oh my love, I am the one who betrayed us!" Roszalia spoke aloud to no one. "How could I have not trusted you, I will bring you home."

Things were definitely not going as planned, Devon thought to himself. Vanessa was still alive. He had not intended to kill her that night. The fantasy of Roszalia was too intense and when Vanessa began to protest to his roughness, he had held her throat a bit too hard. When her flailing had ceased suddenly, he realized he had gone too far, and thought he had killed her. He wrapped her limp body in a sheet and took her down the back staircase and out to the far field, where he dumped her naked body by the deepest part of the ravine. He had figured that the wild animals in the woods would take care of the body before anyone would find her remains. He did not feel any remorse for his actions. She was becoming a nuisance; he had told her what to do to break Gavin and Roszalia apart, and it had worked wonderfully...until she showed up alive.

Devon crossed to the decanter of whiskey he had brought to his chambers and poured another glass. He quickly drained this and stood for a long moment at the side table. He would have to make another plan. He would have to make it appear that he was exonerating his brother's name, as a good and loyal family member. Right now however, he needed make sure that Vanessa never woke up. The plan would have to be flawless this time. He would get his brother out of prison, and then be rid of him finally. The estate would be his and the little gypsy wench too. At this, he put his now empty glass down and headed to dress for his outing.

Roszalia left her room in search of Andrew and Caitlin to show them the incriminating note she had just read. As she rounded the corner, Devon was exiting from his chambers. He had his cloak and riding attire on. She did not advance until he descended the stairs. For if, what she surmised was true, Devon was far more dangerous than she ever imagined.

Devon stood in the shadows at the wharf. Just a man in a hooded cape, faceless to any onlookers. The mangy person he was meeting walked towards him. Handing this man a purse of coins, "The other half will be delivered when the jobs are complete." Giving Devon a toothless grin, he stuffed it in a filthy sack, and told him the first part would be quick. Then he would wait to hear when Gavin would be home, and then complete the job. Devon looked nervously around and told the man to remember he was never here, then took his leave.

The next day word reached Gavin that Vanessa Burke died sometime during the night. The charges were changed to First-degree murder. Gavin was incarcerated in Cork Prison. The cell in Cork Prison was cold and rank, with the smell of mold and vermin permeating his nostrils. He was a man accustomed to discomfort. On the long sea voyages many times living conditions were less than desirable, but the crew were his family and made it tolerable. Here in the dark stone surroundings, he felt more alone than he ever had. His mind went back to Roszalia's last words. *I believe you and love you.* He did not know why she had shunned him before but he needed to believe she loved him now. And he did not know what event made the barrister think he had done harm to his daughter? He could not think straight right now, his father just barely laid to rest and this atrocity.

The guards had been very apologetic for the situation. They

did not believe that Gavin could have committed such an act, one had gone so far to say, "Now if we were hauling in 'is brother, I'd throw away the key." Yet there was little anyone could do. He pressed his eyes shut and forced Roszalia's face to appear, her hair, her lips, oh god he had to get back to her.

Only Andrew and Barrister Ausby were able to visit and communicate with Gavin. Roszalia had given Barrister Ausby the note from Marie, but he explained, unless they could find the girl and she would testify, the note had little meaning. Anyone could have penned it, and it would be perceived as a motive. Gavin would look guilty that he may have caused the girl harm so she would not tell you of the event. Caitlin had been in shock when they told her Vanessa had passed away. She could only think of the courts finding Gavin guilty and sentencing him to death. Barrister Ausby went to confer with Gavin.

"It seems that Roszalia is willing to testify that she was with you the night of Miss Burke's attack. If this is true, then she could be your alibi." Gavin shook his head vehemently,

"No, I will not have her perjure herself, or put her virtue up for all to talk about on public display. We will find a way to clear this up." Though now sitting in the rank cell, he felt less than sure.

The days and nights following the passing of William O'Connor and Gavin's arrest were somber ones at the estate. Roszalia had been trying to keep as much of this from the children, yet they could feel the tension and asked her often where their uncle Gavin was. Andrew and Barrister Ausby were trying every avenue to change Barrister Burke's opinion to no avail, he did not forget his daughter's accusations years ago. And when her last words were O'Connor and Devon having a solid alibi, he vowed someone would pay.

Roszalia made sure the children were ready for bed, then, to ease their concerns, she told them their uncle had to go away for a time and would return as soon as he could. She decided to go to the kitchen and get a glass of warm milk for the evening and entered her room from the far stairs. A faint scent lingered in the air in her quarters, tobacco, and whiskey. As she headed over to the drapes to pull them shut, a movement caught her eye and she spun towards it. Devon was sitting in the large wing back chair in her sitting area, staring at her. Her eyes darted to the door she had just entered and realized she had walked right past him in the shadows. The other door to the stairs descending to the children's room was behind where he sat. Devon, sensing her desire to run, rose and closed the open door. She heard him turn the lock before he faced her again. He stood motionless for a moment then turned up the lamp on the table.

"Devon, please, not now, everything that has happened, please do not make it worse." Roszalia's words held a slight hint of fear and helplessness to them.

He shook his head, and with an insincere hurt tone said, "Ah Roszalia, it is a shame you think me such an evil person, but nevertheless, I did not come here to upset you." Roszalia found his words hard to believe, given the note she possessed and all his past shameful behavior. Devon moved closer, taking pleasure in the way she recoiled in anticipation of his actions. *Not yet*, he thought, tonight he would leave her be, he would have her soon enough.

"Roszalia, I have a proposition for you," he paused to light a cigar. Roszalia narrowed her eyes. Anything he proposed could only be for his benefit.

"Come sit," he motioned to one of the wing back chairs. She felt she had no choice. She held her head high and sat down. Devon made no effort to hide his roving eyes, he took in every inch of her as she sat he watched the materials of her skirt slide up her ankle before she smoothed them back.

"Yes, Devon, please, I am weary, what is it?" she mustered between clenched teeth. She wished Gavin were here. She had to listen, if it could help her love, she would agree to anything, even with Devon. After he had taken a long draw on his cigar, he leaned forward.

"Roszalia I am going to be very honest with you," she raised an eyebrow, knowing honesty was not a virtue that he possessed. "I have wanted you for a very long time, I usually take whatever, and whomever I please..." he paused long enough to emphasize his last statement, "whenever I wish." He sat back and crossed his legs, "But you see...there is a problem," Devon paused, "My dear brother. With your alibi and my sister's, there is a chance, slim but a chance, he will be acquitted." Taking a long puff on his cigar before continuing. "I would have to make sure this did not happen, rest assured I can do this." Devon never taking his cold steel grey eyes off Roszalia leaned back casually. "It would be tragic if my brother met with a fatal accident in prison." Roszalia stifled her hatred for this beast in front of her. "He is a problem that needs eliminating."

Roszalia clenched her teeth. Wanting to tell him how she detested him sitting so comfortably in her rooms planning harm to the man she loved. Instead, she sat still, her hands clasped tightly in her lap. There would be more, she knew.

Devon, seeing that he had made his point clear to her, continued, "I did everything I could to separate the two of you. I counted on Gavin returning to sea and then I thought if the two of you were separated he would leave for good, but none of these seemed to work out."

Roszalia thought he seemed to be talking to himself, like a dangerous animal whose attack had failed and did not understand why. She felt she should speak to cut his dangerous train of thought, but choose her words carefully,

"Devon, everyone is under stress, with your fathers passing, but you know I love your brother..." She noticed his fist clench and stopped speaking sitting tensely not knowing what he would do next.

"Love!" he spat the words. "I have loved you ever since I saw you, yet you have rejected me. I could show you love, but you choose him!" his fist came down hard on the table and sent the small picture of her mother flying. Roszalia sat stone still, she was in real danger, and she needed to calm him. "Devon, please, what do you need from me?"

He stood up and turned his back to her to compose himself, she looked so beautiful with her dark hair in the flickering lights was driving his emotions in a dangerous direction. He could take her now, he thought, but he would continue with his plan and then she would be his. He finally would have won over his brother, the one true possession that he loved.

Devon turned, the anger in his voice gone, but the danger in his eyes remained. "Roszalia I am, in my circle, an influential person, I have many high ranking people, should we say, in my debt. I am sure with a word to the right people we could exonerate Gavin of all these charges and he could be free within a fortnight." He stood, pleased as he saw the look of hope on her face. She now stood up and faced him as he looked down at her. A sadistic smile appearing. "But, of course, all good deeds have a price," at these words, he grasped her shoulders lightly, she must agree to his terms. "You see what I need from you is simply…well, you, and a promise you will never be with my brother again."

Roszalia shrugged his hand off her, detested by his touch. "Devon, you know I will never consent to this!"

He looked into her eyes and she saw the menace return and something else, deadly and cold. "Oh I think you will. You see, I am asking this of your own consent. I can also say the word and my brother, your lover, will hang by the neck until his breath is snuffed out. Now, it is your choice." At this, he knew he won, triumph on his face.

"Devon, I will say I was with Gavin that night, I am his alibi." Devon laughed out loud and spat,

"Oh yes, the gypsy wench who everyone knows is pathetically in love with the heir of the estate, what a reliable alibi you would be! Besides, Gavin has already denied this to save your reputation." His tone became deadly even, "Now who do you think can persuade these powerful people? I have knowledge of their deepest darkest secrets that could ruin them in family and business. Think Roszalia, you agree to be my mistress and I will agree to make sure Gavin is a free man. He can live anywhere he chooses… just not with you."

Roszalia, reddened by his comments, choked out through the tears that she refused to let flow, "Gavin will never allow it. He will kill you before he allows you to take me!" her fear and anger mounting.

"Ah yes, but only if you protest, but you will not, you will agree willingly. I will set you up in an apartment in town, and there you will be in wait for me." His smile told her he had won. She would agree for she knew he could make Gavin's trial go either way, and she had to save the man she loved no matter what it entailed of her.

"Alright," she whispered

"What did you say, do you agree?" Devon's voice held a sickening triumphant tone.

"Yes, you can have my body but you will never have my heart or soul. They will always belong to Gavin, and in this you have won nothing!" her eyes burned with hatred. Devon took her in his arms in a flash and kissed her deeply, Roszalia remained as rigid as ice as the revulsion rose in her throat.

He dropped her, stood back, and laughed. "Your body my dear is good enough, for now... as for your soul and heart, I do not give a damn about those."

With that, he opened her door and stepped out, not bothering to close it. She sunk into the chair and let her defeat flow through her. She had given in to Devon. She straightened and wiped her eyes. She would have to remain strong, for herself and Gavin's child within her. Nevertheless, the man she loved would be free.

CHAPTER TWELVE

On the morning of Gavin's trial, Roszalia had readied herself early, she wore a simple dress of grey linen, and she pulled her hair in a severe chignon, covering it with a scarf. Caitlin and Andrew were already in the carriage when Roszalia came down the stairs. Devon stood in the doorway, looking rather smug,

"Ready, my dear? This should be quite a show. I was in town most of the night," he hesitated, and then added. "Let's just say, making arrangements."

Roszalia looked at him and said evenly, "Be careful Devon, you may need to explain a few events yourself, just keep your end of this bargain."

"And you, the same, though I have to say I shall enjoy reaping the rewards immensely."

To those not privy to the meaning of their conversation. It would seem they were politely exchanging pleasantries. But sickness rose in Roszalia's stomach at the thought of her future. Ignoring his charming smile and extended arm, she strode out the door towards the carriage, her head held high as to show him he would never have her spirit.

Devon stood for one moment to compose himself. *Impudent bitch,* he thought. He had arranged so Gavin would not hang, and he also knew that his brother would never leave the estate or Roszalia, as long as he was alive. Therefore, he had a plan in motion that would eliminate his brother shortly after his release. With this, he retrieved his coat from the butler and made his way to the awaiting carriage. Roszalia looked away as Devon climbed in and sat next to her, she felt a deep resentment that he would even dare to come to the trial and wished he would not. She choose to stare out the curtained window, feeling the pressure of his thigh against hers and a new revulsion arose in her, remembering what she had agreed to. She forced herself to think only of Gavin, and saving him from a possible death sentence.

The family arrived at the courthouse and sat in the third row. The courtroom was already filling up with supporters from all classes, many of the men from the docks stood against the walls showing their solidarity for their captain. Roszalia saw the tall figure of Gavin in front of her, sitting upright, proud, announcing his innocence. She noticed the hurried shave he had received, the dark lines under his eyes spoke of his lack of sleep, yet she had never thought him handsomer nor loved him more.

Devon sat right next to her, this she did not want, and it made her uneasy. Was he purposely trying to unnerve her, to dare her to break her promise? He had set Vanessa up in Gavin's bed and god knows what else he had done to her afterwards. The thought made her shudder. Was this to be her fate also?

Barrister Ausby entered the hall and took his seat next to Gavin. A troop of assistance came in also and set out an array of papers. All were quiet as the presiding Magistrate Breen entered the room. The congregation rose, and then sat when instructed. A disturbance ensued in the back of the room as a rotund man spoke to the guards, then proceeded forward to the bench, nodding as he passed Barrister Ausby and Gavin. He spoke in hurried tones, gesturing wildly, then gave the magistrate a pouch and papers. Gavin looked at Barrister Ausby,

"What is this about?" With concern on his features Ausby began to rise.

"I do not know, but will find out." The magistrate was telling the man to wait and motioned for Barrister Ausby and Barrister

Burke to approach the bench. All looked on and mumbled in hushed tones as the three men conversed. At one point, Barrister Burke looked back at where Gavin sat and scowled.

Roszalia sat as puzzled as all in the courtroom. Only Devon seemed to have a knowing glint in his eye. He reached once for her hand and gave a snicker as she quickly retracted it. Barrister Ausby returned to his seat as the magistrate put his hand up. He rapped his gavel for order.

"Silence." It seems we have had a last minute development occur. "We have a confession of guilt from the actual perpetrator of this crime. We have the evidence of the belongings he stole when he raped and brutally beat Miss Burke and a signed confession in hand." At this, the barrister struck his gavel and stated, "I hereby dismiss all charges from Gavin Edward O'Connor, you are free to go, and God speed." He rapped his gavel once more and stood to leave the bench.

The courtroom sat in frozen silence, then Devon stood, "Well, what a good fortune, we have reason for celebration, I do believe."

Suddenly everyone began speaking and hugging Gavin. Roszalia sat dumbfounded, and as she glanced at Devon, she saw him staring at her with the same sly grin on his face. He had done it. Whoever he had paid or blackmailed had come through and Gavin was free. Gavin was in front of her, he took her hands and brought her to her feet she threw her arms around his neck, they kissed, the room spun, and she did not care. Gavin murmured his love in her ear and she clung to him as if he would once more vanish. The room crowded in on them and the friends and family began to move them towards the door. Caitlin was crying and laughing at the same time, Andrew slapped Gavin on the back, and Barrister Ausby had more emotion than anyone had ever seen. He offered Gavin and Roszalia the use of his carriage so the couple could have privacy on the return trip to the estate. Before she entered the door, Devon caught her hand and bent low to whisper,

"Enjoy your ride home, but remember you are now mine. I held up my end, I can turn the tables just as fast."

She pulled away and with an icy glare said without emotion,

"I know what I must do," and entered the carriage.

Gavin looked suspiciously at Devon, he could not hear his words, but he wanted Roszalia away from him. "Roszalia, I know what you intended to do for me."

Roszalia held her finger to his lips, "Gavin, I have been a fool, but no one needed to do anything, you are free." Gavin kept silent, he felt her tremble, moving closer to the man she loved and rested her head on his shoulder, this was enough. For this would be the last time she would be able to touch him. After today, she would belong to Devon.

The night was bitter sweet for the family. Friends and the household staff were pleased with the turn of events. Now all felt that William O'Connor could rest in peace with his eldest safe at home.

Roszalia had left Gavin in the entry hall to go get the children and then made her excuse to go change. Instead she was going to take a few belongings and go to Agnes's until Devon summoned her. She could not face Gavin, he was safe, and she would now fulfill her part of the deal. He would find out eventually and would detest her, for surely Devon would make him think it her idea. He would find another, a woman of social standing. She changed into her traveling clothing. Closing the wardrobe that held her uniforms, for she was no longer going to be living or working at the estate. She took a picture Caitlin had given her of the three O'Connor siblings. Her friend had brought her the photo after the upsetting news of Gavin's disappearance at sea. Staring at it now, she creased the photo and tore it between Caitlin and Devon, leaving the latter in the room, and then she placed the remaining picture in her satchel. Carefully, she laid the necklace Gavin gave her when he asked for her hand, on top of the silk lining in the box. Folding a note, she closed the lid, as she ran her finger over the inlaid silver crest.

She gave a loving look at the room, put the box in her pocket, and then went down the hall to the stairs leading to Gavin's chambers. She entered his room, knowing he was downstairs with the others, and placed the box on his dresser. The door opened and Roszalia spun around as Gavin entered the room and walked over to her. He took her in his strong arms and kissed her. Unwillingly, she threw her arms around his neck and returned his kiss with passion of her own. Never letting up on his kiss, he picked her up laying her on his large bed, the cotton cover felt smooth against her arms and calves as her skirts rode up. He let her go for only a moment. Roszalia, suddenly aware of what was about to take place, started to protest, but the words would not come out. The man she dreamed of, loved and wanted to live for was about to make love to her. She had almost lost him forever, and soon would never see him again. She needed this moment.

"You are so beautiful," he murmured. "You are the only vision that kept me believing and my mind sane." He bent to kiss her, and she turned, tensed, for reality came flooding back. She no longer was Gavin's, and she now had an obligation to Devon. The thought of Gavin returning to that awful cell, or worse, provided her determination of what she had to do next. "Gavin, I cannot stay here now." Roszalia sat up, with the pretense of smoothing her blouse so he did not see the tears that threatened to fall. She had to leave and honor the arrangement made to save him from the gallows.

Gavin sensed the turmoil within her and decided he had had enough surprises. Moving in front of Roszalia, he said, "You are not leaving this room Roszalia, until I know what is going on."

Looking at his creased and tired face, she stood up and smoothed a lock of his hair, "Just know I will always love you, I must go to see Agnes. It is important." She felt guilty to lie to the man she loved, but she had to leave before Devon found she had been with Gavin.

Raking his fingers through his hair he said, "I do not understand, but I will respect your wish. After tonight we will stay together, I will not let you alone again. I will see you to the stables."

Roszalia protested. For she did not want him to see the bag with her belongings she would have. "That is not necessary, everyone will question where you are. Please for Caitlin s sake,

you know I love you but now I must be on my way before…"
she hesitated wanting to say before she could not leave him. Instead she said, "Before it is too late to arrive before dark."

Roszalia gave him one last kiss, the very last, she thought.
And fled the room.

CHAPTER THIRTEEN

Agnes met Roszalia at the door to the shop. She had foreseen trouble coming her way. When she entered, her distressed look and common attire confirmed her feelings. Taking her niece's hand, she led her to the sitting room, sat her down, and poured each a cup of freshly brewed tea.

They sat in silence, then Roszalia's tears began to flow. All the pent up sadness for Barrister O'Connor, the anger of her arrangement with Devon, and her heart breaking for the man she loved but could not put in danger. Agnes wrapped her arms around her niece, smoothing her hair and let her cry. After a moment, she straightening up and wiping her eyes with the handkerchief her aunt offered she began,

"Oh Agnes, what have I done, I told Devon I would be his mistress, he said he would exonerate Gavin from the terrible things they accused him of doing to Vanessa. He kept his part of the deal, but how can I be with a cruel man like Devon? My being with him will hurt Gavin more than I can bear." Roszalia covered her face in shame, and the tears fell again. Agnes sat back in her chair, *a grave situation indeed,* she thought. Devon has an evil spirit, and no doubt, he could be cruel, even deadly.

"Child, I do not mean to distress you further. However you

need to be aware. I have had a disturbing vision…there will be bloodshed, whose I cannot foresee. At this comment, Roszalia's mind cleared, for she also had feelings of impeding tragedy, but given all the heart-wrenching events that had recently occurred she had suppressed these feelings.

"As you are aware, I cannot see details when it comes to anything involved with your life. But I feel it does affect someone close to you." Roszalia sat upright. She had not thought of this.

"You must tell Gavin of this arrangement. He cannot hear it from Devon; for I do fear then, Gavin *will be* guilty of a crime." As Agnes began speaking, the feelings all resurfaced. *What if Gavin was so angry he did harm Devon? Oh, what a mistake I have made!*

"What can I do? Devon will know if I tell him, I am afraid for us all." Agnes went to her desk, took out a parchment, and scribed a note upon it. Sealing it with wax, she told Roszalia to stay put. There was a delivery boy a few stores down. Finding the boy at the shop, she handed him the note and a coin telling him to hurry, for it was urgent. "Now, we will have Gavin here within a fortnight and then we will work this out." Roszalia hugged her aunt yet did not feel reassured as of yet.

The errand boy rounded the corner, headed for the stables when a tall looming figure stopped him. He had been following Roszalia and stopped outside Agnes's shop. Lurking in the back, he witnessed the exchange between the woman and the boy.

"You there lad, I could not help over hear. I am heading to the O'Connor Estate now. I can take that and save you a night trip." His smile seemed genuine. The boy hesitated until he produced three coins. Giving a quick glance around, the youth handed the note to this stranger, snatched the coins, and took off in a run, not looking back.

Devon opened the note, made a disgruntled remark, then crumpled it and stuffed it in his pocket. He would have to speed up his brother's demise. He headed to the tavern to make these arrangements. The man was already there. Sitting at the long wooded bar he waved for ale. Devon, did not like meeting with him in such a public place, decided to hurry his business and be gone, forgoing the drink. He sat hunched over and spoke low to the man, "I need the job done in the early morning. My brother shall not see the midday. Am I clear?"

The man grinned, "Aye, did not take long to snuff the girl. This should be no problem...in and out." The man made a motion with his hand then gulped the last of his ale.

Devon restrained from showing his disgust for this vile man and his ignorance to mention Vanessa. Right now, he needed him. He would eliminate him later.

"My brother will ride early in the morning. He grooms his horse so there will not be anyone inside... Just make sure he is dead, no errors." At this, Devon placed a bag of coins on the bar. The man snatched them with dirty fingers and extended his hand. Devon glared at him with disdain, stood, and left.

Just out of sight on the landing, little Marie hid when she heard Devon's voice. Taking the job at the Alehouse, she never expected to see Devon again. Staying hidden, but was close enough to hear the conversation that took place. Devon was planning on doing in Master Gavin, Marie's already fair, mousy features turned paler. She had to tell someone. But whom? Her employer was a mean man and probably in alliance with Devon. She then thought of Roszalia, she would tell her, she heard she was at her aunt's right here in town. She began to feel a bit better, for maybe she could do right and clear her conscience for her part in not telling anyone what she knew about Devon drugging Master Gavin that evening. Taking off her apron, she made it out the back unnoticed and headed down the street in the direction of the apothecary shop. Marie was feeling uneasy, being out on her own with the day light fading. She hoped Roszalia would let her stay for the night. The deserted streets caused her to jump at every sound. Finally, she came upon the apothecary shop. Seeing the closed sign on the front door, she hesitated, and then decided she would go round to the living quarter's entrance. Marie rang the bell and waited, her eyes darting up and down the alley. A thin woman came to the door.

"Yes? May I help you?" Agnes peered at the girl.

"Beg your pardon, ma'am, but is Miss Roszalia 'ere?" Marie asked in a frightened whisper.

Roszalia recognized Marie's small voice and sprang to the door. "Marie, come in."

Agnes opened the door and led the girl to the parlor. She seemed like a frightened mouse, her eyes darted from one window to the next. Roszalia went to her and took her hands.

"Thank you Marie, I received your note, it made my heart happy to hear Gavin did not forsake me."

Marie looked at Roszalia, "Oh no, miss he did not know nothing. In fact, I am sorry once more, but I was forced to not say nothin 'bout the drug in his brandy 'da night of the, er' ya know, with Miss Vanessa. He did not know a thing. He loves you fierce, we all could see it." She began to sob, and Roszalia put a shawl over her shoulders, as she continued, "I was scared, miss, the devil that Devon is. He would do to me what he did to poor Vanessa." Roszalia and Agnes glanced at each other but held their silence for the girl was strained enough.

Agnes spoke up then, a foul feeling was in the air, "Child, why have you come to find Roszalia?"

Marie looked at them and through a sob said, "A terrible thing, I 'erd im, at the tavern, scared I was, but I 'ave to try."

Roszalia's patience was wearing thin and she asked, a bit strained, "What did you hear? About Vanessa?"

"No, No 'bout Master Gavin, his brother plans on 'aving 'im killed"

Roszalia jumped out of her seat and faced Marie. "Are you sure it was Devon? When, how? Marie, please tell me everything you saw and heard."

"Oh yes," her eyes even wider now, "I could not see 'im but I nev'r fergit that devil's voice. He told this man to do away with his brother, no mistakes. He said something 'out he rides in the mornings." Marie looked at the women, "I wanted to help, makeup for the terrible thing I done!"

Agnes patted the girl's hand. "You have, now have some tea; you may stay here tonight if you choose." Marie nodded. Roszalia was up and putting on her cloak.

"Child, you cannot go back tonight, in the dark." Agnes felt the urgency also but the cover of night was not a time to ride through the countryside "First light, set out, I will send word to the authorities of what is going on."

Roszalia knew her aunt was right. If misfortune befell her in the night, Gavin's fate would also be set.

"Agnes, please take care of Marie tomorrow, I fear for her safety if Devon finds her." Agnes nodded and then remembering her vision, somberly said,

"Roszalia, be careful my child." She knew nothing she said would deter her from tying to save the man she loved. Roszalia went to her small room and lie on the soft ticking mattress, and thought of what Marie had told them. Devon had planned to eliminate Gavin even after their agreement. Her eyes began to get heavy and the last thought she had was looking in Gavin's eyes and saying. I will love you, for all eternity.

She awoke with a start, she heard, no, felt something sharp in her chest, but it was only a branch scratching the windowpane. The sun had not risen yet, a misty fog hung in the air, but the moon shone bright enough to light her way. She felt she must go as quickly as possible to Gavin, for she had also seen the vision of doom for someone that Agnes had, and had a dreadful feeling that was growing by the minute.

The next morning when Gavin awoke, he found the necklace and letter on his dresser.

My one true love,
I do now what I must, I do this in body only, my heart and soul shall be yours alone. Please do not think ill of me. All my love– for neither man nor time can keep our love apart.

Roszalia

He went in search of Truda, but she only knew that her niece was visiting Agnes, she did not have any idea for how long. Gavin saw Caitlin coming down the stairs and headed towards her. Since Roszalia had not come to get the children for breakfast this morning, she assumed her friend had spent the night in her brother's room. When he approached her alone, she was surprised to see the distraught look on his face.

"Caitlin, I do not know what to think, Roszalia told me she had to visit Agnes. I assumed she would return today. When I woke, I found the necklace I gave her and this letter." Caitlin took the folded paper, and after reading the note, she looked up at her brother.

"Gavin, something is terribly wrong, after Roszalia found that letter Marie penned, I thought all would be straightened out."

Gavin looked at his sister, "What letter? What are you saying?" Caitlin went to the library with Gavin close behind. She retrieved the letter that Marie had written Roszalia. Barrister Ausby had put it in the desk for safekeeping.

Gavin read it. His jaw began to twitch as anger welled up in him. Suddenly, Gavin thought of the yellow ribbon on his chair, and then another image came to mind, of a yellow dress, and a frightened Marie carrying it from Devon's room. He was the one, what had he said to Roszalia? And what had he done to Vanessa? Anger gripped his very core. He turned to his sister and asked, "Where is Devon?"

Caitlin shook her head. She felt an icy chill run down her spine, the look in Gavin's eyes was one of pure hatred. She tried to restrain him. "Gavin, please, you do not know why Roszalia went or where she is, she may be in any moment?" She knew her words were spoken to deaf ears.

He would first go to town and get Roszalia. Devon was dangerous and Gavin needed to protect her. Then he would take care of his brother.

"Caitlin, do not let Devon know where Roszalia has gone, I will go to Agnes's and bring her home. Tell Andrew my plan." She gave him a pleading look. Then to assuage her fears,

"I will not do anything foolish, my only concern is Roszalia's safety."

She felt she was forcing her mare to push through the paths

towards the estate too hard but she could not afford to stop. Agnes assured her Gypsy would be fine on the ride after she fed her some special oats, as she called it. The skies remained dull and gloomy as she rode on, the rain that had been falling for the last hour, now gave way to a damp fog. Roszalia could not even think that she would not make it to the estate in time to thwart Devon's plan. She would tell Gavin everything, Devon had a hand in Vanessa's death, and he needs to be stopped.

The estate was only a few hundred yards away now. She had ridden for hours. The dawn had long since risen over the horizon, yet the heavy fog remained, giving the land an eerie cast. The stables were in sight and Roszalia headed her horse in its direction. Catching a glimpse of a cloaked figure entering the side door, her heart began to pound. This dreadful premonition threatened to overwhelm her. It was still too early for Gavin to be riding yet. She decided she would tether her horse on the side porch to save time and enter the house to warn him, even if it meant seeing Devon in the process.

Not wanting to waste any more time than necessary, Gavin decided he would ride to town to find Roszalia. A heavy fog covered the morning ground as he headed out the door towards the stables, a light flickered within, and he thought the groom was up earlier than usual.

Seeing his brother leave through the kitchen door, Devon waited until he was far enough away that he would not look back and see him watching. He felt a renewed energy. Soon all of this would be his. He dropped the curtain and turned to see Roszalia standing in front of him, dripping wet, her fists were clenched at her sides, her eyes burning with hatred as she looked at him. For a moment, he felt an impending sense of doom, ever slight, and quickly it passed, but he did not like it. Regaining his composure, he asked, "What are you doing here, and what of your appearance?"

Roszalia looked at him steadily and said, "It is over Devon. Where is Gavin?"

Devon, now faced with a challenge, rose to it, "Over? Oh no my dear, it has just begun, as you will soon see."

Roszalia felt an icy chill run up her spine, then a vision. She saw a flash of a cloaked man and a bright fire–and then she knew.

Before Devon could reach out to her, Roszalia pushed past him and out the back door and ran towards the stables. She entered through the open side door. Gavin about to mount his horse, turned as he heard the sound of footsteps and saw Roszalia. His initial smile turned to confusion as she cried out his name in panic. The shot from the pistol echoed as it traveled towards Gavin. Roszalia reached the safety of his arms just seconds before the bullet did. She stopped, and her hazel eyes widened. As she felt the warm sticky feeling spreading across her back, her throat constricted, and then she collapsed in his arms as the searing pain ran through her.

Holding Gavin with what strength she had left, her vision began to dim until she only saw the look of terror in his amber eyes. Gasping for breath, her voice faint, she never felt more like one with Gavin and knew their love was true. Coughing as the blood mingled with her words, she whispered, never letting her eyes leave his, "My love, our souls will be together always." A racking cough made her body quake as Gavin desperately kissed her lips; a jolt ran through him, his salty tears mixing with her blood. He was saying he loved her. Still looking in his eyes her world went spinning into blackness.

Devon had run after Roszalia and upon entering the stables stood with a look of shock as he saw her lifeless body in his brother's arms. The hired gun was supposed to shoot Gavin. Soon others heard the shot coming from the stables. When they saw who had been injured, one of the stable hands ran back to the house and alerted Truda. As Caitlin and Andrew came down the stairs for breakfast, they stopped a servant who seemed in a fluster to inquire about what the commotion was.

"There has been an accident in the barn, a shot was fired. Master Gavin was in the barn." Caitlin fearing the worst did not stay to hear any more. She hurried towards the barn. When they arrived, they saw Gavin holding Roszalia's limp body, a deep red stain spread over his shirt from her wound. Devon was on his knees with his hands over his face. Truda and Andrew rushed over to Roszalia as Caitlin went to Devon and in a panicked voice asking who did this. He just shook his head. Gavin had not moved since Roszalia lost consciousness and slumped in his arms. Looking up he saw Truda and the others.

"Gavin," Andrew spoke urgently as he applied pressure to the wound and checked for a pulse, "There is a weak pulse, we must get her inside now, please." He knew his brother in law was in shock, but he nodded. Lifting Roszalia in his strong arms, he rushed to the house, carried her into the parlor, and laid her on the divan. He refused to believe she might perish, she looked peaceful and beautiful, as if asleep. Andrew pushed Gavin aside and went to work, doing what he could to stifle the bleeding from the wound. He was not optimistic; her loss of blood was extreme.

During all the excitement, no one noticed a cloaked figure leave the stables and enter the woods.

Agnes knew as soon as the bullet entered her niece's body. She had felt something terrible would happen this day, Agnes felt the pain and saw through Roszalia's eyes, she was looking into Gavin's, and there her soul would remain, bound by their eternal love until they could free it. She did not wait for the news, she immediately sent for a messenger to take a note to the O'Connor Estate and retrieve Gavin. Time meant everything if they were to save Roszalia.

Devon sat in the corner of the room. Caitlin was crying on Andrew's shoulder and Truda went to tend to the children. Gavin finally let Roszalia's hand go and turned to Devon.

"Brother, I pray to god you had nothing to do with this. Did you see anyone?"

Devon looked up; the grief in his face was genuine. Because of his lifelong jealousy for his brother, he might have caused the death of perhaps the only woman he would ever truly desire.

"Of course I did not! I heard the shot and came running. The perpetrator must still be nearby. He could not have gone far." He was not sure if Gavin believed him, but he had to shift any suspicion off himself. He knew that Gavin would kill the person responsible. Gavin still not trusting his brother's innocence said, "Then mount your horse, we will find him."

"Gavin, please…" He looked at Caitlin, with tear falling as she pleaded, "Please let us call the authorities. No more bloodshed!"

Gavin went to his sister and knelt beside her, "Caitlin, I will find the person and he will tell me who sent him to eliminate me." He stopped as he looked at his beloved lying so still on the divan. "I must do this," he kissed her and turned to Andrew.

"My friend, please save Roszalia," he choked on her name. "Make sure her friends and family know of the situation, I will return as soon as possible."

Devon knew he had to find the man he had paid to kill his brother first. Or he could implicate him in this mistake. He left the stables as soon as he was saddled. Gavin saw him ride out as he entered the door, Damn fool, he thought, even for this he feels he must best me.

Gavin headed Samson towards the woods. The morning fog covered the paths, making it difficult to see. The clearing up ahead showed signs of recent travel. Sampson began to get skittish as Gavin saw another rider ahead.

"Easy boy," he whispered, keeping his pistol ready. There was a man slumped forward on his horse. Gavin called out, "You there, announce yourself." He received no answer, the man's horse whinnied and stomped, and the rider fell to the ground. Gavin galloped over and saw the man's open–eyed stare looking up at him, then saw the knife wound gaping in his chest. The dagger was still embedded. Dismounting, he leaned over the lifeless body. He removed the hood of the cloak, and then extracted his dagger. He did not recognize the man staring up at him then he heard hooves approaching through the brush.

"Good God, brother, what have you done?" He turned to see

Devon and two guards looking at him from their horses.

Gavin narrowed his eyes, "You set this up."

"I do not know what you are saying. I am not the one standing astride yet another lifeless body, with the murder weapon in your very grasp." Devon shook his head in mock despair. Gavin knew the guards were eying him closely, he also knew these must be men whom were on Devon's pay. Cautiously, he made his way to his horse.

Devon motioned to one of the guards. "My poor dear brother, it will seem that you would meet a terrible fate when you came across the person who shot Roszalia. It seems you have already retrieved the dagger. I, of course, found both bodies, one with a fatal knife wound and the other with a hole in his heart. This will finally work to my liking. Alas, losing Roszalia was not in my plan." Devon gave Gavin a bow and then instructed the guards with a wave of his hand, "Shoot him when I am out of sight, and make sure he is dead this time."

Devon kicked his horse into a gallop. One guard was dismounting as the other retrieved his pistol. Eying the distance between the two men, Gavin lunged for the closer. His footing still not on the ground, the man stumbled, grabbing for his own pistol. Gavin wrenched it from his grasp and flung it deep into the woods. The other man, from the murky darkness of the trees' cover, pointed his gun in the direction of Gavin, and fired. He heard the grunt as his bullet hit its mark. Rushing over through the fog, he found the other guard lying face up with a smoking bullet hole in his forehead. Turning around, he then stopped to listen – not a sound. He carefully made his way to his horse, but before he could mount, Gavin's strong arm encircled his neck, depleting the air from his lungs. A guttural sound escaped him and Gavin let his loose and the man fell forward, gasping. Now weaponless, he remained motionless. Gavin slapped the guard's horse, causing it to gallop away through the fog. He then mounter Samson and looked down at the guard.

"I spared your worthless life so you can make up for the stupidity of your alliance with my brother. Go now. Tell Barrister Burke that Devon has caused the deaths of innocent people, possibly one of them his daughter. Perhaps this will repent your soul, or may god help you." Then snapped the reins and Samson set to flight.

In his retreat, Devon heard the echo of the gunshot, and with a sadistic smile, he headed towards town to reward himself at the Inn. He planned to return the following day to the site where he had set the trap for Gavin's demise and bring his brother's lifeless body home to the estate. He would say they separated to cover more territory in their search for the shooter. When he backtracked, he made the tragic discovery. He would be the perfect grieving brother. After all had settled, he would take his place as the head of O'Connor Estate.

Chapter Fourteen

Gavin rode his horse mercilessly to find his brother with no avail, and realized it was for the best, he now knew it had all been his doing, and Roszalia lie near death by his hand. If he had come upon him, he would kill him. He turned Sampson around to head back to the estate. As he entered the road, he saw a lad standing beside his horse. The hour was early for a young lone rider. With caution, least this be a trick of his brother's, he approached the lad, though he did not have time for delays. As he neared, a gash in the animal's left hind leg was visible.

"You, lad, what has happened?" the young man nervously stroked his horse's mane as he spoke. "Sir, I was on an errand to deliver a message to the O'Connor Estate when a shot spooked my mare. Gavin dismounted to check the leg. He walked the horse around and determined she would be fine. "A message for O'Connor's you say? I am Gavin O'Connor."

The boy retrieved the letter from his saddlebag and handed it to Gavin. "This message is for you. Ms. Agnes, from the Apothecary told me to give it to Gavin O'Connor, and she said it was…life or death, so I was pushing my mare too hard."

The mare whinnied to be on her way. Gavin stroked the animal's neck as he thanked the boy an assured him his horse would be fine to ride. Watching as the boy retreated towards town he wondered of the coincidence of meeting the messenger as he entered the road. Tearing through the wax seal, he opened and read the note, then swiftly mounted Sampson and headed, not to the estate, but in the other direction, towards town. He again road hard, not wasting any more time, and ended up in front of the Apothecary. Agnes was like a mother to Roszalia, she was there only the night before. There was no way Agnes could have received the news of Roszalia's situation so quickly. He wondered of the rumors he had heard of Agnes's gypsy magic, and being able to foresee the future were indeed true, and then he thought of the words on the paper:

Gavin,
Urgent – come to my shop, Roszalia's soul and life depend on it. Agnes.

He tethered his horse around back and rapped on the door impatiently. No sooner had his hand drawn back to deliver another knock, when Agnes opened the door.

"Come in, come in. Close and lock the door behind you, we must hurry." She spoke as she led him into the back room. A second door let to a smaller room stacked with books and bottles. There were a few scattered pieces of furniture, and Agnes led Gavin to a chair.

"Sit, rest, I will get you a drink. We must talk." Gavin did not need to talk, but when Agnes handed him the glass filled with whiskey, he gratefully took a large swallow. For the first time in hours, he felt he took a breath, and the thoughts of the day began sinking in. His hair was soaked with sweat, as were his clothes. Agnes gave him a towel and he wiped his face. He finally looked up at Agnes and she saw the look of despair in his eyes, but she could not allow him to wallow in those thoughts right now, Roszalia's life depended on this man.

"Gavin, my boy you must listen to what I say." She took his hand as if he were a child, "Gavin, you must understand!" She repeated a bit harsher

"Understand? The only woman I will ever love is barely holding on to life, and this arranged by my brother. What more is there to understand?" he replied in an agitated voice. "And I do not know what I am doing here. I should be by her side."

He attempted to stand, but with strength he did not expect, Agnes pushed him back in the chair. "No, you are wrong, Roszalia's body may be on the verge of death, but her essence and her soul is still very much alive." Gavin looked at Agnes with disbelief. She sighed, "Yes, it is hard to understand, and I do not have the time required for teaching you these things. Believe me, your love for Roszalia and hers for you has bound your souls together."

Gavin shook his head. A bit harsher than she intended, she spoke, "Do you have any idea how old I am?"

Gavin looked confused. "I do not know what that has to do with..." he trailed off as Agnes gave him a cutting glare.

"I have lived over three centuries, no, not this body, but my soul and spirit. I am what people might call a shaman, a gypsy, a soothsayer, and many names throughout history. Roszalia possesses the same quality as I. She does not know these things...yet, but her ability to renew her soul lies in you right now. Gavin did not understand, but as crazy as this woman's ranting seemed, if Agnes had a way to save Roszalia and bring her back to him, he would listen.

"Good, I see a spark in your eyes. Come over here, sit." She motioned to the table."

Reluctantly he obeyed, for he was sure the news of Roszalia had sent the woman senses amiss, Gavin went to the table where Agnes had set out a vile containing a thick purple liquid, similar to the one he had noticed in the glass case in the front of her shop, a book, and a candle of some pungent scent. "Now, what I tell, you will have a hard time believing. All I can say is believe with your heart and love for Roszalia as she would for you." Agnes opened a book, it was leather bound. In the pages, Gavin saw photos of his family, his home, things about his life.

"What is this Agnes?" he was paying close attention now.

"You see Gavin, by this book," she opened it to the cover

sheet and pointed to the words. 'Prominent Families of Nine-teenth Century Ireland', published edition nineteen–ninety five, England. Gavin leaned forward and held the book. "This book proves you will be there, Roszalia's soul will enter her reincar-nated body, the one in the twenty first century, and you will en-ter that time to save her life here."

Still trying to grip some semblance of reality, he said, "I have never known of a family book such as this." Once again looking at the date.

"And you will not in this time. For you see this is the book that shall lead Roszalia back to you." Gavin continued to flip through the pages, the book was something he had never en-countered, the pages were of a shiny texture, the type stood bold and even, he turned the next page and saw a portrait of Roszalia, and under it read, *betrothed to Gavin Edward O'Connor*. Gavin had never seen the photograph of Roszalia and presumed that Caitlin must have arranged it when he was at sea. As Agnes went to a table on the other side of the room, he silently and carefully tore the page with the photo out of the book. Folding it, he put it in his vest pocket. He did not know why he did it, but felt this may be all he had left of his love. He did not turn the page, instead, closed the book.

"Agnes, I am a man of patience, but I feel I need to return to the estate." Still barely comprehending, yet desperately wanting to believe he could get his love back, he asked, "If you can tell me, how do I get Roszalia's soul back and breathe life into her?"

"Yes, well that part is not easy, you see we must go to pas-sage tomb in County Meath." Gavin's eyebrow shot up. Agnes could sense his reluctance and his disbelief. It did not matter if he knew how they would accomplish saving Roszalia's soul, only that he would go agree to do what she asked, so she spoke quickly. "We must be there by the time the moon is full in the sky. We only have a seven–minute window where you will enter Roszalia's current time in the twenty first century, and reunite with her and win her love. She may then return with you here, but your time is limited, for your body will grow weak and you will have to return, with or without her."

Agnes was getting impatient, for each moment they delayed. Her niece's soul chanced being lost. "Gavin, there is not time, do you or do you not want Roszalia back!"

Gavin looked at the serious little gypsy woman, "Aye, what do I do?" He did not know why he agreed to this, something Roszalia had once asked of him, if he believed that love could last lifetimes. If it was possible, he was willing to do whatever it took. He had heard rumors and mystical folk tales of these ruins and passages.

"We need to make haste to get to Boyne Valley. There, we must enter the passage. The pagans believed it would transport their loved ones souls to another plane, this is true, but it has another purpose, one we need. You see it can also transport a live soul through time. It is powerful, and it will take you to your last thought, so you must only think of Roszalia. We must be careful, they have started excavating it, it is now visible to the public, but there is the entrance that no one knows of where we will enter. We will make our way through the maze to the center. There, at the moment the full moon rises its highest, you must drink this," Agnes produced a vile with the swirling purple liquid that he had seen in the locked cabinet. "You will feel light, dizzy, and then sleep. When you awake, you will be in a strange place, a different time, things will be very different, and nothing will be familiar. In fact, you will not even be in Ireland, for Roszalia...Rose as she is known in her time, will be living in America."

Gavin inhaled deeply. "Alright, Roszalia asked me once, if I believed in eternal undying love, I hesitated then, but not now." Agnes told Gavin to go to the stables, get her carriage, and meet her back in front of the shop. "And Gavin, leave Sampson there. Make sure my two grey mares are hooked to my carriage, they can take the journey without rest."

Gavin looked questionably at Agnes, "It is over two hundred kilometers. It will take us all of a day to arrive, I do not think..." He suddenly ended his sentence as Agnes stood with hands on hips shaking her head glaring at him.

"With all you know, and all that I tell you, you question how we will get there on time?" Agnes began speaking in Hungarian, and Gavin could just imagine its meaning. "Now go, get the carriage, I will collect what we will need." She shooed him with her hand and headed to the front of the store. Gavin decided he would not question, he would just follow her directions. He would do anything to save Roszalia, even if it meant following Agnes. He entered the stables and met the same boy who had delivered the note to him earlier.

"Ms. Agnes's carriage is ready." Gavin looked at the boy as if to ask how he knew why he was there. He seemed to understand. "I always keep it ready. Ms. Agnes goes on last minute journeys a lot. Ms. Agnes sent me a note two days ago saying to have her mares ready for a trip soon."

Gavin followed the boy to the far side of the stables. There at the rear door stood the carriage. It was nothing out of the ordinary. The interior had seating for two, and the single bench in front was for the driver. Gavin did not know what he expected, but the reined two small dapple mares did not seem sturdy enough to make such a long trip, pulling them in the carriage. Nevertheless, as he was finding out, as strange as they seem, he should not question Agnes's methods.

As he pulled the carriage to a halt in the front of her shop, Agnes stood waiting with her shawl and a small satchel. She entered the small interior and told Gavin to head north towards Dublin. Again, he was about to ask, but she said, "The mares know the way, they will stop in a bit, and I will explain, but let us move now."

She shut the door and he headed the carriage north. The horses rode hard. The sun was in the west and he guessed they had ridden for at least two hours when the mares slowed and turned into a side trail, then came to a stop. There were no homes or farms, or even signs of livestock in this area. Only green pastures and the heavily wooded area they had just entered. Agnes quickly opened the door and exited the carriage, coming around to the horses.

"There are my beauties, good girls. Now, I have your treats, you can show your true spirit today."

The two animals began to stomp and whinny, knowing what to expect. She produced a small leather pouch and a corked vile. She added half the vile of liquid to the pouches contents. Carefully splitting the grain into her palms, she offered it to her mares. Gavin watched with awe as the mares seemed to grow right before his eyes, their flanks strong, their eyes glowing with determination as their muscles rippled. They stood at attention, waiting for their commands. Agnes returned the items to her satchel, then looking in Gavin's direction.

"Gavin, please come inside the carriage, the next part of our trip will be rather …" she paused, "Well, just come inside if you will." He did as asked. He was now sure every strange tale he had heard about Agnes, with her gypsy magic, was true, and he had no reservations that this woman would do everything in her power to save her niece.

"We will be traveling very quickly from here on, so all that I can tell you is … this is just the beginning of the strange things you will encounter."

She gave a shout in Hungarian to her mares and they took off. Gavin was apprehensive that there was no one at the reins, but after what he was experiencing, he put his trust in Agnes. She had pulled down a type of shade that was in the carriage, it let light in but seemed to be made of metal, and he could not see out. He felt the bumps in the trail as they made it back on the main road, and he could feel a speed he had never known a carriage to produce.

Agnes spoke again, "Gavin, I know how difficult this all is to understand, but as I mentioned, I have been around a long time and have learned many things." She paused as a look of regret passed over her features, just as quickly, it disappeared. "You see Roszalia was meant to be my student and my predecessor. She has all the gifts I possess and many more. But her heart chose another path in life, and now I pray it will not cause her end."

Gavin took Agnes's hand in his. "Agnes, all this may be strange to me, but my love for Roszalia is real, and love is the strongest magic there is…so I will find her and win her heart.

We will save the one we both love dearly."

Agnes looked into Gavin's soul through his eyes and there was only love. After only a few hours passed, the carriage slowed down, Agnes rolled the strange shades back up, and in the distance Gavin viewed the partially exposed mound, Brug Na Boinne. They continued at a slow pace until the carriage stopped in a wooded place west of the megalithic site. The air was still, and Agnes told Gavin to follow close.

"Unfortunately my boy, there is no magic to help our walk through the passage, we have about a quarter of a kilometer before we enter the ruins."

In front of them, camouflaged by the enormous jagged boulders and tree roots was an opening to a cave. Agnes removed some of the brush then entered, motioning Gavin to follow. He had to bend down to enter, but soon could stand erect in the musty earthen passage, He could feel them descend as he followed Agnes closely. A lantern lit their way, but soon a green phosphorous glow illuminated the walls. She extinguished the lamp, saying over her shoulder, "Not much further."

Gavin noticed that the walls of their passage were now made of smooth sandstone, and he caught glimpses of strange circular and diamond shaped designs scribed deep within them. They came upon what seemed like a dead end. Solid rock blocked their way. Agnes gently pushed on the upper right corner of the stone, and to Gavin's amazement, it pivoted as if it weighed nothing. They entered a large, square, chamber room,

"We have arrived. We must hurry, the sun is setting."

She began pulling things from her satchel: a tallow candle and the vile of purple liquid that he had seen earlier, it now was definitely glowing. He wanted to ask, but instead, he just watched as the older woman set things out in an order that he felt she was very used to doing. Finally, Agnes looked up. "We are ready, you must sit and drink this, the sun will set and the moon will rise, you must finish this before they cross." She looked at the corbelled ceiling and said a prayer in Hungarian as she blessed the vial. "Now, drink the entire contents, I will meet you on the other side."

"You will be there, in the future?" he said incredulously.

Agnes gave an abrupt laugh. "Dear boy, I would not leave my niece's life to you alone, now hurry– drink, Roszalia awaits us." Gavin closed his eyes and in his mind, he saw her face. He drank the foul liquid and within moments when darkness enveloped him.

When he woke, His head was pounding. He remembered having a horrible nightmare. Roszalia had taken a bullet meant for him. He knew he had to be on his way to town to bring her back and straighten out the misunderstanding. However, before setting out, he would need to find Truda and get a mixture for this head pain.

"Well, he finally awakes!" a vaguely familiar voice was saying, his focus still adjusting, drink some hot tea, it will help your head."

Gavin recognized Agnes's voice and wondered if he had ridden all night to find Roszalia. Drinking the warm sweet tasting tea, his vision began to sharpen. The room was dark and the furnishings were odd. Agnes went over and flipped a thing on the wall and the room lit up. Gavin squinted, the illumination came from the ceiling and the tables, there were no oil lamps, but the room glowed brightly. Sitting very still, Gavin looked towards Agnes his eyes still adjusting to this new light. She sat back down in the chair on the other side of the room. Her appearance seemed different. She wore men's breeches and a long shirt.

"Agnes…" he began slowly, "where is Roszalia?" At her name, Gavin began seeing images. "Just let the warm tea set in, then we will talk, you will begin to remember in a few minutes." As the pain decreased in his head, his thoughts indeed returned and with it, the painful memory of Roszalia, lying unconscious in his arms.

Agnes saw that he was struggling with these thoughts and intervened, "Alright Gavin, do you remember our conversation? You have traveled far, today is March fifteenth, and the year is two thousand and thirteen."

Gavin shook his head, Agnes told him to take a moment, his

mind and memory would clear. He stood and crossed the bright room to a window. Looking out he could see rooftops of buildings up and down the street. One familiar sight and scent caught his attention. The ocean and its horizon were just beyond the mess of concrete that littered his view. Just knowing it was there was reassuring, of what, he did not yet know.

He began to hear strange sounds, loud horns, and voices. He saw automobiles, not like the few he had seen in the large cities of Dublin or England; these were shiny metal boxes in an array of colors. As he looked at the people, he saw women barely clothed crossing streets, men with only torn off trousers and carrying long fin shaped planks towards the water's edge. All seemed so vibrant and alive, happy and full of energy. There was nothing drab or dreary here. He turned back to where Agnes still sat and waited, after another moment she began.

"My dear boy, we have much to do in a few short weeks. You will encounter everything imaginable, and to you, many things unimaginable, in this time, but remember why you are here. You must meet with Roszalia and she must remember the love she possessed for you. She must feel this with her soul to be reunited. She must make her choice." Gavin looked quizzically at her, and began slowly with an arched brow.

"Her choice? What do you mean?" Agnes stood her full height only reaching Gavin's mid–chest. "She will have to choose her love for you, or her life she now knows, and Gavin, if she chooses not to return with you, Roszalia's soul will perish in the past. You will return to the tomb passage alone," she said. Gavin seemed taken off guard by this new revelation.

"Ah, a minor detail forgotten to be told!" Agnes just shrugged. "Would it have mattered? As long as you could see she is alive and well?"

Gavin, knowing it would not have, nodded, if he could only have but a moment with his love again.

"Where do I begin? Gavin, you must be careful not to do anything rash, for this Roszalia, Rose, does not know you. You are a stranger to her." She hesitated, and then decided to tell Gavin that there was another man involved in Rose's life. "And I know this will upset you, but Rose lives with a man. He is a tyrant and she is not happy, but you must be careful, the decision to return with you must be her own."

Gavin felt his jaw tighten, the thought of another man with his love. He would need all his composure if he ever were to come face to face with him.

CHAPTER FIFTEEN
Del Ray Beach, FL. – Present Day

Rose looked in the full-length mirror, tonight's choice of the dark shimmery dress made her smile. Yes, Donovan would hate it. He liked her to wear flashy provocative clothing. Tonight she really didn't care what he thought. In fact, she hadn't cared what he wanted from her for the past few years. She knew for some time that it was time for her to move out and start a new life.

Rose had met Donovan McVie five years earlier. She had been working for an exporting firm in the city and had gone to a holiday party given by one of their clients. She always hated the parties because all the men who attended were usually there to show off how much money they made, or to show off their mistresses. The wives that did go would discuss their latest nips and tucks, and eying the young interns for their next affair. Rose went because her boss had told her to, plain and simple. Show up, be polite, and then slip away when the drinking got heavy so no one would notice. This year however, a young partner in the firm had caught her eye. They met over appetizers and spent the rest of the evening in conversation. Donovan was charming, sophisticated, and as they began spending all their time together, she found herself very attracted to him. It felt like their relationship progressed with whirlwind speed, but never having much to call her own and no real home or family, when he made the offer for her to move in with him in his ten–room home on the ocean, she could not resist. They lived together, yet had separate lives. Rose did not think she ever truly loved this man, she always felt there was someone else she was destined to meet, and she had just gotten too comfortable. She knew Donovan wanted a possession and did not like her independence, especially when she opened her shop with her old roommate, Maggie. He would spend long weekends away on business trips. She suspected he was having affairs but never accused him. Not until this year, four years after the fact, did she lose all respect for him. She had learned that he used the intimate knowledge she had told him about the firm she had worked for to put it in ruins. After this there was no question, she had to get out of his home and him out of her life. Rose shook her head to clear her thoughts, picked up the tortoise–handled brush, and pulled the strands of hair from its bristles, a habit she had, and began to brush her hair again. She was tense tonight, a strange apprehensiveness had enveloped her and she could not shake the feeling that something significant was about to take place. "Silly!" she thought out load, shaking her head as she replaced the brush gently on the table. She then opened the small box that contained her most prized possession, a necklace she had bought while she was on a shopping trip with a friend, rummaging through antique shops. Rose clasped the necklace and ran her fingers over the stone. It felt warm and somehow comforting. The chain was of fine gold strands and from it hung a teardrop emerald encased in gold. An inscription was once on the back, long ago worn off, now all but the words 'forever' remained.

She remembered the day she found it. While her friend was arguing with the shopkeeper over some furniture, she was idly rummaging through what looked to her like junk when she came across a curious piece – a small trunk. It was very musty and filled with mostly linens, junk jewelry, and silver items from an estate in Ireland. Rummaging through it, Rose felt a small wooden box. As she extracted it, she had the same strange sensation she was experiencing tonight, an unexplainable feeling that she was about to make a very valuable find. At first, the box seemed empty. As she closed the lid, it caught a piece of the silk lining. Opening it again, she tugged the material to straighten it, and her eyes widened as a necklace slid out and onto the bed of silk, now yellowed and frayed. She felt a small tingle go up her spine, not caring if it was valuable or not, she had to have this piece. The owner of the shop saw Rose holding one item.

"Miss, it is the entire trunk, all or none." She quickly closing the case, and placed it with the other items.

"Of course. I'll take it." After paying, she left, feeling somewhat giddy and anxious to look at her find more closely.

Along with the necklace, there was the tortoise–handled brush, why she chose to keep this she could not tell. It was a man's brush, but she felt the same sensation when she picked it up. Also in the trunk, there were old photographs. One in particular fascinated her, a torn picture of a man and a very attractive young woman. The man on her left was intriguing, so handsome, and rugged and relaxed, the kind of man you read about in a romance novel, dark hair to his neckline, his arm draped across the back of the chair the woman sat in. Although very yellowed and faded, she could feel his eyes staring at her, she knew it was a silly thought but still the feeling was there. She had kept this picture for some reason, tucked away in the bottom of the chest. As her thoughts returned to the present, Rose arranged the necklace once more. As she touched it, a flash of that dream came back to her. The dreams started shortly after she purchased the trunk and its contents. She told herself it was from spending so much time looking at the mystery man in the picture, yet recently, they seemed so real. She looked forward to seeing him in her mind and began wishing for a lover that lived centuries ago.

Now, sitting at her mirror, Rose gazed at her reflection. She planned to take an early leave. Tonight was going to be the last of Donovan's parties that she planned to attend. One last brush through her hair and she was ready to face the night.

Leaving her room and heading down the stairs the voices

from the early arrivals floated up towards her. She stood for a moment surveying the room. A few guests she knew stopped to chat then made their way to the open bars. A waiter passed and Rose grabbed a glass of champagne and thought how she hated to endure another one of Donovan's business parties. He was a showman, a big wig in the commercial export world, and his business acquaintances were numerous. Lately however, with all his parties, drunken late night outings, she didn't care if he came home at all. It was more than she could handle. Her solace was that she would soon be away from all this and him. Draining her glass, she set out to look for a friendly face in the growing crowd of people.

Donovan saw Rose come down the stairs, and he noted the drab dress she chose to wear. He also noticed that she wore that necklace again. Over the five years they had been together, he had bought her a fortune in jewelry, yet she chose to humiliate him by wearing a trinket she found in a rummage store. His thoughts drifted back to when they met. He was a junior partner for a large exporting firm. Rose worked at the company that his firm had in its sites for a hostile takeover. After he had won her trust and moved her into his home, she unintentionally provided intimate knowledge of the company's financial pitfalls. At the time the transfer was enacted, Rose was ignorant to her part she played. It had really been too easy and he had to admit, he had taken a liking to Rose, she was stunning, and he did like nice, showy things around him. At first, they attended parties and functions as a couple, then she began to want to go on her own, and then that blonde interfered, putting business notions in her head. He knew she wanted to leave him, but he was the one who would say when he would end a relationship, and he wasn't ready just yet. Donovan's thought was interrupted, as one of his colleagues asked his opinion on merger with an overseas company. He decided not to ruin his party with thoughts of Rose.

She was feeling on edge tonight and she mindlessly touched her necklace for comfort. Quickly withdrawing her fingers, she could have sworn she felt heat from the stone. She shook off the thought. The flush was more likely from the quick drink of the champagne. In the center of the room, Rose spotted Maggie, her close friend since college, and now, her business partner. They saw one another at the same time and both women headed towards each other. Maggie locked arms with her friend and breathed a heavy sigh. She rolled her heavily made–up eyes and said in a half whisper,

"Oh darling, another long boring night of fake smiles, hugs, idle endless business talk and wheeling and dealing. I already have a headache!" Rose laughed in agreement with her friend. They walked to the side of the room and out the open sliding glass doors. They both sat on the bench that faced the ocean.

"Have you been having your dreams again, you look like you haven't slept. Maybe you should go to one of those sleep classes?"

"Maggie, I cannot go to some study program and say I am in love with a dream man who I fantasize about because of an old picture I found!" Rose drained her glass and felt the warmth from the liquid flow through her, or was it the thought of the image of the man in the picture? Maggie frowned and finished her glass of its contents.

"Well you have a point there, so how goes it with Mr. popular over there?" She tilted her head in the direction where Donovan was standing in the middle of a group of men.

"Same," she said, glancing in his direction, not feeling like elaborating tonight on her dead end relationship.

"Okay. Got ya, same 'ol, same 'ol." Her husband was motioning to Maggie from the other side of the room. "Hon, Daniel needs me, he hates these things. I will tell him to go on in the den and watch the game. Some of the guys are in there. I'll be right back."

Rose watched as her friend meandered through the crowd, stopping every other person or two to say hello. This could be a while, she thought, and stood up to survey the room. There were quite a few guests and Rose wondered how many of them were business related and how many were here to make Donovan look impressive. The crowd was a diverse one, some wore jeans, some suits, and one woman, surrounded by men, wore a very revealing, almost see–through sarong. As Rose scanned the crowd, she also wondered how many of these women Donovan was sleeping with. Then feeling amused by the fact that she really did not care.

A waiter passed by with more champagne and Rose took another glass from the tray and took a deep gulp of the bubbly liquid. As she looked up over the rim of her glass, she felt the color drain from her face, fighting to swallow her drink. Across the room – she saw him. He was leaning against the wall, arms folded across his broad chest. His white linen shirt was open at the neck to reveal dark hair against tan skin, he wore a leather vest that matched the black leather pants, tightly fitting and revealing muscular legs. His hair fell casually to his collar. Rose felt her throat constrict and felt she could not breathe. *You are the man in my torn photo*, taken over a century ago.

The room began to spin and the heated sensation she felt earlier was back. Rose was holding the champagne glass too tightly, and she shakily set it on a table, never taking her eyes off this man. Suddenly she realized as she studied his eyes, amber like aged whiskey, dark lashed and very masculine, he was staring at her. At that moment, it seemed all the people in the room faded away, and she thought she heard him softly call her name. How often in her dreams, he had come to her. She watched his lips, full and inviting, a scar over his eye. His stare was intoxicating, and then he raised his own glass as if to toast her, slightly nodding, and smiled. Rose felt her heart would stop at any moment. She was about to cross the room to find out who this man was when she was startled by a hand on her shoulder. Rose spun around, a shiver running down her.

"Donovan, you startled me, I was..." a blush ran down her and she stammered for words to cover her emotions. She felt like he had caught her with a lover, one who has been in her dreams for years.

"Why so jittery, see and old friend I shouldn't know is here?" Donovan goaded her, yet took a quick look in the direction she was facing. Anger flooded her at that moment, that Donovan was watching her every move, said unconvincingly trying to calm her voice.

"No, it is no one I know, now if you don't mind." As she turned her back on him, he muttered something inaudible and walked off. Rose quickly scanned the room for the handsome stranger, but he was gone. "Damn," she muttered just loud enough for the man next to her to raise an eyebrow. She felt so shaken. Was he really here? Was it the alcohol? She went back to sit down on the couch to think. Maggie finally returned and was concerned how pale her friend looked and having a vacant look in her eyes.

Rose finally looked up and saw Maggie standing in front of her with a glass extended towards her. She accepted it and drained the liquid. Maggie's eyes widened and she took the empty glass from her friend's shaking hand.

"He was here," Rose spoke so softly it took Maggie a full moment to realize she had spoken at all.

"What...Who? Rose, are you okay?" Maggie sat down next to her friend, "Christ, what happened? You look so pale, like you saw a ghost."

"He was here, Maggie." for the first time she looked at her friend, "My dream lover, mystery man, whatever, or whoever he is, he was right over there," she said, pointing to the now empty archway.

"Okay, okay." Maggie took Rose's hand, "Hon, maybe some guy looked like your dream lover." Maggie was genuinely concerned. This was out of character for her friend. Rose was the calmest woman she knew, not even that prick, Donovan got to her, and now a dream man is appearing at parties. "Here, let's get some air and take a walk on the beach."

Rose nodded and stood, following her friend out to the patio and down the long steps to the cool sand below. She kicked off her sandals and inhaled as the salt air seemed to sober her. Looking out over the water, she said,

"I know it was him, I don't know how, or who he is, but for a moment our eyes locked. It was like electricity, we connected."

The party raged on behind them, noise and light and music

spilling into the cool blackness of the night air. Rose shivered, but not from the night air, she had made her mind up that if this man was not in her imagination, she would find him, and that thought excited her more than anything.

Gavin cursed himself for being so bold as to come to her home, he just could not resist seeing his Roszalia. He watched as she and another woman came across the room. She was so beautiful, perfect, and she wore the necklace. How did she have it? Did she know its meaning? When she saw him from across the room, he could sense that she connected with him, and then the man appeared. He seemed very familiar with her. Was this the man she lived with that Agnes had mentioned? The anger he felt from another man's hand on her creamy shoulder infuriated him. He knew the risk of coming here, and that he would have to go slow and re–win her heart, but it tore him apart to see her tonight. He thought of how far he had come to get the woman he loved to fall back in love with him, with no guarantee this Roszalia ever would. He had stayed in the hall shadows, watching the encounter with the man and his Roszalia, until he could not stay any longer. He left out the back and walked down to the beach, he wanted to go back to the house, to confront her, but thought better when he heard her sweet voice and saw Roszalia and the blonde woman coming towards him. He looked at the large home as he left and thought that at least she is living well. He hoped that Agnes would still be up because he needed her advice.

In this century, Agnes lived in a large English Tudor style townhouse two blocks back from the beach with an ocean view. Once inside, Gavin went to the kitchen. "Hell where does this woman keep that scotch?" He rummaged through the cabinet until he found a bottle of sherry. "This will have to do," he muttered and poured a generous glass.

"So, when will a man ever learn to heed a woman's advice?" Agnes's voice said from the alcove where she was entering the kitchen. "You went to her house, eh?" Agnes smiled in a knowing way that Gavin had yet to become comfortable.

"Aye, as you probably knew I would!" Gavin took a gulp of the amber liquid and let it warm his insides.

Agnes gave a sharp chuckle, "Doesn't take a fortune teller to know what stupid things a man in love will do!"

Gavin shot her a look. "So what am I to do? I come God knows how far to watch her be fondled by another man at a party so strange I can't begin to comprehend." In an angry and helpless gesture, he drained the rest of the sherry.

"Dear boy, you do nothing, it is arranged. I know the Rose of this century. She will meet with me and tell me all about seeing you at her party. You will meet again, this time arranged by me." Agnes gave him a hard look, "Next time she will be more accepting. Remember, Rose of this time still has the blood of the family running through her. She may deny what she feels and thinks, but she knows in her heart it to be true."

Gavin, feeling little comfort in her words, bid Agnes goodnight and headed up the stairs to lie down and make his own plan to meet Roszalia again, this time away from her home and the man. As Gavin began to drift to sleep, he thought he could smell lavender in the room and hear her voice softly calling him.

CHAPTER SIXTEEN

The night finally wound down around three a.m. Rose could not sleep if she wanted to. Her mind raced with thoughts of the man, she was now unsure she had even seen him, maybe it was the champagne as Maggie had said. The early morning air was chilly. Overhead tars peppered the clear sky like precious stones laid on velvet. Deciding to head towards the peace and serenity of the beach, she absently walked to a place she knew well and sat at the water's edge. A gnawing feeling in her stomach told her that her friend was wrong and the man standing so casually by the arch was real and was there specifically looking for her. If Donovan had not broken their gaze then she would have met this stranger. His handsome image burned into her mind, she kicked at the cool sand with her toes as if to unearth an answer.

Flashes of her teenage years began to creep into her mind. To her they called her gifted. But she also heard the other children and even the house parents' talk, they said she was strange; it made them uneasy that she knew what would happen. She could feel things that others could not. Rose also had a special bond with animals and a gift for healing ailments with herbs. At college, she studied botany, psychology, and parapsychology. Her 'gifts', or curse as she often thought it was. She had the ability to know when events would happen and to whom. Becoming a lab rat at the university did not appeal to her. Sometimes it hurt to watch an event with one of her friends take place that she could have stopped, but Roszalia knew that nature and the universe had its plan and though it provided her a glimpse of this plan from time to time, it was not for her to interfere. Once she did step in to try to save a friend the unexpected heartache when Roszalia knew her father would die in an accident, and although it readied her friend for what would come, the accident happened anyway and not only did her friend lose her father, but she rejected Rose. That lesson learned, and she never again interjected with one of her visions. And with age and practice she had taught herself to control these premonitions. However after seeing the man in her photo tonight, she wondered if the dreams she had been having for these years were not a suppressed premonition of meeting this man.

The morning sky was now fully illuminated as she entered the yard. Rose absently picked up bottles of champagne that had been dropped in the bushes, and tossed them in to the trash. After checking to make sure the main hall door was locked, she passed by Donovan's study. There as a sound from within, annoyed that a straggling guest had decided to camp out, she opened the door and was about to say something when she saw Donovan sitting in a chair, glass in hand. Instantly regretting entering the room, Rose turned to close the door and head up the stairs. Donovan called her name. Turning back, she sighed and faced him, his eyes glazed, perhaps from the liquor.

"Did you enjoy the party?" he asked, not looking at her.

"Not particularly, drunks and braggarts don't impress me. That is your idea of a good time. "She said dryly, swallowing hard to diminish the vile she felt rising as she thought of his so–called friends. He looked at her now, damp hair, and dress. His cold eyes seemed to penetrate her very thoughts.

"Strolling the beach? Maybe I should follow you and see who you go to visit every morning."

"Donovan it is late, or early. I am tired, do as you want, you will be sadly disappointed I am afraid." she turned and walked from the room. Donovan had always been extremely jealous, even though she knew he was sleeping with any woman who caught his fancy. She told herself that soon she would not have to answer to him. All that she wanted to do at this moment was climb into her bed and think of her dream love, as she had so many times before. Getting into her bed and pulling the covers up, she almost thought she could smell a light scent of tobacco, leather, and spice. She was soon lost in her dreams.

He walked towards her. She wore a richly embroidered colored skirt and peasant blouse, low cut and showing off her figure. Red slippers adorned her delicate feet and a bright red sash hung from her long dark hair. Twirling around him, he reached for her, as she avoided his grasp. Toying with him, the music was festive and fun, he finally grabbed her waist and began the dance with her, pulling her close, then spinning her away. They embraced and held one another as the music increased its speed. The tall, good–looking man bent and kissed her red inviting lips, she breathed his scent: spice and leather. She ran her fingers through his dark locks. He kissed her throat as she arched with the rhythm of the music, still twirling around, suddenly a loud shot rang out, then the searing pain, and he held her close as she realized the shot had not pierced her flesh but her lover's heart. As he looked at her, he mouthed the words, "Roszalia, I will love you for all eternity. Come home with me."

Rose sat up with a start, the bed sheets entangled around her legs. Sweat poured between her breasts and thighs, no one ever called her Roszalia, that was her given name but she never knew her real parents, they died in an accident when she was a baby. In the orphanage where she grew up, the other children called her Rose. Only the housemother called her Roszalia, and she had not heard it since she left the home. Why now, would her dream lover call her this? Fully awake now, the clock ticked away, and she knew it was futile to try to go back to sleep. Donning a pair of capris and a short top, she pulled a sweatshirt over her head and set out towards the beach. Even though the sun was up, the air seemed even crisper than the previous evening. She headed in the direction of the distant boardwalk. Walking on the hard cool sand, the shallow waves rhythmically lapping at her toes. The gulls were unusually quiet but as always, the crashing of the surf broke the silence. She pondered her dream, they had become so vivid recently, she never knew her heritage, but the music and the dance of her dream felt right. When she was young, she would dance and spin and twirl until she fell, exhausted but feeling alive. One of the housemothers had given her the nickname, gypsy princess. It was in her blood. She stood for a long moment facing the water, a light breeze rippled through her hair and as she closed her eyes. A very faint musky scent, both soothing and familiar, invaded her thoughts. Slowly turning around, a small inaudible gasp escaped her, before she quickly regained her composure.

Gavin stood behind her, a mere arm's length away, agonizing to touch her. Instead, he stood still, not wanting to frighten her away. He had changed into some clothing Agnes had set out for him. She said that he needed to blend in more, though he now felt more out of place than ever. He wore a pair of denim jeans and a cotton shirt, but insisted on wearing his own boots.

Neither spoke for a moment, their eyes locked in the startled moment of recognition. His of the love he thought he lost and hers of the handsome stranger from an old photo, the same man she had been dreaming of for years. Gavin was too stunned that his early morning sleeplessness would take him for a walk on the beach and find Roszalia. He remembered what Agnes had said, that she did not know him and to take it slow. Looking at her now, she was here, alive, beautiful, the wind was making the loose strands of her hair that had escaped the tie, whip in her face, she brought her delicate hand up to push them aside.

There was a long moment of uncomfortable silence, and then with a smile she nodded, "Good morning."

Gavin began to feel panic slip over him, he had to keep her here, he had to keep the conversation going, and they were so close. Just to hear her voice was magic enough for the moment. He desperately wanted to touch her but dared not get too close.

"Beautiful morning to walk upon the beach," he replied in a heavy accent.

Rose could barely speak what could she say to this man. You look like the man in my dreams. What a fool she would look like, but who was he? She had lived on this beach for five years and had never seen him. Turning back towards him, she took a step forward. The sunlight shown on his handsome face, he did not attempt to move.

"Yes, I sometimes can't sleep and walk in the mornings, have you just moved to the area? I have never seen you here before." Her voice sounded shaky and unfamiliar to her. She wanted to ask if he was at the party.

Gavin wanted to tell her how far he had come for her. Instead he said, "Aye, I am here visiting my…" he hesitated for just a moment and continued, "My aunt for a few weeks."

She looked at him, "From Ireland, Scotland?" she noted his thick brogue, and thought it pleasing.

"Aye, County Kerry, Ireland, near the Ardbear Bay." Your home, he added to himself as he fell in step beside her.

"I have always dreamed of going to Ireland. In fact, I have some jewelry that I bought from an estate over there." Her voice sounded distant in her own ears. Rose felt so comfortable with this stranger, he felt so familiar. She wanted to spend time with him to ask a thousand questions. Instead, she silently sighed as she viewed her beach home.

"I really have to get back to the house now," not hiding the regret in her voice. Gavin walked her back to the gate and as they both reached the latch, their fingers touched. She did not pull away, he closed his large bronzed hand over hers, and for a moment, an electric current ran through them both. Rose reluctantly dropped her hand from under his and let him unhook the latch.

Looking down into her eyes, Gavin smiled, "Have a good day, Roszalia," and began walking farther down the beach, she noticed he has a slight limp. It took a full minute before she realized she had never told him her name, and certainly not Roszalia. He had not mentioned his. An image of swirling in this handsome stranger's arms in a dance came to her. Rose found herself obsessed with a man who she had recently seen at her own home and had walked with on the beach, no longer just a dream, but now flesh and blood.

The next few days were going to be hectic, Rose had committed to speaking at a convention on holistic medicine in Boston. She had to be at the airport no later than four o'clock this afternoon, but since it was not yet noon, she decided a visit to her friend François's antique shop would get the mystery man off her mind for a while. Since François was an antique dealer, she had told him about the inlay on the necklace box. He had called the day before Donovan's party and left a message. His voice excited saying had found the family crest in an old book. The box was in her purse and she gingerly ran her finger over the inlay on its top, remembering the day she discovered it.

At first glance, dust and mold covered the wooden box and it seemed to be very ordinary. However, after Rose took her prize home and began gently cleaning it with an oil soap mixture she had always used on her wood curio cabinet, the luster of magnificent mahogany began to show. The more she rubbed, the grime began to dissipate, and soon, a silver design began to appear, inlaid deep within the wood. Rose surmised by the shape and details that it was a family crest. A strange feeling, a warm excitement, came over her upon touching the design, and she decided to research it further.

François Dubois was a dear friend. He was the person who had gotten her into the love of old and forgotten memories. As Rose drove her mustang down the row of small, but very expensive stores, finding a place not too far from the entrance, she parked the sports car, and walked to the front door, the name on the carved wooden door was, 'Your Elegant Junk.' Rose had to smile every time she read this sign. Behind the sign, advertising junk was a small king's treasure of antiques, jewelry, glass, and vintage items. François once said as he waved his arms

"You can call this stuff antiques or junk chéri, but when the wealthy clients want to find that one in a million piece of furniture I can search the world over and find it. They do not care what the name of my store is." Roszalia remembered the first time she walked into the store. She was fresh out of college making her first attempt at remodeling her small beach apartment. A friend had told her to go visit François. If he could not find what you needed to make your home one of a kind, then no one could. Curious about a man with such a reputation, she decided to stop in and meet this person. When she entered his shop, she was stunned with the disorderly, but impressive array of items. There were antique crystal pieces set under tiffany lamps to catch and send prisms of light everywhere. The rich smell of old wood permeated the interior air and lemon oil invaded her nostrils. The gleam of the wood overcame any of that. Expensive wood, silver, crystal, leather chairs, and divans stretched isle after isle. A gallery in back held its audience captive with small collection of artists' original paintings, and the jewel room was enough to dazzle an empress!

Then there was François himself, a man in his sixties, or 'there about,' he would say. He was slender with a shock of unruly grey hair that seemed to have landed on his head. Quite a contrast to the grandeur around him, yet it was his bright and friendly eyes and quick with a welcome that made you want to get to know this man.

Rose walked through the shop in search of her friend. François was sitting in his large leather chair at his oak roll top desk, piles of invoices and documents of origination for items in the store cluttered every inch, he looked up over his glasses as he heard her heals on the tile approach. Motioning her to sit, François gave her a warm smile and then waved his bony hand at the stacks of papers.

"Have you ever seen a better filing system?" Rose moved to the opposite chair and gave the man a hug before she sat.

"François you are incorrigible, millions in antiques and you do not own a file cabinet," she chided with a teasing scowl.

"Ah, but there you are wrong, I do…but alas," he waved towards another paper pile, "I do believe I lost it in this mess!" Rose laughed and then took a more serious tone.

"François, you said you found something about the inlay on my box? Rose held the wooded box out to François to look at.

The thin man sat up straighter in his chair and took the box from Rose; delicately he began turning it, looking at the symbol and all of its sides. Rose began to feel excitement rise in her,

François looked up. "Come with me," he stood and took her hand. They walked to a back room where François kept old newspapers, documents, and many old books. He rummaged through a huge stack of books until he came to one that was leather bound, with the words, 'The History of Family Crests' embossed on the cover. He stood for several minutes turning pages to find the story he wanted, then in an excited voice he declared, "Yes, yes, O'Connor."

The air in the room made Rose feel claustrophobic, it was musty and stale from the old paper and leather, and she began to feel impatient. Finally, François turned the large book to her.

"There, the O'Connor family, and here is the family crest, just the same as the inlay on your box, and the silk within," he proclaimed with a smile.

Rose took the book from him and stared at the photo in the book. Yes, it was the same design, the family crest of the O'Connor family, County Kerry, Ireland. Suddenly the room seemed to get smaller, Rose felt dizzy, maybe from the heat or the musty odor but she also felt an excitement that that had nothing to with her surroundings.

"François may I borrow this book?"

"Of course, but please keep me informed, I do believe the author is a descendant of one of the children and is a historian in Ireland. Perhaps you could contact them for more information." Rose gave her friend a hug, which in turn made François's smile widen. Then tucking the leather book in one of her overnight bags, she headed for the airport to catch her flight.

She would contact the relative in Ireland, she thought, and this made her mind wander back to the man with the thick Irish brogue. Strange, he had said he was from the same county. She unconsciously shook the idea from her mind. Try as she would, the thought of seeing him again sent a thrill through her, foolish she thought, they may never cross paths again, and once more, she realized he was in her every thought, and still she did not even know his name. "Very foolish," she muttered out load, as she stepped on the gas and took off down the road.

She had not planned to attend this year's conference, but Maggie had suddenly become ill and had a presentation scheduled on holistic treatments. Rose offered to attend and deliver the speech, though she had a suspicion that her friend was not so sick, but rather worried about Rose's behavior lately, and wanted her to go to get her mind on something else.

For as long as she could remember, she had been involved in the natural healing craft, and this was a very familiar subject. She did not particularly enjoy the public speaking aspect or the lime light, but it would give her time to be away from Donovan. She needed that right now. Even with the upcoming event, she could not get the image of the stranger out of her mind. She hoped to see him again, before she moved from the beach.

The flight went smoothly, even landing ahead of schedule. The airport shuttle to her hotel was extremely crowded and she wished now that she had just rented a car. When she finally arrived at the host hotel, the lobby was bustling with convention goers. There were two separate events taking place there this week, people were crowding in front of the check in counter, and to the left, the elevators were straining to keep up with their constant passengers. Rose finally got her room cards and waited towards the back of the crowd at the elevators. When the doors opened, a stream of people and luggage all crammed in tightly. Taking a step back, she decided to find the stairs and take them up to the third floor. The porter had already delivered her luggage to the room, and after sitting in the plane for three hours, some exercise sounded refreshing. Taking two wrong corridors, she finally saw the lit sign above the exit door at the end of the hall and headed that way. A man and young woman had the same thought and entered ahead of her. Hoisting her shoulder bag up, she began the climb. By the time she reached the third floor landing, her calves burned from the effort. She pushed through the stairwell door, and was pleased to see the number on the door in front of her matched her room card number.

After hanging up her few articles of clothing she brought, the thought that she had not eaten all day occurred to her, and she decided to go down to the dining room and see what they had on their late menu. Rose managed to wrangle through the lobby where she found a sign on the other side that said cafe. Inside, the crowd was lighter. Deciding to get a sandwich to take back to the room, she paid the obnoxious fee and headed out. This time she took the elevator.

Entering her room, she kicked off her shoes and shed her travel clothes, taking advantage of the fluffy robe the hotel left out for guests. She pulled her hair back hastily and secured it, then went to the big chair by the table with the reading lamp. She had brought the leather book that she borrowed from François with her. She knew from attending many of the conferences that once the seminar started she would not have much time to relax, but tonight there would be time to look through the pages carefully. Opening to the section where François had found the crest, Rose turned the pages, reading every line of the history of the O'Connor's. All the while, something gnawed at her, a familiarity about the name. She read on about the family heritage and accomplishments, the O'Connor family estate was one of the largest estates that did not fall due to the famine and where an Irish family still lived and ran it. Barrister William O'Connor the Second was an only child and inherited the entire estate. He married a commoner, Katherine Callaghan and they had three children. Gavin, Devon, and one daughter, Caitlin. Gavin being the eldest child. It seemed misfortune had fallen on the family, the father, William O'Connor the Second passed away and soon after Gavin's betrothed was accidentally shot.

"How sad," Rose realized it was her own voice speaking to no one. She read on, about the decedents until it came to the last known decedent as of the published date. Then there was a small paragraph about a family heirloom, a necklace given to the betrothed of Gavin O'Connor, a gypsy girl. The necklace stayed in the family for years.

Rose unconsciously touched her own prize necklace. In the early nineteen hundreds, the adult grandchildren divided the estate and sold a large portion. Caitlin O'Connor Anders, the author's great grandmother, and her husband, a physician and their two children moved to the home left to her in the country. This is where the author of this book still resides.

Rose made a mental note, upon her return home she would call the author and ask a few more questions. The author's notes said she had also written a book on prominent Irish families, including the O'Connor family. Perhaps she could find a copy. Carefully putting the book on the side table, she turned the light off, her mind was still racing, but soon the day of travel took over. Closing her eyes, sleep took over and as always, her dream lovers amber gaze comforted her. *Propped on one elbow, he looked down into her eyes. They lie on a soft feather mattress atop a heavy four–poster bed. He spoke only one sentence. 'Roszalia, I have come to take you home.'*

CHAPTER SEVENTEEN

Agnes decided if she did not arrange a meeting for Gavin and Rose, the fool boy would continue to follow the girl like a helpless puppy until she had him detained as a stalker, and explaining the presence of an over a hundred year old man who doesn't exist would be far too much for her old soul to handle.

The shop on the corner of the road was full of glass bottles and fresh scents, as Agnes entered she was overwhelmed by the smell of lavender and smiled, *Yes, that is my Roszalia* she mused, even time cannot make us forget our past and passions. The old woman only hoped this was true of the girl's heart as well, for Gavin hadn't much time, not long to win a woman's affection, make her fall in love, and then trust him enough to return to a time with very little creature comforts. Agnes sighed and stepped farther into the shop. Maggie saw her and rushed forward. Agnes had been visiting the shop since the first day they opened. She bought her fresh herbs from their store. The three women would spend hours discussing a remedy and drinking tea, and then it would months before she visited again.

"Agnes, I will not ask where you have been, I've learned years ago you are as secretive as some of the potions you introduce us to." The younger woman's blue eyes sparkled with admiration. Agnes held out both her hands and the two women embraced in a hug. Agnes thought of how she had first encountered Rose in this century. When she began having these feelings of peril in her niece's aura back in Ireland, she knew she had to pin point which century her soul would choose to reincarnate. It took many years, but when she found her, she kept a watchful eye on her niece, and was glad she had found such a good soul in her friend Maggie.

"Come, sit, I've a fresh kettle of chamomile tea brewed. Rose will be sorry she missed you. She went to the convention for me. I thought it would get her mind off of her troubles." Maggie waved a delicate hand as if to disperse her friend's problems. Agnes was disturbed she did not foresee this. How could she have missed knowing the two women had switched plans? Her composure never wavered to the onlookers, but her mind was racing. This was not good, not good at all. Perhaps Gavin's blundering intervention, she thought, he has disrupted her bond with Rose, but she also felt there was something else causing a disturbance in the balance.

Maggie was chatting and Agnes had to bring her thoughts back. "Well, my dear, I wanted to invite Rose and yourself and your husband over to dinner. But we can wait, when did you say Rose will return?"

Maggie thought for only a moment and said, "I was scheduled for only one seminar so Rose should be back on Sunday."

Maggie handed Agnes a cup of tea and the older woman sipped slowly, trying to decide whether to confide in Maggie her plan for Rose to meet Gavin. Of course, she could not tell her who he was, but she decided Maggie could be an ally in the matchmaking. Agnes set her teacup down on the small marble top table and leaned close as if to divulge a secret.

"I am afraid I am planning something I do not think Rose will like," a bright sparkle glinted in her eyes and Maggie noticed the smile curling on her lips. Now curious, Maggie raised an eyebrow. "You see my nephew is in town for a few weeks and he is well, a single man and I thought I would try my hand at matchmaker."

Agnes waited for Maggie's reaction. For what seemed a full minute, Maggie said nothing, then laughter rang from her lips, she took Agnes hands, "That is an understatement, she will be livid, but I am game, she is planning on finally leaving that brute she is living with. Yes, this is just what she needs, a distraction from Donovan and this dream man."

Now it was Agnes's turn to raise an eyebrow. "Dream man?" she asked, giving Maggie a quizzical look, hoping she would elaborate.

Again, Maggie swiped at the air with her hand, "Oh, she has been having these dreams of this gorgeous man for years and now they have all but consumed her, she even thinks she saw him at her home the other night." Maggie stood to put the teacups aside. "But yes, we will come over. I'll bring Daniel so if she gets terrible rude to your nephew, my husband and he can always talk football."

Agnes laughed, but was making a mental note to explain the game of football and the importance of it in this century to Gavin. Maggie agreed she would have Rose there this Tuesday, and the two women said their good–byes and parted. Agnes was sure Roszalia would accept the offer, she saw her in her home in her mind's eye. She could not see what would happen much beyond this and that was very troubling, there was some kind of interference clouding her sight.

Gavin had awoken before sunrise. Everything in this time was strange, fast paced and chaotic. He wished he could take a long hard ride on Samson, to feel the familiarity of his families land, the sights, sounds and smells always cleared his mind and allowed him to think. He wanted to go to the beach and see if Roszalia would be out walking. He did not know what he would say this time, but he had to see her. He waited by the rail for hours in vein. She never came from her home. As he left the beach and walked towards Agnes's home, he passed by a small shop with jewelry and hair accessories. A tortoise and silver hair comb caught his attention and he thought of Roszalia's mahogany hair pulled back with the comb in it. On impulse he bought it, he would give this to her when he saw her again.

The thought of her in the house with another man made his blood boil. Something was familiar about that man, though he knew he was being foolish. It was impossible, yet many impossible things have happened within the last week. He was anxious and getting angry just waiting something needed to be done. He thought perhaps when he saw her he should just tell her the truth. Then laughed to himself, and speaking aloud said, "Roszalia, do you remember me? I am your betrothed from the past, come to take you home." Gavin sat down hard in the chair with a defeated sigh.

Agnes entered the living room where Gavin sat. She noted the distraught look on his face. "Patience my boy, she will be visiting my house here soon. She and her friend are coming to dinner Tuesday. I will introduce you two and perhaps she will have a past life remembrance."

Gavin stared at her and said, "Aye, and perhaps I can grab her and kiss her and make her remember that bit of her past!"

Agnes gave him an angry stare. "Gavin we need to not frighten her away, do not make contact until I pave the way." He now stood and paced the room. "Too late Agnes, we met on the beech a morning ago."

Agnes sighed. "And?"

Gavin turned, "And nothing, I was as a school boy, my words were meaningless. We spoke, we parted, and I grieve. I told her I was visiting an aunt, nothing more."

"Good, then we will see what happens." Agnes left Gavin wondering about the dinner meeting. How could he contain his love for the woman who did not even know him?

It was late Sunday evening when Rose finally made it to her house. Donovan had left a note saying he would be gone on business until next week. Fine, Rose thought, two or three days to pack and be gone. She was much too tired from the flights and airport to do more than pour a glass of chardonnay and head for a relaxing bubble bath, then sleep. She had remembered if she called over to Ireland, there was a time difference, and that it would be daytime now. She decided to make the call while her bath was filling. Shedding her travel clothes and wrapping in a warm robe, Rose called international information for the phone number of the author. The phone rang three times and she waited, feeling a bit nervous. What would she say? She wanted to hang the phone up. She did not even know why she was calling.

"Morning," a cheery voice with a deep brogue startled Rose from her thoughts as she realized someone had picked up on the other end.

"Hello I am looking for the author of the book, 'The History of Family Crests'?"

"One moment please, that would be Miss Caitlin. I will call for her." The phone hummed for a moment, and then a sweet voice came onto the line. "This is Caitlin, how may I help you?" The voice had the same thick accent as the woman who answered.

Rose made her introduction, saying she was researching some old estate belongings and had come across a necklace in a box, with the crest of the O'Connor's. Caitlin listened politely and asked a few questions. Rose described her necklace and then, there seemed to be an uneasy silence.

"Are you still there?" she asked.

"Yes, yes, I would love for you to e–mail me a picture of this necklace. You see if it is truly was my ancestor's necklace, then it belonged to another."

Rose began feeling a tightening in her stomach but brought herself to ask to whom the necklace belonged. Caitlin began to tell her the story of her great, great uncles, Gavin and Devon and the gypsy girl they both loved. It was a tragic love, for jealousy drove Devon to arrange for his brother's murder. The girl intercepted a bullet meant for Gavin seriously wounding her. Soon after, Gavin disappeared. The popular folk lore is that her soul was kept alive in Gavin's love for her and he traveled far to bring her life back with gypsy magic. For, even death could not break their love bond.

Rose felt a brief chill as she thought of her dream and the man saying, 'I will love you for all eternity.' Caitlin continued, explaining there was a journal that told part of this tale, and then it just ended. "A colleague of mine found it, and in fact is check-ing its validity. There are others mentioned in it that we never knew about tied to the family." Caitlin covered the phone and spoke to someone. Then she was back on the line. "Devon was arrested and imprisoned, but let free thanks to another man's admission to the crime. It was not long before Devon lost every-thing due to his drink, gambling, and women. They say he final-ly felt the guilt of his actions. He disappeared for a few years. Some say he died in a duel." Caitlin went on to say her great grandmother had inherited the country home in Dingle and had moved there after all of this, along with her husband and their two children. We lost track of the necklace, Gavin had given it to his intended bride," Caitlin finished, "Your necklace as you describe it sounds identical. I would love to take a look."

Not being able to resist, yet feeling she already knew the an-swer, Rose asked,

"Caitlin, you said a young gypsy girl? Who was she?"

"She was just a young girl when she came to the estate, then a few years later became the children's governess. The story is that she had loved Gavin since she first arrived after her mother died. A beautiful girl, long dark mahogany hair, brown & gold eyes with flecks of green." Rose clutched the phone. Her heart was now pounding. Caitlin had just described her. Rose had a feeling the next question she asked was to be the turning point in her life, she continued slowly, trying to calm her voice.

"Caitlin, do you know, are there any of the O'Connor rela-tions living in America?"

"Well let me see, I wrote a book a number of years ago cata-loging all the relations of the O'Connor clan and their descend-ants." Rose heard her cup her hand over the phone and speak to someone again, "I am having the book brought to me…yes, yes. There was a descendent of Devon."

Rose broke in, "Devon, I thought you said he died?"

Caitlin responded, "Well no one knows, he was missing for years, but before he disappeared, he sired two children. Devon wed a socialite, some said he was trying to erase the gypsy that he lost to his brother, but the waif of a woman died in childbirth and my great grandmother raised the child with her own. He also sired another daughter. Her mother lived in the brothel near the harbor. Although Devon gave her financial support, he never let her live in the estate. We uncovered this scandal during our research. The child was a bastard but still had O'Connor blood. This child grew up and took passage on a ship to America. Susanna Petry was her married name. Ended up residing in New York where she had a boy and girl. The daughter had one child. Then there was the male, Donovan McVie. He had a son, whose name is also Donovan McVie. Junior of course."

Rose went rigid, her throat suddenly dry and she felt lightheaded. There had to be a mistake, this could not be her Donovan. The silence on the phone was like a black shroud, and then Rose heard Caitlin.

"Rose, are you still there?" I could send you a copy of this book, if you are interested. There was another descendant of Gavin and Roszalia…." Rose was no longer listening,

"Yes, thank you so much. I will get you a picture of the necklace as soon as I can, and yes, please send a copy to my shop." She rattled off the shop's address, and then hung up the phone. Her legs were shaking and she was numb from the information she just heard.

Of course, now she knew why the name O'Connor seemed so familiar, there was a family history book in Donovan's library. She had been paging through it one afternoon when Donovan angrily snatched it away saying something about his bastard ancestry. The necklace she so loved was an O'Connor heirloom, lost for centuries and he did not even know it. Donovan would never speak of his childhood or family. When she asked about meeting them, he only would say in an offhanded way that his grandparents were Irish immigrants and his family grew up poor. He vowed he would never end up like them and had been on his own since he became legal age, and had no contact with any of them.

With a sudden burst of renewed energy, Rose found her bed slippers and cinched her robe tighter. Her senses were alert and as she shivered, she knew it had nothing to do with the cool night air. She headed down the stairs to Donovan's study. Rose now felt certain the necklace was meant for her to find. She searched the shelves for a leather–bound book with 'Nineteenth Century Prominent Families in Ireland' embossed on its spine. She was thankful Donovan was out of town. Becoming frustrated, she had begun to give up when she spotted the book on the bottom shelf towards the far wall. Her excitement overwhelming, she stroked the leather cover, running her fingers over the letters and went over to the large overstuffed chair. The lights were low but that suited her mood fine. Slowly opening the book, she found herself staring at the O'Connor crest, the same crest François had found in his book, the crest on her box.

Rose turned each page, scanning for reference to the family. Toward the front of the book, she turned to a photo of a regal looking couple, the man was tall and the woman sitting looked frail, but beautiful, even in this old photo, she could see the fire and warmth in her eyes. The caption read, *Katherine and William O'Connor the Second*. Rose turned to the next page and saw a picture of a grand home in Ireland, the O'Connor Estate. Next to this was a young boy in riding dress next to a majestic looking horse, his young handsome features were warm and friendly. Upon turning the page, Rose's heart skipped a beat, and her breath caught in her lungs. The photo that she had found in her chest, a similar one was in this book, and there he stood, the man in her dreams, the man she saw at the party, the man she walked with on the beach. He stood, legs clad in leather breaches, a white shirt, and riding boots, a pretty younger version of lady O'Connor sat next to him, and a taller brooding man stood on her other side, the torn side of her photo she thought, the other brother. Rose touched the page, and then read the words beneath. *Gavin, Caitlin, and Devon O'Connor*. Her breath caught in her lungs. Devon was Donovan's great grandfather, and the resemblance was uncanny, right down to the brooding scowl. This other man was related to him also. And he was here. But how? She turned the page once more and the shock that ran through her was intense. There in a vignette, was a portrait of herself, the name under it read Roszalia Danyovok, betrothed of

Gavin O'Connor. Rose finally exhaled, feeling dizzy.

"How, was this possible?" she asked, realizing she spoken aloud, as if someone could answer these questions. Then she saw it. Around this girls neck was the necklace, her necklace. Rose clutched at the gold strands around her neck and felt the heat rise, unable to tear her eyes away. Finally, she sat the book down. She felt she needed air, she could go to her spot near the water's edge, there she could think, maybe figure out some logical explanation to finding all this. Even though she already felt she knew the truth, and it made her uneasy. *What if I run into this man Gavin; if that is his name.* She had always known and felt things, always feeling she did not belong. She had never known her parents or family history. Being a healer, she has experienced many unexplained things. Therefore, these events should not be so unbelievable to her. She opened the book to the photo of Roszalia. If this girl and Gavin were married, then was she a descendant like Donovan? No, she felt there was far more, she *was* the girl Roszalia in the photo. She could feel this in her soul. Of course, she believed in reincarnation, she often had unexplained flashes of another time and places she had never been. "Has he come for me?" A knock on the door startled her.

"Yes?"

Kitty the housekeeper poked her head in, "Beg pardon, Miss, but is everything alright? I heard a noise and then saw the light on in Mr. Donovan's library," she hesitated, looking at Rose, "you look a bit pale." The frown on Kitty's face made Rose compose herself, she said in a forced steady a voice,

"Thank you Kitty, I am just very tired from the travel, I needed a book to read to unwind," she tapped the book she held, "you can lock up now." Rose left the room heading towards the stairs. Never before had the feeling of apprehension or fear entered her thoughts, yet all of this, there had to be an explanation. She thought again of the beach, but decided she had no idea what to do if she met Gavin again, though she knew she would. She headed back up the stairs to her room, even with her uncertainty of seeing him again. She could not deny the excitement she felt from her newfound knowledge.

Chapter Eighteen

The morning came all too quickly, and now her dream man had a name...Gavin O'Connor. When sleep finally won her over, the dreams took a wild turn. *The dark stranger scooped her in his arms, spinning away. She wore bright skirts and flowing silk blouse, she danced and teased him as he followed her hungrily with his eyes. She spun dizzily but when she fell upon him, it was not Gavin, but Devon's arms that held her. His steel grip crushed against her, his hot and hungry lips burned hers. She struggled to get out of his grip and he only held her tighter, the more she resisted, the more he held on...then Gavin appeared. The two clashed and as Gavin turned to look her way, Donovan thrust a dagger into his chest.*

Rose sat upright, her sheets were drenched in sweat and tangled around her legs, the heavy drapes in her room were drawn, and in the semi darkness, she began to focus.

"It was just a dream," Rose spoke out load to reassure herself, yet it did not have the calming effect she hoped. After a few moments, she began to regain her composure. Returning to sleep was impossible, her nerves were on edge, and she had an ominous fear of how this particular dream would end.

The sun was bright and Rose needed coffee. Donning a fresh,

fluffy, terry robe and a pair of slippers, she headed down the stairs and towards the kitchen. As she started to push the swinging door open, she heard Maggie's cheery voice entering the main foyer.

"Hey hon," she chirped. She already had a steaming cup of expresso from the Cuban deli a couple streets over in her hand. She was dressed in a fifty's style white and red polka dot sun dress with a large brimmed red hat atop her blond hair, looking fresh and stunning as always. Rose had often asked her if she actually got right out of bed looking so perfect. "God you look awful! Wrestling with your dream man?" Maggie was always one to speak her mind, but after the words came out she stopped, her cheery smiled turned to a frown as she noticed there was something terribly wrong. Rose was more than tired this morning, she looked deathly pale and had a glazed look to her usually animated eyes.

"Morning to you too, and thanks, I feel like death warmed over this morning." She gave her friend a pathetic attempt at a smile, "I have to find some coffee!"

"O.k. well, this will either cheer you up or you will want to kill us both, but I accepted an invite to a dinner with Agnes on Tuesday."

Rose ran a shaky hand through her tangled hair. "And why would this be a bad thing? We have had dinner with Agnes in the past." Rose asked, not wanting any more surprises. She was rummaging, looking for coffee, today the need to be alert was intense.

Maggie, noticing her friend's distressed state, took her hand and sat her down. Then she went to the cabinet and took a mug out, looking at the printing on its side, 'This is not the life I ordered' "Isn't that the truth," she muttered, then poured half of her espresso in it and returned to where Rose was sitting at the kitchen table.

"Because Agnes is playing cupid. Her nephew is in town and she wants him to meet some people, so I took the liberty of accepting for both of us."

Maggie grinned like a demon. Rose groaned and took a deep

gulp, not caring that the liquid scalded her throat.

"Maggie, I found out about my necklace, and the irony of it is that it belonged to an ancestor of Donovan's." Rose looked at her friend and could have laughed. Maggie's mouth was agape, and then her crystal laugh filled the room.

"Well, that beats all. The thing is probably worth a fortune and he doesn't even know it, and don't you dare tell him!" She got out between laughs.

"I also found out who my dream man is, he is also an ancestor of Donovan's, yet he lived in Ireland in the nineteenth century, and now he is here." Rose took another drink of the espresso, grimaced, and waited for her friend's disbelief.

Maggie's mirth ended abruptly, "Rose, where did you find this out?" Rose left for a moment to retrieve the book she had read last night. Returning to the kitchen, Rose opened the book to the section on O'Connor.

"I called the author of the book that François had found with the crest from my box. She told me the story of the ill–fated love of the heir of the estate and about my necklace. The woman is a distant relation to Donovan, and told me about how his ancestors came to America."

Rose shoved the book at Maggie, who was still looking at her incredulously.

"This book is why when the woman on the phone mentioned the name O'Connor, it sounded so familiar. I had seen this book a few years ago in Donovan's library. It has the same picture of the man I found in the trunk, the same man I saw at the party." Rose showed her the pages of the book with the photos of Gavin, knowing how insane she sounded. "So now you see why I am a bit frazzled."

Maggie wiped her brow. "Hon, I still think your nuts, but let's say this guy is this Gavin, then, what is he doing here in our century? Not to mention *how*!" Rose shook her head.

"I don't know, but he may want the necklace back, it was for his fiancée." Rose chose to leave out the photo of herself she had found in the book last night. She may have some tie to this Roszalia from the past. "I also ran into him on the beach the other morning. He also knew my name. I never told him, I never even met him before!"

Maggie then said, "Whew, well let's make sure if he isn't some ancient time traveler, we let the local police know you may have a stalker." She could not believe all this about a man from her past, time travel, but was genuinely worried about her friend's safety.

Rose realized her friend could not believe all she had discovered, so she agreed with her and said she would think about alerting the police, then changed the subject to the convention. She would deal with finding out who Gavin really was and where he came from on her own.

Getting back to work at the store had kept Rose incredibly busy. She decided to postpone her plans of moving in with Maggie for a while. She really needed to find out who Gavin really was. With Maggie thinking she had a stalker or lost her mind, she, no doubt would be watching her actions.

It was past one o'clock on Tuesday. Maggie was in the stock room doing some last minute inventory when Rose asked,

"Maggie, I'm going to get a coffee, it's really too late for lunch now, want something?" Maggie turned down the radio.

"No thanks, why don't you get something then head home? We're so slow and I was thinking of closing early, so we can get to Agnes's dinner party on time." Maggie poked her head into the front room waiting for a reply.

"You sure? You've been here all weekend, I could close the shop tonight." Her friend appeared, turned Rose, and nudged her towards the door. "Go already! Give me peace!" she chided, a warm smile on her face.

"O.k., o.k. I do not need to be told twice, see you tonight," Rose gave her friend a quick hug and stepped out the door. The bell on the handle jangled and she breathed deeply as the warm air hit her face. Rose always parked in the lot across from the shop. Today the sun was strong and she shielded her eyes from the glare as she crossed the street. Rummaging in her purse to retrieve her keys, she did not see the tall figure leaning by her car until she was almost to it. It was not Donovan, this man was taller, arms folded, his legs stretched out…it was him. She began to shake inside. Even though she had been extremely busy, his handsome face kept appearing in her thoughts and of course, her dreams. Now directly in front of her he stood in blue jeans, a button down shirt, and his black boots.

Gavin straightened as she neared, "Hello again, I wanted to see you. Your maid told me where the store was. I hope I was not being to bold."

Rose stood looking up at him for a moment, and then replied in a deliberate voice to hide her excitement of seeing him again.

"No, not at all, I was just going to grab a coffee, would you like to join me?" He smiled and accepted her invitation by opening her door to the Mustang, then got in the passenger side. She headed to the street where François shop was and a small café. She was going to find out who he was, and why he invaded her dreams every night. What was the irresistible urge to be near him that overwhelmed her senses?

Gavin sat uncomfortably as she drove. He rode in Agnes's car and had not liked it, this one was even smaller, and he felt like he was in a box. However, he did enjoy the fact she was so close to him. Her scent, Roszalia's lavender, filled the tiny space and he breathed it in.

This handsome man sitting beside her had never told her his name, yet she knew in her heart and spirit that this was Gavin O'Connor. And she knew she had nothing to fear from him. Then an idea came to her and she asked, "So, tell me Gavin, what brings you to America?"

"I am searching for someone I lost." He stated without hesitation. She had almost wanted him to say that was not his name, yet he answered straight forward without hesitation and she felt that this was the way this handsome man lived his life, no hidden agenda, honest. They walked across the street to the café and sat outside, she ordered two dark roast coffees, and they sat for a moment in awkward silence. Gavin broke it by handing her a small package.

"What is this?"

"Just something I purchased after I saw you on the beach the other morning, it reminded me of you." With hesitation, she opened it, a tortoise, and silver hair clip. She looked up, confused.

"I thought it would look lovely in your hair. I was hoping I would have the chance to see you again."

"Thank you, I have a tortoise comb and brush set it matches perfectly." Another coincidence? But she thought not, she had the feeling this man knew she had the brush set, in fact she felt he *knew her*.

"Roszalia," he began, but she held up her hand.

"First, how do you know my given name? Everyone calls me Rose, I never told you, yet you called me Roszalia." Gavin looked evenly at her; she also saw something else in his handsome features, distress.

"If I told you, you would think me insane and probably run and I would not want that." He reached over the small table and put his hand over hers. It felt right, but she pulled it away. This was all so insane, her heart was beating wildly, and she needed to talk to calm herself, to hear her own voice. "Do you have any other relatives over here?" Rose was trying to get him to mention Donovan. She was not willing to get into a discussion about the ancestry book and the photos she had seen.

He only shook his head, "Only my aunt and the one I seek." Rose felt crimson filling her cheeks, was she the one this handsome man sought? She realized that she wanted to be this person. She was here sitting casually at a table with a man who spoke with a deep brogue from another time, and was so distractingly handsome she felt her head begin to swim, she almost thought she heard him say, 'I've come to take you home,'

"Pardon, what did you say?" now giving him her full attention.

Gavin smiled and repeated. "We should be getting back. I have a dinner engagement tonight."

Rose felt like a huge sledgehammer hit her – a date. She wanted to ask with who or where. A surge of jealousy ran through her. With all the composure she could muster, she stood and retrieved her purse, "Well, we better be getting you back for your date!" she spun around towards the car, biting her tongue, knowing how childish and foolish that sounded. Gavin followed, enjoying her anger, a huge grin on his face. She let him off at the beach walkway as he requested, saying he could use a stroll. She was so angry with herself for feeling jealous, she said a brisk goodbye, then spun the tires and left.

"A dinner engagement!" Rose fumed. Last night she was stunned to find out who he was, or so she thought, she even felt she should avoid him, but her thoughts betrayed her, and when she saw him earlier she was excited, and now he has come to the future to date. Why should that be any stranger than believing he actually came to the future for her? She really needed therapy, or at least a double margarita.

Pulling into the garage, she saw Donovan's BMW parked there. "Shit!" she said aloud, "I do *not* need this tonight!"

As she opened the door Donovan was barking an order to the maid, hearing her enter, he turned. He glared, then softened his look, "Oh good, you're home, I was just wondering why nothing had been planned for dinner."

Rose tossed her keys on the cherry burl table near the door and said in a cool tone, "Perhaps because I didn't know you would be home and besides, I have made plans to have dinner with friends."

Donovan's eyes clouded, yet his tone remained even, "I see, anyone I know?

"Yes, Donovan, Maggie and I are going over to Agnes's." He seemed to relax, but he did not believe her for one minute.

"Great, we will both go, since there is no dinner ready and I'm starved. I'm sure Agnes would not mind if you brought your fiancée along." He smiled, but she saw the treachery beneath. Unable to handle an argument or a confrontation, she agreed,

"Come along if you wish, however, you are not and have never been my fiancée." She did not wait for his reply, but turned to go freshen up. "We will need to leave by five. Please be ready," Rose said, never looking back. In her room, the one she had taken a few weeks ago after having enough of Donovan's affairs. Sitting down she thought again of Gavin, frustration and jealousy rose up in her. Was the person he was meeting the one he was seeking? Suddenly this thought reminded her of Agnes's nephew. Oh, this will not look good. Agnes had planned to play matchmaker with her and her nephew, and she had forgotten and allowed Donovan to come with her. Perhaps for the best, at this point she surely did not want to get involved with another man. This brought Gavin into her thoughts again. Her cheeks flared red but she did not care. She could only imagine she was the woman Gavin O'Connor was looking for, no longer a dream, but the man.

Chapter Nineteen

Rose chose a simple sleeveless dress for this evening. She turned inspecting her image. The material clung nicely, enhancing her figure. She tied her hair back, then, decided to let it hang. At the last minute, she remembered the comb Gavin had given her earlier. She reached in her purse and took it out then pulled the hair near her temple back and secured it with the tortoise comb. The last thing she put on was her necklace. Looking in the mirror for a moment a flash of a woman, herself but in a Victorian dress appeared. She blinked and the image was gone

"Now I'm hallucinating, get a grip!" But the quick vision did un–nerve her, she had seen this many years ago when she was just a teenager. As she left her room, flipping the light off, she made a vow she would find Gavin again and tell him she knew everything about who he was. Then let him deny it or tell her the truth, no matter how fantastic it may be.

Donovan had changed into black chinos and a light mint shirt. Rose had to admit, he was a good–looking man and that was part of the problem, he knew it. Again, Gavin crowded her thoughts, earlier as he leaned against her car; he had looked exquisite, muscular, handsome, and strong. She shook her head and willed herself to pay attention to the present. She would plant Donovan in the room in front of the television and he could watch the game and boast of his accomplishments while she spoke to Agnes about all she had found out, and she would tell her about the man, Gavin. She had to know what the connection was. She would have to apologize to her nephew for bringing a guest, and explain that at this time in her life, she had some issues to take care of.

Rose knew from the first time she saw, or felt Agnes's presence in her shop, that she was a kindred spirit, and had a special gift. Rose could feel her power, it was like a ripple between them, and she knew that Agnes could foresee many things. The two women had never discussed this, but she sensed that Agnes, like herself, knew many things others did not.

As they walked up the path to Agnes's home, Maggie came to greet her friend waving a glass of champagne. Her smile froze as she saw Donovan. He continued towards the house barely acknowledging her. Then he saw Maggie's husband and another taller man through the window.

Maggie pulled Rose aside, "Rose, what the hell is he doing here?" Rose gave an exasperated sigh,

"Oh Maggie, please, he was home when I got there with the inquisition and I couldn't deal with it. He thinks I am meeting someone here, I feel terrible about Agnes's nephew, but I just couldn't handle one more thing right now!" Maggie hooked arms with her friend and smiled,

"Sorry to say, you're about to feel a lot worse when you get a look at Agnes's gorgeous nephew. In fact, he looks a lot like the man in the photo you showed me. If this is your dream man, boot that bastard Donovan to the curb now, and you better hold on to this one!"

Rose had a strange feeling start to erupt in her stomach. As the two women entered the room, Agnes greeted Rose with a hug and nodded towards Donovan whispering, "Do not fret child, I understand." Agnes took her hand, led her into the dining room, and said in a cheerful tone, "I would like you to meet my nephew, Gavin." Agnes watched as Rose's eyes became huge, her hands began to shake, and she nervously searched for Donovan. He had already gone into the parlor and was yelling at the team to "go…go." Rose stood staring at Gavin. He had on a pair of kaki chinos and a crème shirt, his dark hair against his tanned face. If she hadn't been so stunned to see him here, she would have marveled at his handsomeness. His broad shoulders and self–confident stance were enough to astound any woman. Suddenly the room seemed to close in around her.

Gavin was pleased with her reaction and surprise at seeing him. She looked beautiful. His Roszalia of this time was so self–confident, poised, and alive. She sparkled tonight, he thought. A brief moment of anger passed through him as he thought of the man she had arrived with, but seeing her here in front of him, so vibrant and beautiful, his mood quickly mellowed. His grin was sheepish as he came across the room to her, taking her small still shaking hand in his. He bent in a bow and kissed it, never letting his eyes leave hers.

"Good evening to my beautiful dinner date," his voice deep and husky, laced with hidden emotions.

Rose was dumbstruck, she felt flushed. She was his date. Oh how foolish was she? She had been green with jealousy this afternoon when he mentioned he had an engagement to attend, now she was fighting with the mixed emotion of elation that Gavin was here in front of her and the sheer panic of knowing Donovan was in the next room. Suddenly Rose felt very ill. Usually, she could negotiate her way out of any conflict or confrontation but she wasn't so sure she could tonight, being this close to Gavin, his scent making her dizzy, his smile unarming her. She placed her hand on the chair back to steady herself. Her eyes searched for Agnes.

"I …I'm sorry, I suddenly feel ill, I think I had better go." Agnes gave her an understanding look, but as her eyes locked with Gavin, he looked crushed. She immediately regretted her words, but she knew with Donovan so close, she would not be able to hide the emotions she felt when she was near this man, and that would cause a scene. Agnes, seeing the glances and feeling the negative energy in the room stepped forward as Rose said, "I will call on you tomorrow Agnes."

As she turned around to make her retreat, Donovan was standing behind her and panic seized her. How long had he been there? Donovan watched the look pass between Rose and this tall stranger. He wrapped his arm around her waist possessively, as if to show that she was his property. His steel grey eyes narrowed and bore into Gavin. The low deliberate way he spoke sent a chill up Rose's spine,

"Why, that would be rude, I don't believe I have met your...friend," he said, drawing out the last word maliciously.

Rose really did feel sick now, she wanted to run, but Donovan had her in a grip, a bit too tight. She saw the anger on Gavin's features with his fists clenched at his side. A helpless feeling began spreading through her.

Agnes, witnessing the two men's mounting animosity, interjected quickly, "Come now," she went to Rose, took her from Donovan's grip, and led her to the table. "Let's all sit at the table and we can get to introductions. Gavin," she snapped at him to get his attention, "you sit across from Rose."

Maggie and her husband, hearing the strained voices, entered the room to see what was going on. Upon seeing the two men's faces and Rose's discomposure, Maggie spoke cheerily to try to ease the tension,

"Yes, pour some wine and let's eat, Agnes, I'll help get the rest of the food." Rose began to get up and Maggie said,

"Rose hun, you're just still stressed from the trip, have a sip of wine. Food is on its way." Maggie's husband sat next to Gavin and Donovan seated himself next to Rose. The two men, as if in a duel, never taking their eyes from one another.

Rose noticed that Agnes had seated Gavin so she had to face him during dinner. She could tell she would not be eating much. How could she have been so stupid to allow Donovan to come along? Agnes was talking, and Rose tried to force herself to concentrate on the conversation. Gavin's presence was electrifying, and her heart beat wildly.

"So, Gavin has come from Ireland to visit me. He is in search of a lost relative." Agnes, disturbed and a bit confused as to why she could not read everyone's emotions, was carefully watching all at her table. Gavin's jaw twitched as he saw Donovan reach under the table and rest his hand on Rose's knee. Instinctively, she moved her leg and shot him a glare. He grinned and she realized he was actually enjoying seeing Gavin's anger.

Donovan had the feeling that Rose and this man knew each other, and not just through Agnes.

Maggie broke the silence, "So Gavin, what is it you do in Ireland?"

"I run a large shipping business, along with other endeavors," he said, smiling Maggie's way. She smiled back, thinking that this man is wonderful and charming, and secretly she hoped he would be the one for her friend. Both men began attacking their food with a bit too much gusto. Each trying to keep their emotions under control.

Donovan, unable to contain his thoughts any longer finally asked, "Tell me, have you and Rose met before?"

Rose, not trusting what emotion her eyes would show, did not look up from her meal.

Gavin, beginning to enjoy the discomfort he was causing his adversary, smiled, "No, but if I had, I assure you I would not be worried about any other man in the room."

Donovan could barely conceal his anger. He did not like nor trust this Irishman. Rose remembered what she had read in the book the other night, the blood tie between Donovan and Gavin, and wondered if this handsome man knew that he was staring at his great, great nephew? Certainly, Agnes would have sensed this. Did she know about the women who resembled her in the past? Her mind was racing when Donovan asked Gavin his last name, Rose stopped and held her breath.

"You see I have a family history back in the border towns in Ireland, maybe you know some of my kin?" Donovan was playing a game with Gavin.

He replied with an even tone, "It is very doubtful I would know any of them." He took a healthy sip of his red wine, allowing his gaze to linger on Rose. "I have been traveling and have not been back to the border land in a very long time." His accent seemed to deepen as he spoke of his home. He added, "My family name is O'Connor." Gavin put a piece of the steak he had cut into his mouth and noticed the color drain from the other man's face.

"O'Connor? Well it seems we are somehow related. You see Devon O'Connor was my great grandfather," and under his breath muttered, "the bastard."

Donovan stuffed a forkful of meat in his mouth, and then washed it down with an excessive gulp of wine.

It was now Gavin's turn to show surprise. The table became deadly silent. Rose glanced at Agnes and realized she did not know about Donovan's ancestry, for there was a brief look of confusion that spread over the woman's features.

Agnes now knew the reason she could not see the events that would happen in this time, the presence of the O'Connor ancestor was crossing with Gavin's energy patterns.

Gavin's amber eyes clouded and darkened. Never wavering, he asked, "And how do you know you are kin to Devon O'Connor?"

"From an ancestry book a distant cousin back in Ireland had sent me a few years back. Seems that my great grandfather Devon, was quite the black sheep of the family, he would have been heir of O'Connor Estate when the first son disappeared in a boating accident, but he returned." Donovan seemed not to know or remember that the first son's name was Gavin. "Guess that makes me sort of a distant high society relation. Perhaps I should claim my inheritance eh, Gavin?" Donovan took a drink of wine and raised his glass in a toast. "To things in common," he was looking directly from Gavin to Rose.

Donovan thought how when he had first met Rose, he had fantasized she was the girl in the book that was to marry the first son before the tragedy, suddenly, he put his wine glass down spilling some of the red liquid on the linen cloth. He realized the name by the picture of the eldest son was Gavin. Was this the attraction this man had, did he know of the history also? Had he seen the portrait of the girl named Roszalia in the book and noticed the similarity in Rose?

Feeling helpless, Rose could only watch Gavin's handsome face at hearing all this. No noticeable sign of surprise or anger showed except for the tightness in his jaw muscle, and the muscles in his forearms twitched when Donovan mentioned Devon's name.

Gavin kept his outward composure, yet to hear this man was an heir of his brother, and now living with the woman he loved. Fate was cruel. He wanted to this man exactly what his ancestor really was, but he had a feeling that he knew the truth. And it seemed there was little difference between them. He turned his attention to Rose as he felt a small foot touch his leg beneath the table. The feeling was like a shock, he looked at her perfect face, and his muscles loosened, she was smiling at him. Then he thought... *she knows*, but how?

Donovan felt victorious at the jab he made to Gavin's past. He had had a bit too much drink and needed to take his leave for a moment. Maggie's husband had retreated to the other room, where Rose could hear him cheering his team on and for some guy to, "Pass the damn ball!"

Maggie, along with Agnes, began to clear the table, leaving Rose and Gavin alone for a moment. He stared at her, she looked breathtaking tonight, and even with the recent shock of who she was living with, he still knew he would have her back, even if he had to fight Donovan for her love. In fact, he relished the thought. Carefully, Gavin posed a question, not wanting to scare her. His eyes softened as he looked into hers, "So, you know," he paused just a moment, "who I am?"

Rose looked at the worried expression on his brow and smiled. "I think I do, how or why I can't even begin to imagine. I thought earlier it may have something to do with my necklace, I found the book Donovan mentioned, I saw you, your family and ..." she hesitated, not knowing whether to mention the portrait of Roszalia with the necklace. Gavin reached in his trouser pocket and took out a folded page. He carefully smoothed it and laid it in front of her.

"And you saw this photo?" he never took his eyes from hers. Swallowing hard, Rose nodded. "I can't believe it, but it feels right." She fingered the stone on the necklace she wore.

"Aye, it should, the necklace belongs to you, and I have not come for it."

"Then maybe you are searching for your great–great nephew?" Gavin gave a disgusted laugh.

"Not likely, that is like seeing my brother, I cannot believe I did not notice the resemblance immediately, and I have no use for him, he is only trouble. I do not think you are safe with such a man." After a moment, he asked, "do you love him?"

She did not hesitate. "No, I don't know if I ever did. Now he just possesses me like a trophy."

"Then why?" Gavin stared at her and began to speak when Agnes intervened, "Come now let's take coffee and pie in the living room."

When Rose got up, Donovan was standing next to her, "It's time we went home." Donovan shot Gavin a smirk as if to say, she is mine, and I am the man taking her home. Donovan went to the hall room to get her sweater.

Gavin quickly brushed against Rose and whispered, "Would you meet me on the beach at midnight? I will wait at the same place I saw you the other morning."

Maggie came into the hall to say goodnight and all three women hugged. Agnes pressed Rose's hand,

"Rose, please call on me tomorrow, we have much to discuss."

"Yes, I will…and I am sorry about this evening." She looked over towards where Donovan awaited her.

"Not to worry, all will be fine. Now go, but be careful." Rose said she would. Donovan thanked Agnes for dinner then turned to Gavin and in a cold tone said,

"I hope you find who you seek very soon, and can return to your country."

Gavin nodded and replied, "I am sure I am close." The two men dueled with their eyes for a moment. She needed to get Donovan away from here. He was drunk. Rose suspected he had taken cocaine earlier and the effects of drugs and alcohol were taking their toll. With luck, he would pass out and she could go to the beach and find Gavin, her dream lover – no, her past lover? Whatever he had meant to her in the past, every sensation in her body was telling her what she wanted him to be tonight.

Rose changed into her nightclothes when they got home to avoid Donovan's suspicion, but he never asked or noticed. He took a drink and headed to his room, without as much as a 'goodnight.' She waited until she was sure the alcohol had taken its effect and he was in a deep, drunken slumber.

She then quickly changed into sweat pants, a white tee and a grey flannel hooded sweatshirt, she did not know if he would still be at the beach. He had said to meet him at midnight, and it was already half past the hour. She did not know what possessed her to go, but she felt she had no choice. Something was compelling her towards this man. Walking through the gate onto the sand without thought, she headed towards the place that she had seen him previously. The moon was bright and as she got closer, she saw his figure sitting near the surf, his back was to her, and as she approached, he turned his head, the moonlight showing his smile.

Rose walked over and sat on the blanket that Gavin had spread on the sand. They sat for a moment in silence and then he reached over and took her hand in his, it felt so right, his large warm hand. He was looking at her and she finally spoke,

"I, ah, don't know what I am doing here." he just looked lovingly at her. "I mean, I wanted to see you, to talk to you again."

"Aye, myself also, I needed to see you alone." Rose noticed the emphasis on the word alone. As she shivered, Gavin took his advantage, he put his arm around her opening his jacket to include her, and she welcomed this as though it was only natural to be so close and familiar with this man. She rationalized to herself... after all she had known him in dreams for over two years. Breaking the silence,

"I don't know why or how, but I know you have come from a very long time ago to find me. I found your picture and your family in a book Donovan has. You, and Devon and your sister," she paused, "and me, or your Roszalia. Since Donovan is a descendant of your family, I thought perhaps he was the one you came to find, but I realized at dinner, you had no idea he was related to your family."

"Yes, the sins of the fathers shall be visited upon the sons." Avoiding mentioning Donovan or Devon's name.

The warmth from their bodies intensified as she looked into his eyes. The stars, the surf, and sand were their only companions this evening. Gavin could wait no longer; he raised her chin up and kissed her lips.

Rose felt a fire began to ignite within her she had not known existed. She wanted more. She wanted to drown in his eyes and his kiss. Her senses screamed to back away, yet her heart said hold on. She returned the kiss with matched intensity and Gavin began stroking her hair. He kissed her neck and her temples. Her skin was soft and sweet, a hint of lavender, her breath coming in rasps as he drank in her texture. Boldly, he reached into her jacket. His touch was sending fire shooting through her, she did not care. She wanted him, here, now. This was insane she knew, but she may never see him again after tonight and it felt right.

Gavin could sense her willingness and the sounds of the surf matched the pounding of his heart. His beautiful Roszalia was here in his arms. He needed to make her his once again now, or he may never have her back. He slowly lifted her hips and slid her pants off. He bent over and kissed every inch of her, slowing as he reached the edges of the lace panty. He felt his own excitement building at the image racing through his mind. Not needing his coaxing, she arched her hips, inviting his kisses. He knew this was his Roszalia, she moaned with pleasure, unable to hold on any longer, he rolled her over and poised atop her but only for a moment, then the two became one once more. Rose dug her nails in his back, flashes of a past she never knew flooded her mind, this man, and a love so intense. She cried for him to make love to her as she had dreamed so often. They clung to one another as the waves of ecstasy flowed through them both, never wanting the feeling to end. Panting and spent, Gavin rolled to his side, still cradling her in his arm, stroking her hair, he murmured, "I love you Roszalia."

Rose closed her eyes and languished in the moment. Yes, she

believed he had come for her, and she knew she loved him in the past and now in the present. Rose, still in his arms, asked,

"Gavin, were you my first?' Gavin rolled over and perched on his elbow to look down into her eyes, his smile genuine,

"Well, usually the lady knows if the man was the first, and judging by your ability to please me beyond my wildest imagination, I would have to say, no… but I will make sure I am your only from this moment on." He smiled as he teased her.

Rose gave him a playful nudge. "You know I was talking about in your past."

Gavin corrected her, "Our past, or my life, your past. And yes, my love, I was your first." She now propped herself on her elbow and pouted at him,

"And was I terribly disappointing?"

Gavin had to laugh at this. "Roszalia, why else would I travel through time to find you if it wasn't the best bedding I ever had?"

She pushed at his chest then hugged him tighter. "I know this is crazy but I know I love you, you are the man I have been waiting for," she murmured. He held her tighter. The sound of the gulls overhead broke their peace and they realized the pink glow over the horizon warned that it would soon be light. Rose had to get back to the house. As she pulled her sneakers on, she touched Gavin's face.

Gavin looked at her and said, "My brother Devon is a very dangerous man, and it seems this Donovan inherited that. I just do not know why Agnes did not warm me. It seems she was unaware also."

Rose looked into Gavin's eyes. "I have been planning on leaving Donovan for some time, but now after, well," she blushed, "tonight, I think it will be immediately."

Gavin hugged her. "Roszalia I was telling you the truth, I love you, and I will protect you. I will go to the house with you." She shook her head,

"No, I must do this on my own, but as strange as it seems, my heart now knows that we have been lovers before and I feel so much love for you now. I now see us together. I have always

227

had a strange gift of seeing things others cannot."

He kissed her forehead. "Yes, and I shall keep that love burning and soon you will have no question." Gavin picked up the blanket and tucked it under his arm walking her to the gate he suspiciously looked at the house.

"You know this kills me to let you go back in there with him." She stood on tip toes and kissed him, smiling, mocking his brogue,

"Aye, I know but I am yours in my heart and soon I will be in your arms also!" She did not feel as brave as she acted and was shaking inside.

Gavin took a deep breath, against his better judgment. He thought of the fate she had met in the past trying to protect him.

Yet he knew he had to allow her do this alone. Still holding her hand, he said,

"I will wait...but not far away." She kissed him again, turned, and ran up the path, for if she did not, she would never leave his arms, and she needed to end it clean with Donovan.

Chapter twenty

The house was still silent when she entered through the kitchen door, she took off her sneakers and her sweatshirt, lingering as she pulled it over her head to inhale the memory of Gavin's scent. She knew she had to leave Donovan as soon as possible, she would tell him tomorrow. Knowing there would be no easy way and that it would most likely end up in a battle. Standing in the kitchen, she decided to make herself a cup of cocoa before retiring for a few hours in her room. She pulled down a white china cup from the cabinet, closed the door realizing that she would not miss this home. Nothing in it belonged to her. She had lived here for almost five years and still never felt the desire to make it hers. Perhaps she always knew in her heart she did not belong here, that another would capture her heart and her soul. Her mind wandered to Gavin and she smiled as she poured the hot cocoa in the cup. Taking a sip of the scalding liquid, Rose turned out the lights and headed for the stairs in the front hall. As she neared, she saw his dark figure leaning against the stair wall. Her heart began to pound and a premonition of danger threatened to choke her.

Donovan looked at her, his grey eyes seemed black and sinister in the dimness. He spoke in a low angry voice, "Did you have a good run? A bit early, even for you."

He stood there, rigid. Rose felt a chill run the length of her spine. Trying to look unflustered by his insinuating tone and her own guilt, she said in a steady voice,

"Yes, I needed to clear my head, now if you don't mind I need to get changed, it was damp out this morning." She attempted to pass, Donovan never moved. Still blocking the stairs looked at her steadily, his dark eyes piercing through her. She began to feel trapped.

"Ah yes, must be why you were naked on the beach in another man's arms?"

He was too calm. He had followed her and had not been asleep. She felt a very real panic as her heart began to race.

"Since you're pretense of going to bed was somewhat convincing, I decided to play along with your game and see where you were headed to. Seems you do know this Gavin quite well."

He had seen them together. She clutched her hot cocoa, as if for support and said, trying to muster all of her strength,

"Donovan, I was going to tell you tomorrow, but I am leaving. I should not have been out there, but I am leaving you. We do not love one another. We are over, you can tell your friends you kicked me out, make me look like the bad person, just let me pass now." Her words held much more bravado than she felt with his stare boring into her. Oh, how she wished Gavin were here.

Donovan took one–step closer and grinned. "Oh, but you are wrong, it is not over. You see, I never lose a possession until I tire of it, and especially not to some foreign relative."

Rose flung her hot cocoa at him trying to catch him off guard hoping it might give her a moment to flee. It splashed in his face, the hot sticky liquid only infuriating him further. He reared his head in disgust, as he wiped his eyes with his sleeve. Rose saw the opportunity to head for the door and took it. Donovan reached out blindly as she attempted to run past and grabbed her by the hair yanking her back viciously, and shoved her down on the tile. At this moment she knew that reason was beyond Donovan, he was not going to let her leave him. He came towards her, fists balled. Searching in the dim hall light for something to protect herself with, her hand felt the table. She grabbed the heavy leaded glass vase of flowers that was on it. Donovan, blind with rage, came towards her like an animal. He grabbed her shirt, and as he lifted her from the floor as if she were a rag doll, to throw her again, she hoisted the vase. With all her strength, she brought it down on his head. It made contact and a she heard dull thud, then the glass shattered and she saw blood from an open wound on Donovan's scalp. His eyes widened with shock and surprise and his grip loosened. He stared at her then fell face forward on the tiles at the front of the door.

Rose was sobbing and shaking uncontrollably. She was scared she had killed him. He deserved it, she thought. Still, she had to check, she turned him over. His face was covered with blood from the wound, but he was breathing. A brief moment of regret and relief flooded her, it passed as she realized she had to leave, now before he awoke, for next time he would surely kill her. His body had fallen in front of the door. Lying there, he was dead weight. Once again, panic flooded her. She had to push him aside to open it. Gripping his ankles, she pulled him forward enough that she could wedge the door far enough open to get out. As she began to turn the knob, Donovan's hand reached out and grabbed her ankle. Rose screamed and kicked wildly at his tight grip. The next instant the front door flew open. Gavin stood there looking at the scene. Before Rose could open her mouth, he had Donovan on his feet in a tight chokehold with one arm bent behind his back.

He knew he could easily crush this man's windpipe. Instead, he bent close to his ear and said softly so only he could hear,

"If it were not for Roszalia watching, I would kill you here and now. I have crushed much better men than you," he wrenched his arm up until Donovan face contorted with pain, "and make no mistake, if you ever come near, or attempt to contact Roszalia again, I will kill you before you have a chance to take your next breath. This I promise you, great–great nephew!" Gavin let the man slump to the floor, gasping for air.

Donovan looked at Roszalia and spat, "Take her, but you will not always be there to protect her!"

Gavin in return grinned and said, "There you are wrong, and I have heard that many years ago by another."

Taking Rose by the arm, Gavin led her out the door. He picked her up as she buried her face in his shirt, still sobbing, and shaking, but now she felt safe.

The kitchen door swung open. Agnes turned to see Gavin carrying in a battered and bloody Rose. "Oh no child, come in, come in." Agnes looked past her, shut, and locked the door. Gavin laid her on the sofa. Rose took the old woman's embrace and the tears streamed down.

"I shouldn't have come here. I do not want to involve," she hesitated, "anyone in my problem."

"Oh my child! This was never supposed to happen." Because of the past and present O'Connor's in the same proximity, she could not see the trouble Roszalia would be in. It was time to tell her everything, and let her choose her own destiny. "It is time I involved you, I need to tell you everything. Are you strong enough to hear it?'

Rose nodded her head. Gavin squeezed her hand and went to retrieve a damp cloth and some aspirin for her. This moment he dreaded, she must choose. The older women sat perched on the edge of her seat and with a small sigh, she began. "What I tell you, may be hard to understand, but it is true."

Rose wiped at the trickle of blood that had run down the corner of her mouth, Gavin returned with the cloth and gently wiped her lip. He then sat next to her and took her hand in his, so strong and safe. As he did, Rose had a flash of images, almost like watching a slide show flicker by too quickly. Then Agnes sat back in her chair and began telling Rose the events that took place to bring Gavin here. Rose stared at her old friend, yet not in disbelief. She truly believed it was magic that brought her Gavin. The fact that this man had come so far to win her heart filled her with love she could not even begin to describe.

Then Agnes told her of the tragic accident. Rose could feel Gavin tense as Agnes mentioned how he held her and with his love, kept her soul alive to be reincarnated into this century. His hand tightened on hers and she could see the pain in his eyes reliving the event.

Rose moved closer to him as if to show him she was not going to disappear. A little shaken herself at the revelations she asked, "You mean, I am dead, well Roszalia is dead?"

Agnes shook her head, "Yes and no, Roszalia's body is in a state of suspension, right now her body is barely alive, yet her soul, her essence remains trapped within the love that Gavin has for you."

Rose sat up to the edge of her seat and Gavin put his arm around her shoulders. She looked at him and said in a soft voice he had to strain to hear, "You love Roszalia, I am not that girl."

He held her tighter. Agnes came and sat beside her, "Rose, you are Roszalia, Roszalia is Rose. A soul can reincarnate a number of times but the sum of the memories and experiences are kept in a deep secret place, the heart, you know this child, you feel it too, I know you do."

Rose once again felt the salty tears on her cheeks. She realized she had known for a while what Agnes said is true, she looked into Gavin's amber eyes and felt, no saw, a handsome young man, a picnic, children, a beautiful estate, and realized how much she loved him, now, before and forever. Agnes also saw what Rose had seen and knew she had the special gift of sight, remembrance. Agnes was speaking again, and Rose forced her attention back to her.

"You see, when you selflessly were willing to trade your life to save your one true and pure love, your final kiss sent your soul to him, and he has so much love for you he would not let it die. You have been reincarnated in this century, possibly because of Donovan's blood tie to the O'Connor's, it makes sense now. Everything is a circle, a path to our destiny." Agnes took both of Rose's hands.

"Donovan's blood tie to Gavin is why I could not see him, or certain events. Roszalia, neither you nor Gavin were meant to die that day. Fate took a wrong turn, but you can still get your lives back to what should have been."

Rose, now dry eyed, "How?"

"You must decide if you could give everything up in this life you know and love, your home, your friends, and you must return to nineteenth century Ireland with Gavin." There was a sense of finality in the older woman's words...there was no compromise.

The young woman's face paled ever so slightly and she asked, "And will I remember this time?" Agnes shook her head, "For a time."

Rose looked at Agnes and spoke softly, "Will I know you?" Agnes hugged the girl. "Yes, dear you are my niece by blood, and we love each other. That is a bond time cannot change."

A deep voice cajoled, "And why else would she have put up with a brooding lout like me through time." Gavin stood, looking sheepish, not knowing what Roszalia would decide.

Agnes had laid the path, now she made her excuse to go brew some tea and let them talk.

Gavin looked into Roszalia's eyes. Those beautiful hazel eyes, he could only hold his breath. He would abide by her decision. If she chose to stay, he did not think she needed to worry about Donovan, but if she chose him, he would dedicate his heart and soul to her. Unable to stay silent any longer,

"Roszalia, do you understand, life in the late nineteenth century is very different, but I will promise to protect you with my life this time, for the rest of our natural lives. I love you Roszalia." His voice held an edge of fear to it as he said, "If you do not go back, your body and soul shall cease back home. I must go back, I was never meant for this time, but the thought of not having you by my side, my existence will be hollow." His eyes showed pain at even the thought of this. "Once, in our lives before, you asked me if I believed in everlasting love, a love so strong neither time nor death could end it. At the time I did not know what to say, but I do now, and I believe with all my heart Rose, you are my beautiful gypsy soul mate."

This was the first time Gavin had used her present name. His strong hands were shaking, Rose felt so much love for this man, she knew at this moment, without hesitation that she was the same woman from the past. Looking into his eyes, she leaned close and brushed a kiss over his lips, "You must promise to marry me as soon as we are home!"

A moment passed and Gavin's smile broke wide. He grabbed Rose and swung her on his lap and buried his face in her hair, then found her soft salty lips and drank deeply. In a husky voice, he said,

"As the head of O'Connor Estate, I swear I shall oblige my lady with everything she wishes." He drank of her sweet lips.

Agnes was relieved to overhear it all, her niece would be re-united, and all would be well. She returned to the living room,

"So, then, it is time to prepare for your return. Rose, you must take today to say your goodbyes. This will be hard, I know. And then tonight, after dusk, you will drink the potion, and work your way back." She took a breath and thought how all this was getting harder on her each time she traveled.

"Gavin, since Rose will be traveling back, and she has the gift, you will not awake in the passage we came from, you will be at her last thought before the potion takes effect that will place you in your return location."

Gavin rubbed his chin, "But Rose does not know her past, how can she place us in any location," he held onto her hand as if to not lose her again.

She looked at the worried crease on his brow, yes, she thought, this man would give his life for me, as I was willing to give mine for him. She kissed him, and a vision crossed her mind, as vivid as a movie and as quick as a flash, but clear.

She looked at her aunt and she was smiling. "I know where we will re–enter, but Agnes, will Gavin remember?" Rose had an unspoken concern, as did Gavin.

"Agnes, if neither of us remembers the past or present then how can we stop events from repeating themselves?

Agnes sensed what her question was. "You will for a while, or forever, I do not know. But as your lives settle, the future will seem like a dream, like when you wake and the dream is fresh but as the hours go by the dream fades until you question if you ever had it. Gavin you must remember when you go back- do not allow Roszalia out near the barn, keep her by you inside the house at all costs."

"Aye, this lass shall never leave my side again," Gavin spoke with determination and love as he brought her closer.

"Alright," Agnes waved a hand as if to shoo them, "I have work to do, so go give your farewells."

Rose took Gavin's hand. "Will you come with me? I only have two people I need to talk to. And I need them to know I will be happy."

Rose's smile was genuine, and Gavin again felt his heart would burst with joy. First, they headed to François shop, she introduced Gavin to François as her fiancée, and the older man raised an eyebrow. Rose handed the man the copy of the book she had borrowed and then wrote the name of the book that Caitlin was sending her.

"François, please get a copy of this book and read it, I do believe it will explain everything. I am returning to Ireland in the morning with Gavin."

The older man suddenly hugged Rose so tightly she lost her breath. "Yes, crazy young lovers! I see you have found what we all dream we will find. Be happy and I will think of you always," he wiped a tear from his crinkled eyes and walked the couple to the front door. "Take good care of her son, I may be old but....." He waved his cane as his voice trailed off. Gavin smiled and shook the older man's hand,

"Not to worry, I will treat her like the lady of the land!"

Maggie had finally begun to believe Rose's strange tale of Donovan's ancestor coming through time to find her. After the evening at Agnes's, she decided to read the book, that Rose had shown her of Donovan's ancestors. Upon seeing the photos of Gavin and then the portrait of Roszalia, she knew that the man she had met at Agnes's, and this Gavin O'Connor from the past, were one and the same. She also knew her friend was destined to be with him, her years of dreaming of him had come to reality. How or why, she did not question.

Gavin and Rose headed the car towards the shop where she would have to say goodbye to her best friend. Suddenly the knowledge that she would never see Maggie again overwhelmed her and tears threatened to escape as sadness filled her. Maggie was more than a friend, she was her business partner and more important, her family.

The bell on the door jangled as Gavin entered first, Rose in tow behind him, Maggie looked up to see the look on her friend's face, and knew the time had come.

"Maggie it is all true, I know it is hard to believe, but Gavin is the man I have been dreaming of all these years." Rose and Maggie clung to each other, not saying a word but tears flowed freely.

When they finally separated, Maggie looked at Gavin and said in a cracked voice, "I know, I read the book of the family and saw your picture. What I do not understand is why you came to get Rose."

Gavin looked into Maggie's concerned eyes and said, "I love her, and we will continue with our lives as they should have been lived, together and happy."

"So you two are going…" she waved in the air, "somewhere, and I will not see you again?"

Rose took Maggie's hands in her own. "Yes, please be happy for me, I just know the Roszalia from that time and I are the same person, we share a soul and that soul is entwined with my love for Gavin." Rose needed her friends blessing.

Maggie burst into a fresh stream and hugged Rose tightly. "I will miss you so much, this is all so unreal, but I know in my heart you are meant to be together." She looked from Rose to Gavin and saw the love in both their eyes. After more tears and hugs, the two friends parted. Now the only thing to do was to re–enter the past.

CHAPTER TWENTY– ONE
1880 O'Connor Estate – Ireland

Roszalia saw the stables ahead and turned her horse in that direction. She caught a glimpse of a cloaked figure entering the side door, her heart began to pound, it was too early for Gavin to be riding yet, so she decided to go to the main house and warn him there, even if it meant seeing Devon in the process.

Devon watched as a light flickered in the stables as the cloaked man entered. He felt a renewed energy, soon all this would be his, he shut the curtain and turned to see Roszalia standing in front of him, dripping wet, her fists were clenched at her sides, her eyes burning with hate as she looked at him. For a moment, he felt an impending sense of doom, ever slight and quickly passing, but he did not like it. Regaining his composure he said, "What are you doing here, and what of your appearance?" Roszalia looked at him steadily and said,

"It is over Devon." Devon faced with a challenge rose to it.

"Over? Oh no my dear, it has just begun, as you will soon see."

Roszalia felt an icy chill climb up her, a vision. She saw a flash of a cloaked man and a bright fire. Devon seemed to sense her next move and stepped towards her. She turned for the door but before Devon could reach out to her, a strong arm came around and landed a forceful blow to his face. He slammed his fist once more into Devon and as he buckled over, one last punch sent him to the floor. Roszalia stood rooted to the spot. There was a commotion outside in the barn. Gavin approached her and took her in his arms. She looked at him with question. "Is he?" she stammered, but could not say the word.

"Unfortunately, he is only knocked out." He brushed a lock of wet hair from her face. The back door flew open and Barrister Burke and two officers stood there. Gavin pushed Roszalia behind him in a reflex.

The older man strode over to Gavin and extended his hand and in a deep husky voice said, "Gavin, my boy, I have a great apology to be made to you, we have caught this vermin in the barn with the intent on killing you, the weasel told us everything, including Devon being the one who set it up. And just a short time ago I received a letter delivered by a Marie, she said she was a friend, it explained everything."

Devon had begun to stand when the two officers brought him back to his knees. His face was expressionless, but the hate in his grey eyes was unmistakable. The barrister barked an order to get him out and into the darkest hole they could find in prison. He took Roszalia's hand, gave it a kiss, and then nodded to Gavin, who returned the nod. Apology accepted.

Devon glared at the two of them and stumbled out to the awaiting armed carriage. The rest of the household was beginning to come around to see what all the commotion was about. Gavin took Roszalia's hand and led her towards the library. As they entered, he looked at her with a question, "Letter?"

Roszalia began, "Yes, I thought to write down what I had found out, and dear little Marie told all she knew. Agnes rushed it to Barrister Burke as soon as I left to come here. She did well."

"She did, and we are here together," he hugged her tightly and then kissed her sweet lips, holding her close, he stroked her hair.

Roszalia relished the moment, his strong muscles felt comforting and warm and she felt safe. Reluctantly she pried away and at arm's length looked up at him. She smiled at his handsome face, she was happy. As she looked deep in his eyes, she asked a question, "Gavin you do want a family?"

He took a step back still holding her and took his turn at laughter. "Aye, shall we start right now or after the wedding?"

She smiled widely. "We already have."

He looked bewildered for a moment, then noticing her hand on her abdomen. He raised an eyebrow as what she said became clear. "Do you mean?" His voice trailed off with the question and she shook her head yes. She snuggled close to him.

"Yes, and I think we should name her Maggie." Gavin gently pushed her back, looking intensely in her eyes, remembering that Agnes told her she might not remember her other life.

"Maggie? Why do you say that?" Smiling again she said,

"After everything we have been through, I am, after all, my gypsy aunt's niece, and Maggie is my best friend."

Gavin hugged her tight, and whispered in her hair, "Are you all right with your decision to return with me?"

Still hugging him as to never let him go again she whispered, "Yes my love, all is exactly as it should be."

Epilog

The bell on the entry door jangled as someone came in. Maggie looked wistfully at the door as she had been doing for the last few days, she knew Rose would not return, yet still she hoped. Peering over a tall stack of books, she could see the logo of the overnight delivery truck parked out front. She stepped forward just as the driver rounded the shelves of books. He had a small package for Rose. Maggie took the wrapped package and said she would sign for it and give it to Rose when she returned. Sadness engulfed her, knowing in her heart she would never see her friend again. The deliveryman left and she walked back to the counter.

The package was the size of a hard cover novel, and its postmark was from Ireland. Maggie carefully tore open the brown wrapping. Inside was a copy of the book Rose had told her that a distant relation of Donovan's was going to send her on the O'Connor family. The cover was white with a photo of Rose's beloved necklace displayed from one end to the other. There was a piece of notepaper sticking out of one of the pages. Maggie opened the book to this chapter. The note simply read, 'Hope this proves interesting to you.' It was signed, Caitlin.

As Maggie refolded the note and was about to close the

book, her gaze froze on the page that had a portrait of a family. The tall handsome man was standing next to a beautiful dark haired woman, sitting in a high back chair, holding a little girl on her lap. The caption read, *The O'Connor's, Gavin, Roszalia, and daughter Maggie*. Maggie began to cry, but this time her tears were of happiness for her friend. Her dream man had finally found her.

The bell played its melody again. With a sigh, Maggie looked up expecting to see that the deliveryman had forgotten a package, instead she looked into the eyes of a tall handsome man. His curly brown hair and his dimpled smile were captivating. After a moment, she gained her composure.

"Oh, I'm sorry, can I help you with something?" The man gently laid an item on the counter and without a word he carefully undid the twine and opened the cloth wrapping. Maggie looked at the antique leather book. Scribed on the cover in faded black ink were the words. The past...the present...the future...of Roszalia (Rose) Danyovok O'Conner. It took a moment, then, Maggie's face showed the recognition of her friend's name, and handwriting.

Looking up, she met the stranger's brown eyes again, now serious as he said, "My name is Phillip. We need to talk."

THE END

Gypsy Soulmate

Maranda Marks

About the Author

Maranda Marks grew up in the Hudson Valley of New York State. Her career took her to work in the field of marketing and public relations in New York City, Washington DC, Florida, and finally residing in the Great Smoky Mountains of Tennessee to begin her writing. The author enjoys helping her readers become her characters. Maranda quotes: "I love to transform my readers to a time and place they have never experienced. I want them to root for the hero and heroine and also have a love - hate for the villains. Add a bit of fantasy to make my readers think… *what if that could happen...*" The author is currently working on the sequel to *Gypsy Soulmate*. Book Two in the Destiny Series.

Maranda Marks